152

THE LAST OF LAZARUS

Books by Robert C. Goldston

THE EIGHTH DAY

CATAFALQUE

THE SHORE DIMLY SEEN

THE LAST OF LAZARUS

THE LAST OF

LAZARUS

ROBERT C. GOLDSTON

Random House **New York**

In Memory of

JAMES WINSTON WHITE

THE LAST OF LAZARUS

IRST of all, I am not ill; I am empty of spleen and therefore attractive. My liver, which used to cause me atrocious headaches, is now pacified. If I have any complaint at all it must be spiritual, for I have complete confidence in my doctors—entirely too much confidence for my peace of mind. I no longer suffer from pain and have no fear of the pain to come.

This lack of pain—this is a phenomenon that Stein and The Foundation imagined to be temporary, a somatic manifestation of psychic shock. How excited they would be to realize it is permanent. I imagine hundreds of white-smocked technicians rushing around amid a maze of tubes, microslides, vials and tiny slabs of my body. And Stein himself! I can see him, his uncontrollably predictive face even now tortured into a thousand different expressions, waving his balloonlike arms in a frenzy of discovery. But this is something they may never know.

I think what has happened to me is simply that the tiny

surface nerves remain alive (I can taste my food, can feel and respond with undiminished repulsion to the tip of a hypodermic syringe), while something has happened to the deeper nerves that transmit pain. They are dead perhaps, or their signals are being misdirected. I sometimes wonder whether all the pain they should be communicating to the base of my spine is not being stored somewhere else and will one day explode into an agony so violent that my heart will burst of it. So far I have been very lucky.

I am forty years old, and I once taught history in one of the better Eastern universities. Although this institution treated me shabbily I see no reason to blacken its name by mentioning it. I have always been fascinated by history. Even as a young boy I heard and thrilled to the trumpets of Charlemagne. The Sun of Austerlitz was warmer to me than the sun of midsummer Chicago. And in emulation of Rothschild's agent at Waterloo I even kept pigeons, dreaming and praying for some great regional calamity the news of which should be borne exclusively by one of my carriers. I used to place messages such as *Northern Illinois inundated by Lake Michigan tidal wave, millions drowning, send help!* in their claw tubes and dispatch them from the Loop to our house on Clifton Avenue.

I had over thirty pigeons back there in Chicago. Besides carriers I also had seven prized white-tufted tumblers. I had accidentally crippled one of them by clipping his wings too short, and he could no longer fly. In fact, he could not even walk properly but staggered around our back yard like a drunken hod carrier. I repentantly put up a board so that he could climb into his cage, which was one of a row of orange crates faced with chicken wire. He was murdered one day by a large black cat who lived in the alley behind our house. I discovered his body one afternoon while I was looking through the garbage cans to find used prophylactics. One of my friends had recently told me that my mother and father did It. I rejected this accusation with considerable righteousness; I was six years old at the time. But my friend, who, though no older than I, came from an even poorer neighborhood, showed me a long, limp rubber he claimed to have found in our garbage can. I was an only child and I accused him of putting it there himself. He laughed and I hit him (the only effective blow I have ever struck) and he went home singsonging, "Webster's folks do It, they do It, they do It." So my search for discarded prophylactics was not purely morbid. I was gathering evidence. And that was how I discovered the remains of my crippled pigeon, a small heap of broken bones mixed with feathers, on the blood-stained pavement just beside the garbage can. There was something so forlornly unjust about those pathetic remains that I burst into tears. It seemed terribly unreasonable that so unoffending a bird living so deprived a life should have suffered such a cruel death. I could imagine his ultimate panic, his clumsy attempts to waddle away from those implacably sharp claws, that suggestively fanged mouth. When my mother found me sitting in the alley crying I held out to her a used and soggy rubber I had also discovered, and screamed, "That's why! That's why!" And yet I had had no religious training whatsoever.

You must not think I offer this recollection gratuitously. It seemed, even at that time, amid the chaotic churnings of my childish imagination, very important that love be pure—that love was too important not to be pure. Then why was I so eager, so relentless, in my attempt to prove

it selfish, mundane? I think perhaps because I *dared not*
risk disillusionment in something so vital. Of course my
ideas of purity and of love and of human beings have
changed and expanded since those days. But I have never
lost the sense of desperate importance—the distinctly
physical thrill of my nerves, the wild excitement tingling
in my mind—before the impending glory of love in a fellow human being. As coldly as I have protected myself by
demonstrating its essential falsity, even more eagerly have
I searched for it, hoarded evidences of it. I am speaking
not merely of sexual love. I can be moved to tears by a
military parade. And even though, like you, I have
learned to discount hope, to mask my deepest responses,
to dam up the turbulent stream of generous gladness
when it threatens to spill forth (if there is a principle of
evil in the world, *embarrassment* is its symptom), I still,
like you, treasure the hot, vital springs of love, the an-
archic source of life.

I believe I was a good teacher. Until I was victimized
by the University Establishment I had a brilliant future in
the History Department. I have never been much interested in the theory of pedagogy. The use of such words as
"awakening," "participation," "creative," "permissive,"
arouse in me a deep suspicion of the speaker. I know him
to be anesthetized against the emotional truth of teaching.
For the real relationship between student and teacher is
one of intellectual flirtation spiced by an inescapable
sadism. The recognition and acceptance of this is the
psychic core of all learning. It may also help to explain
why so many excellent teachers enjoy ruinous marriages.
For myself I have often wondered how much of the
potency I might have dedicated to my relationship with
M was drained away in the lecture hall.

You needn't hasten to psychoanalyze me just yet. I am a passionate man. I have been told that I died with an erection and I remember that to be true. My memory has, after all, been trained for many years. For example: King Nectanebo of the Thirtieth Egyptian Dynasty lived from 378 to 332 B.C. And I am not a specialist in ancient Egyptian history. I will not try to explain this phenomenon of memory. I leave that to the marvelous Dr. Stein, the benefactor, the savior, the unwitting assassin, of the human race. I have been reading his notes, which he has kindly left with me. I cannot disagree with Stein's claims, for I have never had the slightest interest in mechanics, let alone medicine. I know that Stein is unaware of certain things; he does not know the whole truth. But the honors he expects to be heaped upon his bald head will not be for knowing the truth; they will be for mechanics.

How my intransigence must torture Stein! It is as if Pasteur's cow had given nothing but sour milk after being injected against the pox, as if Sir Alexander Fleming's patients had all developed cancer from the penicillin that cured their infections. Oh, my condition cannot basically alter Stein's achievement. He can and will publish it to the world and reap his rewards. But what will be the effect of the living evidence? It will be as painful for Stein as I can make it, and an object lesson to the entire human race.

I will withhold nothing from you. I will tell you just what happened to me. If you think I am lying I can only insist that what I tell you happened to *me*. Nor will I stoop to present vouchers for my sanity. All such credentials are necessarily forged nowadays.

I had been sick for a long time. My blood was turning to water. Stein and his accomplices call it leukemia S—a rare form. They have conveniently obscure names for every natural process. But the simple truth is that my blood was turning to water and my internal organs were no longer functioning properly. My blood was dissolving back into the elemental sea from which all blood has evolved. The slight impurities that mean life were vanishing from it. I do not know how I contracted the disease. Stein insists that it is not a disease but rather a chemical fault. But why should such things not be communicable? It seems unnecessarily coincidental to me that my blood began to melt into water almost the very day I discovered M's betrayal, and that the first notable sign of the revolt of my internal organs should have occasioned my dismissal from the University. Just as M became an impurity in my life, so I became an impurity in the academic body. As I purged M, so the trustees purged me—and so I purged my blood. But it took time. Years. Five years over all. And for the last three of these, while I devoted myself entirely to my work of vindication, living in poverty and loneliness in a Bronx tenement while I struggled to amass facts, to interpret the currents of human interaction, to bring to completion *The Theory of Place and Decay*—a work that will one day liberate mankind from the burden of guilt it has borne for thousands of years—while, as I say, I was engaged in this most important life-consuming and life-liberating labor, my blood was secretly and persistently betraying me. But I have grown used to betrayals.

I was sick then. And I was entitled to be cared for by The Foundation. That was the result of a contract I had made during my academic career. It was one of many mistakes. I sold my body to The Foundation in return for free hospitalization. But it seemed a logical thing to do years ago. What were my motives? I had absolutely no religion in my background and so did not believe in survival after death. But I must admit I secretly hoped The Foundation might have some interest in preserving my brain. Then, too, I realized that on the pittance with which society rewards its liberators I would never be able to afford proper medical care should I ever fall seriously ill. Nor do I pretend that my motives were purely objective. I was well aware of the ego implications of that action. But all such ruminations belong to the past. When my disease was finally diagnosed as leukemia S, I had all but forgotten my contract with The Foundation. It was only an accident that it fell fluttering to the linoleum from a copy of Sir Wallis Budge's *Egyptian Magic,* which I was consulting in relation to my chapters on deserts as decay factors.

I truly believe that when I first set eyes on The Foundation building, which stands at the head of Central Park, I experienced a premonition. The building is tall and absolutely rectangular. It is constructed of grayish glass ribbed with anodized aluminum, and surrounded by a small oasis of carefully manicured trees and bushes. Clouds and sky are reflected from its translucent face in pallid, colorless serenity. I saw it as a gigantic tombstone set at the head of a monstrous grave.

But as I entered the building through glass doors that opened silently at my approach, I dismissed my fears as mere aspects of my condition. Yet I felt another thrill of uneasiness when I walked into the vast reception hall. Here the walls were all gray marble speckled with gold, reaching up to a black glass ceiling from which the glow of indirect light filtered down to illuminate furnishings that were uncompromisingly modern and uncomfortable. Although the floor appeared to be made of some sort of glasslike tile, footsteps did not sound upon it. The many passing white-smocked nurses and doctors and blue-uniformed technicians seemed to float silently. Nor did their voices ring within that huge hall although they did not whisper. It was this absence of sound and the over-whelming sense of infinite power that unnerved me. This was not like any hospital I'd ever seen. But why, I asked myself, should I expect it to be? The Foundation was, after all, a research institution only incidentally con-cerned with hospitalization. In fact, as I approached the reception desk—a white plastic ovoid that appeared to float a few inches off the floor—I even wondered (how very hopeful I was in those days!) whether I was not too far gone to warrant admittance. I felt distinctly un-clean.

I need not have worried. As soon as I showed my con-tract to the black-haired, plastic-faced young girl who presided over the desk, things began to happen with be-wildering speed. Within thirty minutes I found myself stripped, smocked, tagged and bedded in a private room overlooking the park from the tenth floor. I will not bore you with all the details of my examination and confine-ment. I suspected nothing. A small measure of hope was doled out to me by the doctors and by Stein himself, who visited me on the third day. I paid little attention. I settled down to conserve my energy for the battle against death—or more probably, against life. For I did not intend to linger through the years sustained by drugs and transfusions. I recoiled into myself and willed my body to a conclusion. And in this state I remained until the second week of my confinement.

The nurse, Miss Williams, had just left, assuming that I was asleep. But I was awake. She was a wonderfully endowed woman, Nurse Williams. She could not have been more than twenty-two or twenty-five and her hair was a deep rose-mahogany color—a bit darker than M's. When she bent over me to take my temperature or count my pulse I could see the very fine reddish down that ran like a rivulet down the nape of her neck. Her body was slight but her breasts and rump might easily have graced a much larger woman. During the time I was supposed to be asleep she would curl up in an armchair at the foot of my bed and read a magazine. And always, sooner or later, after glancing at me to make certain I was asleep, she would remove her shoes and bend down to examine her lacquered toenails. When she did this I could easily see down her uniform to the shadowed cleavage between her breasts. And I never saw any evidence of a brassiere. It was the brassiere I was looking for. It seemed to me impossible that a Foundation nurse could possibly report for duty without wearing a brassiere. My interest was purely sumptuary.

I was pretending to be asleep as she left my room that morning, no closer to a solution of this problem, when Dr. Stein entered. That was one of the many things I came to hate about Stein. He never walked into my room but always entered it as if preceded by a flourishing fanfare of trumpets. Of course, a man of his reputation, a man who for thirty years had been a director of the most richly endowed research organization in the world—such a man was entitled to preserve a proper dignity. But at some time in his life Stein had unwittingly crossed over the thin line separating dignity from pomposity. You will have seen photographs of him in the newspapers, or perhaps even one of his rare television appearances. But nothing so shallow as a photograph or so diminutive as a television screen can possibly convey the "presence" of this man. He must weigh not less than three hundred and fifty pounds, but his movements are so quick and light that he resembles a huge plastic balloon. His head is oversized even for *his* immense bulk, and completely bald. And his face—his face is round, pink-skinned and dominated by a fleshy nose supporting a pair of gold-rimmed spectacles through which innocent blue eyes naïvely contemplate you. His face is that of a baby elephant—but with a sinister quality that cannot be conveyed by mechanical reproduction. That quality is the ability, even the compulsion, to translate predictable responses into anticipatory facial expressions. His features are as malleable as rubber, and they are informed by a terrible preknowledge. For example, if he informs you that you must die tomorrow, his face has already assumed an expression—of, say, grief, horror, joy, what you will—that would be appropriate for *your own* face a split second before you assume such an expression yourself. So that when talking to Stein your own reactions become essentially superfluous. It is a colossal presumption, all the more irritating for being completely unconscious with him. As I knew Stein better I tried to fight against this by assuming irrelevant and unpredictable facial responses to his remarks. But gradually he began to outwit me at that game, too.

"Good morning, Professor Webster," he said, in a voice that was, as always, gratefully free of sympathy, compassion or professional grooming. I must admit that his voice is natural, though unexpectedly shrill for so large a man. But you see, he knew I was awake although I had been pretending sleep. That irritated me so that I did not return his greeting. I was also annoyed by his use of the title "Professor." He knew very well that I had never attained any rank higher than assistant professor at the University.

By insisting on the larger dignity he was reminding me that just as my title depended on his courtesy, so my very life depended on the charity of The Foundation. He stood with his chubby hands locked limply on his stomach, and stared down at me beside my bed. "I understand that you wish to leave us."

The remark chilled me. I had expressed no such desire but had been considering the move for several days. And as he put it into words I realized that I did indeed want to leave The Foundation. My annoyance at his perception increased. "Yes," I said sullenly.

"But you realize that yours threatens to be a terminal case. You cannot possibly receive proper care at home."

He knew very well I lived in a tenement, and a condemned one at that. Oh, my room was suitable enough. It included a kerosene heater for the winter and a double gas ring for cooking. But there could be no question of calling such a place "home." By using that word Stein was reasserting his superiority. He was indulging me in a presumed shame of my previous condition—as if I felt any shame at all or had even begged such a kindness. But two can play that game.

"I have no fear of the word 'death,' Doctor," I replied. "Calling my case a terminal condition makes it sound like some sort of commuter problem. In any case, I prefer to die in my room up in the Bronx. My books are there, and my work."

"We've brought all that down here for you." His patience seemed wonderfully out of place to me. His face betrayed nothing except flashes of annoyance predictive of my own responses. It was disconcerting.

"I prefer to go home," I said, and instantly regretted the slip. "It's home to me, anyhow."

His face compressed into a look of irritation as if *he* had just bitten *his* tongue. He nodded sympathetically. "I can understand your feelings, Professor, but as your doctor I really must forbid such a move. If you wish, we can move you into a larger room with your books and work."

"It isn't simply a question of my work." Stein's face wore the very look of pleading I had banished from my own.

"We could even set up your ah—kerosene stove here for you if that would suit you better." His indulgent smile exposed a golden eyetooth.

"I'm afraid I prefer to go ho— to my own place." The realization was slowly dawning on me that Stein must have seen my room, that he was conversant with every detail of my shame. The expression of frosty superiority on my face slipped into place a second later than it appeared on Stein's. I clenched my hands beneath the sheets and felt them moist.

"I'm afraid that will be impossible." He glanced at his wristwatch as if that ended the matter.

"And I'm afraid you don't understand, Doctor," I said slowly. "I am going home. Yes—home! I am going home this afternoon. Please have my things ready for me."

He sighed, removed his spectacles and rubbed the bridge of his nose, while his eyes shut tight as if in pain. "I think you have forgotten something, Professor." He replaced the spectacles and eyed me innocently. "In return for the very excellent and extensive medication you have been receiving here at The Foundation—and at no expense whatsoever to yourself—you long ago agreed that The Foundation should receive your body."

"After I die," I said softly. "After I die you can do anything you want with my remains. But at the moment I am going home."

The anger on Stein's face—a mere prediction of my own—vanished and was replaced by a look of kindly understanding. "I'm afraid you haven't read the terms of your contract with us." He drew a folded document from the inner pocket of his white smock, opened it and commenced to read: " 'When the Party of the First Part shall, upon examination by competent authority as defined in paragraph four above, be deemed to suffer from a terminal disease, then such termination shall occur within the jurisdiction and competence of the Party of the Second Part, withersoever removed.' "

"I'm willing to die under your competence," I remarked sarcastically, "but I prefer to do it at home."

"You fail to understand the operative phrase here?"

"I understand it all per—"

"The operative phrase here, Webster, is 'withersoever removed.' Now, you have been removed to The Foundation headquarters. It is here that our competence is to be exercised." His voice was patient, exact, as if he were explaining something to a child, an illiterate.

"I'm going home!" I shouted.

"Please do not disturb yourself so, Professor." Stein's face was stricken with *my* panic, *my* anger.

"You can't keep me here. I'll call the police. You're trying to kidnap me. You're covering something up. You're trying to kill me!" I paused for breath and was horrified by the reflection of my own rage and hysteria on Stein's face. "Stop doing that!" I screamed.

"I can't help it," he said nervously, as he made an unsuccessful effort to compose his features. "In any event, you must remain here. I'll have your papers and books brought down. If you insist on hysterics I will not hesitate to place you under restraint. We are doing everything possible for you, you must understand that. But a contract is a contract." He waved the papers and then stuffed them back into his smock. "Try to sleep now. All this will soon be over."

For the first time in my memory, which is quite exact, I found myself speechless. All this would soon be over, would it? Try to sleep now? I watched Stein's immense, balloonlike body float gradually to the door. Just before he left, Stein turned to smile at me. But I surprised a look of my own sickly impotence on his face. Then he was gone. I stared numbly at my surroundings—the dull white plastic walls; the huge, gray ceiling-to-floor window; the neutral drapes; the cuplike armchair; the indifferent bedding—and recognized for the first time my tomb.

But I knew myself well enough to understand my anger was not caused by any mere superficial fright such as fear of death. That I had learned to recognize, rationalize and live with. No, this was more personal. It was fear of my relationship to Stein. From the very first moment I had felt a terrible bond between us. There was something fated in our meeting and in our subsequent relationship. It was a deep blood-knowledge that we shared silently— an instant recognition between our eyes, a slight but definite shock or encounter between our brain waves perhaps. And there was an all-pervasive sense of doom in this mutuality that frightened me. Because I had experienced the same sensations once before, with hideous results. I remembered Harry.

I'd first seen Harry making up small, neat bundles of garbage in the hall. But perhaps I should explain. The unjust and detestable event that severed my connection with the University also deprived me of the apartment I had rented in one of their off-campus residences. Not that

I could have continued paying the rent in any case, nor that I would have been willing to continue any association whatsoever with that corrupt institution. For instantly upon my dismissal I decided to devote my life and my small savings to the justification of my theories the defense of which had already cost me my position, my friends, my future and the very roof over my head.

In response to an ad in *The New York Times* I found myself on a wide and shabby boulevard in the Bronx at six A.M. Of course by that time the apartment had already been rented. I was trudging back to the subway entrance when my eye was attracted by a crudely lettered sign pasted onto the ground-floor window of a tenement: ROOM. The building was five stories of crumbling red brick. An iron fire escape like a jagged scar ran down the aged face of the wreck, and some of the windows were boarded over. The whole visage of the structure resembled the face of a drunken, leprous, scarred and patch-eyed pirate. But as our Dean of Men once wisely remarked, "New Yorkers cannot be choosers." So, suppressing a shudder of revulsion, I climbed the short flight of stone steps that led to the open entrance door. My nostrils were instantly flooded with the stale odor of worn linoleum, blocked toilets, vermin and decaying garbage. I breathed as much as possible through my mouth. Ancient and yellowing wallpaper hung in shreds from the walls of the short corridor; it was paved by tiles slippery with slime and it terminated in a crumbling wooden staircase that ascended into upper darkness. The whole was illuminated by a dim electric bulb. In its shadows, at the far end of this corridor, I noticed a hunched human figure muffled up in a shabby overcoat that reached to the floor, pottering around a row of three overflowing garbage cans.

Presuming he was the superintendent, I said, "Good morning. You have a room to rent?"

The figure whirled about, assuming a crouching, defensive position. A lean, wizened, ageless face squinted at me in abject terror. It was at that moment—when our eyes first met—that I experienced the premonition of doom, the feeling of deep, fated and inevitable relationship between this improbable caricature of a human being and myself. The sense of it was so sure, so powerful and so inexplicable as to be hypnotic in effect. And I have often wondered since that moment whether Harry experienced the same. Did he recognize in me the appointed agent of his destruction? Did this precognition explain his terror? Or was that his normal response to human contact? At the moment, in any event, the look of fright passed from his withered features and was replaced by a crafty smile that revealed a toothless mouth. "No, I ain't got no room to rent," he hissed. I later learned that this hissing quality in Harry's speech was due to his lack of teeth and advanced asthma.

"But you have a sign in the window—"

"What makes ya think so?" He picked up three brown-paper parcels from the floor next to the garbage cans and pressed them to his chest. His smile had widened into a leer.

"I saw it."

"Yeah—but what makes ya think it's mine? Answer me that!"

"Aren't you the superintendent?"

"No, I ain't." He doubled over in soundless laughter that soon turned into a coughing fit. When he could control himself he wiped the spittle from his chin on the sleeve of his overcoat and edged toward me, his head cocked to one side pugnaciously. "I ain't the super, see? But I like to keep the place clean. So I just run a few packages of garbage down to the corner now and then, see?"

"Oh." I stepped back.

"Gotta keep the place clean." He edged after me. "We could all die of disease, see? Sonofabitch Suskind doesn't give a damn. I do it all. Run 'em to the corner, see?"

"I see," I agreed weakly.

"Bastard Suskind don't do nothin' around this dump. Nothing! That's his name, Suskind. Know what it means? In Yid it means 'sweet child.' But there ain't nothin' sweet about him, see? He stinks. Whole goddamned building stinks!"

"Uh-huh."

"You rent a room here you're crazy. Crazy! The conditions!"

I had already reached a private agreement with this conclusion and was about to flee the building (yet in deepest truth was it not rather Harry I was about to flee?) when the old man gripped the sleeve of my jacket.

"Rent's cheap," he hissed. "You keep your own place clean and your own part of the hall clean and it ain't so bad. We gotta stick together. See? My name's Harry. Me, I do a lot of work around here. Know why? Because I don't work days. I work nights. What d'ya think of that? I throw down the bundles of newspapers from *Daily News* trucks, see? Keeps me up with the world. You wanta see the super?"

His eyes, watery, rheumy, encased in yellow, wrinkled lids, held me fast. I nodded.

"He's down in the basement hunting."

I was still trying to digest this last bit of information

and to think of some delicate way in which I could pull my jacket sleeve from between Harry's clawlike fingers when a sharp explosion rumbled from some depths within the building.

"Got one! Got one! Good old Suskind, he's a good shot!" Harry very carefully set his packages of garbage down next to the three cans and threw open a nearby door. "Hey, Suskind, you got one?" he hailed down into the blackness with a quivering voice.

"Get two alla same time," a voice called from below in a vaguely familiar singsong accent. The voice was followed by a heavy tread upon creaking stairs. Harry backed away from the door, rubbing his hands together and making slight, furtive bows, while a smile of abject adoration spread his lips.

A figure so short, so fat, so yellow and so hairless as to resemble a basketball labored up to the doorway holding a double-barreled shotgun in its right hand. The faint but sharp smell of gunpowder cut through the sodden odors of the hallway. Slanted, almond-colored eyes stared at me shrewdly. I now identified the singsong accent. But the slightly contemptuous grin trembling on Suskind's liverish lips told me he was amused by my surprise. "You mebbe never see Chinee before?" he demanded in a quiet, sibilant voice.

"Not with a name like Suskind," I said, summoning as much genial indifference into my voice as I could muster.

Harry chuckled but then lapsed into sudden silence as Suskind's eyes met his own. "This old bastard is anti-Semite," Suskind said slowly.

"Now, that's not true," Harry whined. "You know that's not true, Mr. Suskind. I say let everybody be equal no matter who they are is what I say."

"Shurrup!" Suskind barked abruptly. Then to me, "What you looking for?"

"Oh," I said with a deprecating smile, "nothing really—"

"I got him, I got him!" Harry interjected quickly. "I got him while he was passing by. I told him about the room, see? It was me that got him." His eyes darted a pleading glance to mine.

"You wanna see allabout loom?" Suskind demanded suspiciously.

"Well, as a matter of fact—"

"You come with me." Suskind turned and walked down the corridor, still cradling his shotgun over one arm.

When he reached the last of a row of three cracked and paint-peeled doors he kicked it open with his foot. I hesitated but then felt Harry prod me in the small of my back. "Please," he whispered.

Now, you must not suppose that my mind, still reeling from the shock of precognition between Harry and myself and under the assault upon reason this entire scene stimulated, had ceased to function. I had never imagined such a clear and vivid example of the influence of place upon decay could be found within the confines of the city. But what, after all, did I know about the Bronx? I had never been rich, but had I not always lived safely within the boundaries of the bourgeoisie below 120th Street? Here I could explore other social strata.

The room was exactly square, measuring about seventeen feet on each side. Its one window looked into the eternal twilight of an air shaft. There was a brass bedstead and a rolled-up cotton mattress, several wooden chairs and a large table upon which rested a two-burner gas ring. The wallpaper had long since faded into a neutral gas-yellow and the linoleum had subsided into pale brownish-green. There was a sink and an electric bulb.

"For you I make lent four dollahs a week. OK?" Suskind's eyes were inscrutable. "Lectlicity flee. Gas too." He pursed his lips and sighed. "All light, you dlive hard bargain. Make it thlee dollahs fifty cents a week, not

"Say, that's a real bargain!" Harry exclaimed joyfully.

In spite of Harry I could not deny that it *was* a real bargain. At that minimal rent, and with gas and electricity included, my modest savings would last quite a while. And what right had I to expect anything better? I thought of Karl Marx struggling through his life in a dingy London boarding house. Was my own work less important? Could I afford to demand from fate more than it generally doles out to genius? "Where's the bathroom?" I asked.

Suskind rested his shotgun against the wall, walked back out into the hall and unpadlocked another door. He pointed wordlessly to a toilet in what was little more than a broom closet. "No bath," he said. "You mebbe take bath at Gland Centlal Station like evlybody else."

"I'll take it," I said, feeling myself in the control of powers beyond the pale of reason.

"You pay now two week advance," Suskind said.

"Good for you!" Harry cried, dancing a little jig as I handed over the cash.

Suskind flipped through the money expertly, pocketed it, handed me a key, picked up his shotgun and said, "*Mazel tov!*" as he walked away.

"It'll be good to have company," Harry said as he too left.

Poor Harry! Whatever intimations of mortality he may

have felt when first he saw me were quite lost now. It was as if fate had given him one warning tremor and would vouchsafe no more. Nor did this feeling of doom again occur to me.

Within a short space of time I had arranged my room into a very comfortable studio-bedroom. I bought from the Salvation Army, and soon assembled a livable, if discarded, suite of furniture. Besides that, my books now entirely hid the moldering wallpaper and I had hung drapes over the useless window. I plunged into my work. Mornings and afternoons I spent at the Public Library, evenings I worked over my notes. I rarely went out except to an occasional film. I never met any other tenant of that building and I grew to suspect that there were no others. I'd meet Harry in the hall, he with his inevitable bundle of garbage, I with my inevitable bundle of books. "Fine day, ain't it?" he'd inquire. "Just running some of this stuff up to the corner. You got your garbage under control? Good, good."

As the months passed and winter approached, the problem of heat became critical. I have already mentioned that I had a kerosene heater in my room. But that did not heat the hall toilet. It became torture to relieve myself on cold winter nights. Because it is so central to the matter, perhaps I should describe this toilet in some detail. It was a cubicle not more than four feet square. The walls were painted an obscure brown color and the floor was tiled. The toilet bowl itself was set exactly in the center of the compartment. It was of ancient manufacture, with a water bowl high above it. Both this water bowl and the pipes that fed it leaked steadily and directly onto the head of any occupant. You see that this tiny closet was too small to introduce any normal kind of heating apparatus into it. And no matter how many sweaters and scarves I wore beneath my overcoat when I entered that wooden cabinet, still there were parts of my body that suffered near-frostbite.

But one day I had an inspiration. Why not hang an electric heater—one of those small, round reflecting devices—in the toilet? I could easily run a line from my room across the hall. I broached the idea to Suskind the next time he came to collect the rent.

"What should I care about it?" he shrugged impassively.

With this tacit approval I set to work and had soon rigged a reflecting heater upon the wall facing the toilet bowl at the level of a seated man's head. Of course, the heater was necessarily so close to the bowl that its effect was very intense upon the occupant. And since the pipes and water bowl continued to leak steadily, one had the sensation of being basted while sitting there. But still it was preferable to the arctic climate that had formerly prevailed in that cubicle.

One day not long after I had completed this arrangement, I met Harry making his morning collections from the garbage cans. "Good morning, Harry," I said.

"Good morning, good morning," he replied briskly. "Say listen, I hear from Suskind you got your john warmed up." He cocked his head to one side.

"I've got an electric heater in it."

"That's great, great." He paused and contemplated the garbage cans. "I could help you out with your garbage, see? I mean I could run it up to the corner for you."

"I don't have much."

"Uh-huh. Yeah. Well—what there is of it . . ."

I realized then what he was after. "You want to use my john, Harry?"

He smiled toothlessly and nodded. "I got bad arthritis."

"Well, go right ahead. I'll get you a key from the hardware store this afternoon."

So casually, so thoughtlessly, do we advance to the lip of the pit!

I gave him a key and let him carry away my garbage daily for the sake of his pride.

There was only one minor note of discord which ever sounded in the symphony of my relationship to Harry. Of course it had to do with M. I had foolishly left the transcript of my divorce trial open on top of my desk. I found it necessary, from time to time, to go over certain portions of the testimony. I was still prosecuting but no longer knew whether M or I was the defendant.

I had gone to the toilet, leaving Harry behind stirring his inevitable cup of coffee. When I returned I saw him slithering back into his chair with a look of embarrassment on his gruff face. Of course there was no rational explanation of my reaction. I knew instantly that he'd been looking into the trial transcript. And that was, after all, a matter of public record already. But my instinctive response was to rush over to the table and grab up the green leather folder, clutching it to my chest in something very close to panic. "You've been prying into this!" I hissed angrily, an unreasoning fear chilling my bowels. "You've been prying!"

"Well, uh . . ." He glanced around the room, avoiding my eyes, as if seeking a way to escape. "I *did* take a little look-see. I mean I didn't know what it was. I thought maybe it was something uh—else. No offense, is there?" His eyes met mine and then shifted away again with a look of alarm.

"How much did you read?" I demanded harshly.

"Not much—really—I swear—not much."

"How much?" I cried.

"Well, uh—just about something to do with beer or something like that—I didn't understand it, honest I didn't!"

Harry's evasiveness had changed now to open fear. From the expression of terror on his face I suddenly realized that my own must be a mask of fury. I swallowed deeply, tried to control my breathing, forced something like a thin smile to my lips. But when I spoke my voice cracked slightly. "Well," I said. "Well, it doesn't matter, Harry. It doesn't really matter. I'm sorry I got so excited."

"Oh hell," he said eagerly, "I understand. Hell yes, I understand! A man don't want all that stuff dragged out again. I understand." He got up warily, still watching me as if he expected me to spring at him. "Well, time for the old truck," he said with faint heartiness. "Be seein' ya." And he scurried quickly from the room.

The trial report still clutched to my chest, I stared after him, aware I had wounded him, aware also that my reaction had been completely spontaneous, helpless.

As soon as he had gone I sat down at the desk and opened the transcript to the pages he might have seen. Could he possibly have understood them? Could he possibly see my justification behind all the legal verbiage? That trial, taken at face value, could give a totally erroneous impression! I studied the section he might have read with the desperate avidity of the unjustly accused.

Q. Are you in the habit of drinking alcoholic beverages in the morning, Mrs. Webster?
A. Does that include beer?
Q. Beer is generally regarded as an alcoholic beverage.
A. Some people say it's very good for you—very nutritious.

Q. Do you consider it nutritious, Mrs. Webster?
COUNSEL: Objection.
COURT: Sustained. We are not interested in Mrs.
Webster's opinions as to the nutritive value of vari-
ous beverages.

What would Harry have made of that? Could he possibly have pictured M sitting demurely in the witness
chair, her innocent face a study of regret, her invitingly
plump figure modestly sheathed in a gray tweed suit, her
usually uncombed mahogany-red hair neatly swept up in
a fashionable way, while she deliberately suborned the
court?

Could he know what even the Court never realized—
that beer was M's prop, her crutch, her solace? Not that
she was an alcoholic. She definitely was not. It was more
an addiction than a complusion. It was something that
soothed her nerves, something to which she turned in
moments of stress. And mornings were definitely full of
such moments.

Q. Is it not true, Mrs. Webster, that for the last three
years of your married life with Mr. Webster you
never once made breakfast for him?
A. He never wanted more than a cup of coffee in the
morning.
Q. Would you please answer simply yes or no, Mrs.
Webster?
A. Well then, no. But you don't understand—
Q. Thank you, Mrs. Webster. I think we understand.
A. But he was only interested in the principle of the
thing, not in really eating anything. It was part of his
campaign to—
Q. Will the Court kindly instruct Mrs. Webster to
confine herself to answering direct questions?

COURT: I must caution you, Mrs. Webster, to confine yourself to the questions. You will have an opportunity to elaborate under further direct examination by your own attorney.

COUNSEL: Will the Court please instruct Mr. Webster to stop gesticulating toward his attorney?

COURT: Mr. Webster, I must ask you to restrain yourself.

Of course, all this seems incomprehensible in the bleak abstractions of the court record. For example, the reason I tried to attract my attorney's attention here was simply because I was fully prepared to answer M's allegations on their own ground. I felt no need of hiding behind obfuscating tactics. Yes, indeed it *was* the principle of the thing. And by that I do not mean the principle of wifely obedience—nothing so barbaric. No, I mean simply the principle of demonstrating concern in these ancient and symbolic ways. For I needed such demonstration— needed it more and more as time passed. It was certainly mental cruelty on M's part to withhold it. Oh, she would claim that this craving of mine was exaggerated, that I threatened to drown her personality with it, but that certainly was never my intention.

For example, I would awaken in the morning to see her wandering around in her bathrobe, sipping beer from a bottle, humming some snatch of Bach (she was a violinist), utterly removed from me, indifferent to my needs. And yet I myself awaken in a state of glad welcome to each new day, my feelings unruffled, my temper under leash, a smile in my voice.

"How about some eggs?" I'd suggest hopefully.

"No oil," she'd reply, closing the bathroom door behind her although she might have known I needed to go to the bathroom more than she did. But this was merely another evidence of her indifference. And by saying there was no oil she hoped to throw me off the track and into a discussion of the relative merits of oil and butter for cooking eggs. The truth was that she had no intention of cooking anything whatsoever. I do not deny that I had no intention of eating anything whatsoever, I merely point out the indifference in her manner.

"Well, how about some coffee and peanut-butter-and-jam sandwiches?" I called through the bathroom door, giving her yet another chance. "Hurry up, I've got to get out of here."

"Coffee's made. Since when do you eat peanut butter for breakfast?" Her voice, which was low and on the inside, could insinuate ridicule without actually committing it. I could picture her sitting in there drinking beer and reading through some musical score, my very existence forgotten.

"Well, I suppose I ought to just have a bottle of beer?" I asked whimsically.

"Beer's good for you. Even babies can drink beer," she replied.

"It seems to deaden the brain," I remarked, pulling on my trousers.

"What do you mean by that?"

"Nothing. I don't mean anything by that." My collar button was probably missing—they usually were—nor could any amount of pleading induce M to take up needle and thread. How many times I had attended important faculty functions with my collar held together only by my tie!

"Come on out. I've only got ten minutes left," I pleaded.

"Mmm." And she would, if she felt like it, emerge to
dress. Here again she showed either a complete lack of
feeling for my needs or a demoniacal desire to upset my
natural emotional stability. For she knew that I could not
remain indifferent to her dressing.

It is, I suppose, a matter of taste. But I have observed
that female rumps are built in two standard ways. There
are the upswept or duck-built and the downswept or ski-
slide-built. I prefer the ski-slide to the duck. Now, M was
well aware of this when she let the bathrobe slip from her
shoulders. You must remember at this point that she never
did anything coquettishly. She was a practical dresser, her
movements addressed always to an efficient slipping on of
brassiere or stockings, but this was only an example of her
basic sexual contrivance, Passive Pursuit. I say she would
do this sort of thing purposely in the mornings, knowing
that I had to go to the bathroom, knowing that I had but
ten minutes to make my first class, knowing my stomach
was empty and my collar unbuttoned. She even made
some slight gesture of resistance as I pulled her back onto
me, but her defiance was always mitigated by laughter—
at my predicament!

My arrival in class late, disheveled, exhausted and
stunned became such a regular occurrence as to excite
comment among the faculty, which led finally to a reprimand from Dean Halvorsen.

"Webster," he said, stuffing his inevitable pipe, his eyes
avoiding mine, "you seem to be living it up a lot recently.
Staying out late at night these days?"

Late at night! I could only suppress a bitter laugh and
swallow my improbable explanations.

And when I mentioned this to M she simply widened
her innocent blue eyes, brushed a strand of red hair from

her forehead and coolly replied, "Well, why don't you just get to class on time?"

"How can I get to class on time when you spend all morning in the bathroom?"

"I spend less time in the bathroom than any other woman I know."

"And I'm always looking around for a shirt with a collar button."

"What you want is a mother, not a wife."

"And what you want is a bartender and not a husband!" She knew just how to prick my anger with illogic until it exploded.

"Well, at least he might treat me as an individual!"

"Then why didn't you marry him, for Christ's sake?"

And these lashes, whether administered or received, were the sharpest of all. For the truth was that I had never fully satisfied myself that M was no longer attracted to Tony Buono.

Tony Buono. Very large, very strong, very hairy—yes, everything I was not. Also very sentimental and excruciatingly stupid, and these were other things I was not. He was a bartender down in the Village, in one of those saloons that attract the younger members of the artist-bohemian fringe. I knew little enough about him. He was Italian, of course, and unlike his customers he'd been born and raised in the Village slums. He would easily have passed for just another young *mafioso,* or perhaps for one of the Bleecker Street Goths, except for his fascination with the bar's clientele. It was this unnatural association with on-the-make artists, writers and musicians that had lent him a second-hand knowledge, a borrowed sensitivity, a shaky appreciation of a different and, to him, glamorous world. And of course the combination of strength and earthiness and this gloss of artistic appreciation made him fascinating in turn to women. He also played the cello, poorly but perseveringly. It was this, combined with his dispensing of beer, that had no doubt brought him and M together. And in spite of her constant assurances that their relationship had been purely studious, platonic, I could never rid myself of a secret conviction that it was his other and truer self; the tough, rooted, beetle-browed air of masculinity, to which she'd been drawn. And if that was the case . . .

All this being a fragment of her past it was none of my business, you say? Of course not. Nor did it unduly disturb me. It was only her use of his existence that had the power of arousing a rage in my breast. I could not bear to imagine her in his dirty embrace—for that was the overall impression I had of him: huge and dirty. If forced to sum up my feelings in a phrase, I would have said that I considered him *unworthy* of M. Try as I might to control my feelings, the mention of him on her lips always left me speechless with rage, weak with resentment.

But how could Harry have possibly picked any of this essential background from the bare bones of the trial record? As I closed the green leather folder I found that my eyes were wet with tears. And this made me angry. What had I to regret? My complaints had been justified, hadn't they? Of course there was infinitely more, there was real and solid evidence, a towering edifice of rational justification. But somehow I took no pleasure in going any further with the transcript. Harry's glance at it had undermined the satisfaction I used to derive from it.

It took several weeks of concentrated thoughtfulness, kindliness and invitation to overcome Harry's skitterish suspicion of my violent emotions. But in the end I succeeded in re-establishing our friendship on its ancient foundations of mutual trust and mutual need. If only I hadn't!

I have promised to withhold nothing from you. So I must not try to mitigate my responsibility by an act of omission. I have explained my precognition of doom as being almost subconscious. But I cannot deny that I had more explicit warnings. For besides collecting garbage and throwing bundles of newspapers from trucks, Harry had one other interest in the world. That interest was in executions. How many times had he sat in my room of an evening, on his way to work, sipping a cup of coffee and indulging his fantasies on that subject.

"They still shoot ya in Idaho if you want. Know that?" he'd reflect. "I once saw a hangin'. Some say hangin's the best. But you know what? It ain't only that you might not break your neck but just strangle like. No. I once read about a guy out West he was so fat that when they come to hang him he didn't die of no broke neck and he didn't die of stranglin' either. You know what he died of? He died by having all the blood vessels in his neck stretched so far they popped. He died of drownin', see? What about that? I guess maybe the gas chamber's best. But who knows? Does anybody know? Maybe at the end there it gets you like—you know what I mean? For me I like the big knife. I mean the gullyteen. That one's for sure. That one's for damned sure. I'd like to see old Suskind's face after they chopped his head off. Boy, would I like to see that! Once there was a guy who's head talked after it was chopped off. I read that somewhere. But I don't believe it. What I say is they wanta kill ya they're gonna kill ya and so what? See? Well, thanks for the joe. Gotta get down to the truck."

Such conversations grew to be almost nightly occurrences between us. And I failed to read the signs. Of that much I am guilty. But that is enough. I confess it before man and God.

The day it happened I was sitting at my desk reading an account of the reign of Amenhotep IV (can such things be coincidental?) when suddenly the light went out. I got up, made my way to the door and saw that the hallway too was plunged into darkness. Then I heard the cellar door open.

"Fuse blow," Suskind said in a tone of deep disgust. "You lectlic funny business blow fuse, *schlemiel!*"

"Nonsense," I retorted.

"You open door please to john," Suskind continued impassively. His bald head faintly reflected the light that filtered through the street door into the corridor.

I fumbled in my pocket and produced the key. But as I tried to open the toilet padlock I found it gone. "The padlock is gone," I said stupidly. Something was turning weak within my bowels, something cold had invaded my stomach.

Suskind pushed past me impatiently and threw open the toilet door. Then he stopped short and hissed.

I felt my knees quivering and an icy sweat break out on my forehead. For there, seated on the toilet bowl but slumped into the heater, was Harry. There could be no doubt of what had happened. The curled-back lips, the clawed hands resting limply in his lap, the acrid smell of electric fire—Harry had been electrocuted.

Suskind hissed again, glanced over his shoulder down the hallway and then whispered, "You help me please to belly him now."

I stepped back instinctively as if he had just offered me

a particularly foul piece of fish. "But that's against the law," I said shakily. "We'll have to report this to the police."

"Alla this 'gainst law too," Suskind said impatiently, waving toward the heater and the concealed electric line that fed it. "Maybe police gonna get you for manslaughter, *schmuck*. Maybe you gonna go to jail plenty long time!"

"Nonsense!" I cried. "Maybe I'll be fined for an illegal electric connection—" I stopped as I realized that the look in his eyes was one of real desperation. I thought suddenly of the shotgun. "Why is it so important to you, Suskind?"

"No lectlicity connected in this building. Gas too. I connected flom mains in stleet. More. Alla building condemned. Nobody supposed to live here. Police come they gonna close down building plenty quick. We both gonna go to jail anyhow."

"But what about the other tenants?"

"No other tenants. Why you *hocking me chinocks?*" Suskind returned my stare of amazement with open belligerence.

I could picture it all too well. I had always suspected there were no other tenants. That left just Suskind and myself for the police to blame. Would they accept the word of a Chinese Jew and a disgraced outcast? Would they not enmesh us in a deadly trap woven out of our improbable explanations? And, above all, did it really matter? Harry could be buried decently. Nothing could bring him back now. Whose business was it anyhow? "All right," I said finally.

Suskind gripped Harry's feet while I supported his shoulders. We dragged and carried him—surprisingly heavy for so slight a man—down the steps into the basement. It was the first time I had ever entered this subterranean hunting ground. A stench vaguely animal but filthier than any animal smell pervaded the utter blackness. I experienced a small shock when we dropped Harry to the floor and I realized that it was dirt. No wonder the building was condemned!

"You hold this please," Suskind muttered, pressing a flashlight into my hand.

I switched it on and swept the beam of light around. Instantly I felt my gorge rise. The building supports were heavy wooden pillars beneath wooden joists. And hanging from these joists, in orderly array as in a trophy room, were rows of dead rats, tied by their tails to nails. Each was the size of a small dog, and all bore the terrible wounds of the shotgun to which they'd fallen victim.

"Please, over here," Suskind hissed.

I illuminated a patch of floor and saw that he had secured a shovel from some corner. He began to dig quickly, expertly. Watching him I suddenly wondered how many of his tenants lay buried beneath us. He made no comments. His heavy shoulders pressed into the work until he had scooped out a grave about four feet deep. Then he rested on his shovel for a moment, surveying his work with a critical eye.

"It seems a little short," I observed.

"He just fit," Suskind muttered between labored breaths. "Put him in now, please."

I helped him lower Harry into his final resting place beneath the basement of rats in the Bronx. Suskind was right; Harry's emaciated body fit just exactly into the pit. Suskind quickly filled in the dirt on top of him and then smashed the floor flat again with the back of his shovel.

By this time my horror of the situation had changed imperceptibly into a horror of Suskind himself. The absolute coldness, efficiency and apparent indifference with which he accomplished his ghastly task roused feelings of desperate rage and revulsion within me. And yet, it was not I but Suskind who suggested the final and fitting ceremony with which to complete the interment. There was a delicacy of feeling in Suskind that I had not expected.

When he had finished, Suskind tossed the shovel into a corner and turned to me. "Alla same, ole Hally had plenty *chutzpah*," he hissed. Then he walked over to a pillar and picked up his shotgun which had been resting against it. "We give him one last salute," he said. "Turn out light."

I flicked off the flashlight and waited in the impenetrable darkness. Then I felt the hair on the nape of my neck begin to rise. In the almost nonexistent light that filtered into the basement from the hallway above, I could now see hundreds of flaming, tiny eyes staring at me from various corners. I heard Suskind sigh. Then an ear-shattering explosion rocked me back on my heels. It was followed by another. The smell of gunpowder singed my nostrils. I heard a squealing, scrabbling sound, and then silence.

"Now you turn on light, please."

The beam of the flashlight revealed Suskind holding the smoking shotgun. And in a far corner lay a heap of dead rats.

"For Hally I give both ballels," he said. Then he turned and led me back upstairs.

As we mounted to the world of light above, I examined my memory and my conscience. By the time we were once again standing in the hall I could honestly say to myself that never had I heard a simpler, more heartfelt or more meaningful remark than Suskind's last. I offered him my hand. He shook it sincerely. We parted to go about our business, and never again mentioned Harry. I was later to learn that Suskind had depths to him undreamt of in my appraisals.

But for myself, I thought of Harry often. I remembered his little kindnesses, his cleanliness as regards the garbage, his generosity in offering to dispose of mine—fatal offer! And above all, when I was not immersed in my books and notes, I considered the fatality of our relationship, and I did not hide from myself the precognition I had felt. It was this singular circumstance that terrified me.

And it was this same precognition about my relationship to Stein that terrified me now. To compound it was the feeling of being smothered, trapped; and the weak outrage of being helplessly victimized by legality; and the bitter self-contempt I felt for having elected this position in the first place through idle illusion and carelessness. All these emotions overwhelmed me as I lay in my bed at The Foundation.

And yet my feelings were not quite justified. For it was undeniably true that although Stein was unreasonable, he was logical. He derived his powers from a logically constructed clause in a logically constructed contract. The Foundation was, *must be* after all, susceptible to the processes of analysis and reason. One had only to make the insane assumption that their rights in my case were based on an equitable claim, and work from there. But all people nowadays are used to making such assumptions.

So I banished emotion and reason from my bed and welcomed cold logic to it. I thought deeply and systematically about my position.

Item: I had not demanded to see Stein's copy of the contract. That omission must be corrected.

Item: I was completely unarmed and absolutely unequal to any great physical exertion.

Item: The Foundation was powerfully armed, staffed with unquestioning servants, vastly wealthy and able to summon a collective intelligence far superior to my own.

Item: Institutions, even powerful ones, have been overthrown in the past. Or if they have not been overthrown, clever men have escaped them.

Recent examples flooded my mind. But old-fashioned uprising (I had a sudden vision of myself leading nurses and technicians armed with pitchforks and axes in an assault on the executive suites) was clearly improbable. The Foundation no doubt treated its employees well. As for escape, in my condition it was not to be dreamed of.

And then I remembered Mohandas K. Gandhi.

Had not the frail Mahatma almost single-handed secured freedom for an entire subcontinent—simply by starving himself? Of course I did not compare myself to Gandhi. I could not claim the spiritual adoration of multitudes, nor did people throughout the world hang on my digestive processes. But just as the English, due to their overdeveloped sensibilities, could not allow such a man to kill himself on their very hands as it were, so The Foundation, which was, after all, a place of treatment and mercy, could not allow one of its patients to starve himself to death.

Nurse Williams brought me my tray of grayish mush at five-thirty that evening as usual. I recall thinking it was much easier to refuse that abominable garbage than it would have been to turn back a hot curry—one of my

favorite dishes—and wondering if the English had not
tempted Gandhi with *his* favorite food and concluding
that if they had, then that was some slight measure of his
spiritual superiority to me. I waited until she had completed her ritual. First the long gray curtains were drawn
across my wall-length windows. As she reached up for the
cord I noted how her right breast weighed freely against
the stiff whiteness of her uniform. For the moment I became completely absorbed in my old problem. A breast
properly trapped within a brassiere could never have
moved so freely. Or could it? What, after all, did I know
about modern underwear? Perhaps some clever stratagem
involving hinges . . .

"Good evening, Professor," she said, in a voice I had
long since learned to detest. It was bright, hopeful, a
winsome chirp of a voice, a professionally tutored singsong. It reminded me of a 33⅓ r.p.m. record played at 45
r.p.m. "Here's our dinner." (hoo)

Now, like all the lower employees of The Foundation,
Nurse Williams had been taught to speak in the first-
person plural conspirative. Although this grated on my
sensibilities I had never previously questioned it because
I had been too fascinated by the movement of her very
soft and round lips to wish to silence or even interrupt
them. They caressed every word that escaped them and
always formed an entrancing oval at the end of every
sentence as if they were appending the word "hoo" or
blowing out a distant match. But because of my present
irritation I said, "Are you eating with me tonight, Williams?"

She smiled professionally as she wheeled the table over
the foot of my bed and up to my chest. "No, Professor,
we're not allowed to eat with patients." (hoo)

"Then why do you refer to it as 'our' dinner?"

Her breasts were within one foot of my nose as she arranged the plates on the tray before me. With a simple movement of my hand I could resolve the great mystery . . .

"Oh, it's just a manner of speaking." (hoo)

"Well, it is more inappropriate than ever tonight. I refuse to eat." I watched her reaction carefully. Her smile seemed to lose a tiny fraction of its spread and her wide green eyes to narrow imperceptibly.

"We aren't hungry?"

She had failed to hoo and I noted the fact. "It happens that we are so hungry that even this detestable slop seems appetizing. But we refuse to eat."

She smiled conspiratorially. "Did we know that we have a surprise tonight?" (hoo) She walked over to the far table and pulled open a drawer. When she turned she had a bundle of note folders clutched to her breasts. So surprised was I by this sudden digression that I did not at first notice that they were familiar—that they were in fact my own.

"Where did you get those?" I cried, my voice quivering with anger. "Those are mine! Give them to me!"

"Doctor Stein thought we'd like to have them here to give us something to think about. Doctor Stein is so thoughtful." (hoo) She carefully placed them on the table beside my bed.

"Where are the rest? Those are only a small—"

"Now, we mustn't worry. There is an entire trunkful of folders like these upstairs. And lots of books. And a kerosene stove. I just picked out the first ones on top. I thought we'd start on these." (hoo)

I recognized the folders containing notes from American Indian cultures and also certain personal papers. "Have you read any of those?"

"No, it's all much too advanced for me." (hoo)

I silently cursed Stein for being right. I *was* relieved, interested and in some sense revivified by the sight of even this small fraction of my work. But I determined to push my plan through regardless. "You can take the food away, Williams."

"Not eating isn't going to help our condition now, is it, Professor?" (hoo)

"It will undoubtedly kill us within a very short time. That is our intention. We are being held prisoner here. Very well, we are on a hunger strike. Unless we are released immediately we will commit suicide by starvation."

My sarcastic usage was lost on her. She folded her hands together and looked down on me with benign pity, her smile however a mere phantom of itself.

"We are really serious? We really refuse to eat?" (hoo)

"Please," I moaned, "I am not unfortunately a part of you. I am an objective being. Please call me 'you' from time to time just to reassure me."

A slight frown of incomprehension furrowed her brow and then quickly disappeared. "If it is that important to us we will certainly call us 'you' from now on, you." (hoo)

Her smile regained its bland gaiety and she busied herself wheeling the table away. There was something entirely too indifferent in her manner, something that could not be attributed entirely to training, indoctrination, simple-mindedness. It was as if she had anticipated, even welcomed, my decision!

"Doctor Stein will be worried," I suggested.

"Oh, we could never trouble Doctor Stein with such a small detail of administration." (hoo)

"I imagine Doctor Stein will not regard it as a detail when he realizes that one of his patients is considering suicide."

She lifted the tray and paused before the door, turning that sunny smile full on me. "I do not think we could disturb him about it. He has so many more important things to do." (hoo)

"It will make excellent news: 'Professor Webster starves himself to death while a patient at The Foundation,'" I warned.

"The Foundation never permits news of its clients to reach the mass media." (hoo)

"Now wait a minute, Williams! This is serious. I'm threatening suicide. I'll do it, too. The news will get out. The publicity will be terrible. The public will learn everything—everything: how you've kept me prisoner here, how you laughed when I starved myself to death, how—" But my voice died away beneath that steady, pleasant, vacuous stare. She was right, of course. No one would ever hear of this. I would die. My body would be dissected or submitted to whatever humiliations Stein planned for it. Most of me would be cremated or buried. And who would ever know of it? I had no family. If news of this ever reached M she would only laugh. My only friend in all the world was Suskind. And he was too cautious to even inquire about me.

"I've changed my mind," I muttered. "Bring back the mush. I'll eat."

Nurse Williams opened the door to leave, still bearing the tray of food.

"I said I'd eat," I called out irritably.

She turned to hoo at me once more and then quickly left the room, pulling the door shut behind her.

"Eat!" I shouted. "Wait a minute! You can't starve a patient! You—"

Suddenly I felt very weak, and very tired.

I believe it was that very night that time disengaged for me. There were long stretches during which it seemed to be idling. These were periods of pure and simple duration. Nothing occurred within them, although I had not lost my memory. Then there were other occasions when time slipped back into gear, but into an unimaginably high gear that rushed my entire life-memory through events in the past and present toward some not too distant collision. Try as I will, to this day I can remember almost nothing of this period, save only the dream.

The dream occurred several times and never differed in pattern. I was always lying in bed, half-stupefied with drugs yet somehow aware that it was late at night. The door would open silently, cautiously. A man dressed in a pale-blue uniform devoid of insignia would tiptoe into my room. He was short, stocky, had black curly hair, a large nose, an aggressively square chin, puffy cheeks and strangely pale, blue, reflective eyes. He always clenched an unlit pipe between his teeth. He would scrutinize me from the foot of my bed, examine the clip board of charts that hung from it and then glance at his wristwatch and leave. The first time this dream occurred, so vivid was it that I asked, "Who are you?" But my dream figure did not, of course, hear my dream voice. I had this dream many times until finally I wondered if the figure was Death itself.

I never mentioned my dream to Stein or Williams. I had lost interest in them. I think I had lost the will to live. Whether they fed me or not I can't recall, nor whether Nurse Williams referred to me as you or we, nor for that matter whether she even visited me regularly. All that lost its importance. I was withdrawing into myself. And as I vacated outlying emotions, sense, cares, I became more and more outwardly impersonal. This is difficult to explain. But I have promised you the truth.

It was as if I was a scattered army retreating from the scene of a disastrous defeat. As the soldiers fled they joined together for warmth and protection. But they gradually lost all remembrance of their former outposts. They were weary; they had stood sentry duty for too many years and no longer cared if the enemy infiltrated their abandoned lines.

But that is not all. Now forget, if you will, the retreat of this army. Think of your mind as a carnivore. It has been feasting for years at a well-laden table. Now it loses all appetite for this external food. It begins to devour itself, forgetting that it has ever known any other sustenance, losing its appetite for the objective as its hunger for the subjective increases.

And to these two conceits now add that of a tarantula awakening and seeking to leave its burrow beneath a cold stone. This tarantula is something that has grown within or behind your subconscious for many years. Every hair on its body is a forgotten memory. It exists in a cavern into which you have carelessly thrust all the life-experience for which you had no need. It is made of this material. But you never realized that it would grow into a shape, achieve form, coherence. Now it is scraping at the crumbling walls of its cavern, at the stone above. It is being born although it has been aborning for years. And you watch its emergence impersonally, with little subjective curiosity but with much objective fear. You suspect that this tarantula will live after you have died.

All this was happening within me to a consciousness that became more and more indifferent as it retreated into the deepest core of my being. But the old me, the supercharged I, at least solved one problem before it was extinguished.

I have been told that I died on September first. I must accept that on faith, since I had long since been washed away from the shores of time. I recall opening my eyes and seeing Nurse Williams standing at the foot of my bed. She was studying the clip board in her hands intently. She had removed her starched white cap, which was lying on the armchair, and the soft golden-red of her hair gleamed in the shaded reflection of the night light. Next to her stood a young intern staring at me with insolent curiosity. It may have been his attitude as much as anything else that determined me to cast caution aside.

"Williams," I said, "I can't seem to feel my pulse."

She glanced at me in some surprise, then quickly at the intern. He nodded and left the room.

"That isn't surprising, Professor. It took me one whole month of training before I could take a pulse properly." (hoo)

"But, Williams, I've felt everywhere. I'm worried." My cunning was informed by urgency. For I had awakened to a chill in my legs that seemed to be moving upwards. It would soon reach my groin, and before that happened I wanted to—

"We mustn't worry about something like that." (hoo) She replaced the clip board on its hook at the foot of my bed.

"Still . . . would you mind very much?" I held up my wrist limply.

"Oh, all right." She came around to the side of my bed

and bent to grip my wrist, glancing automatically at her wristwatch.

As she bent forward her breasts swelled, spreading open a gap between two buttons of her uniform. *She wore no brassiere!* The problem was solved!

And those shadowed hemispheres were within reach. I pulled her down onto me suddenly, ripping open the line of buttons that ran down her uniform with one hand while the other explored the softness of her thighs. I could feel every round inch of her body struggling against me through the thin sheet that separated us.

"Professor!" she yelled.

Then, before she could mouth another word, I smothered her lips with mine. But she wriggled free and jumped back from the bed, her figure enticingly revealed behind the ripped fragments of her uniform. Her eyes were wide with shock and she wiped her lips with the back of her hand. Then she began to back slowly toward the door, one hand fumbling behind her for the knob.

I tossed aside the bed sheet and jumped up. "I'm not as sick as you think, Williams," I snickered. "Not as sick as all that. Try your hoo on this!" I pointed triumphantly.

She stared in mingled shock and horror as if it were a snake. Then she had opened the door and was running down the corridor, shrieking, "He's up! He's after me! Help!"

As I followed her into the corridor I felt the sudden cold of the tiles beneath my feet and paused. But then I laughed because I knew that she could not escape. Every door on this corridor was locked except one. And at that time of night, who was there to hear, let alone interfere? I had no need to run. I walked deliberately after her, conscious of my dignity.

She pounded hysterically on the locked doors of empty rooms, a hopeless quaver informing her screams. When she reached the end of the hall she turned and crouched like an animal at bay judging my approach. When I was within a few feet of her she suddenly darted past me before I could catch hold of more than her uniform, which now fell into a little white heap on the floor beside me. As I turned after her my thigh brushed against the cold tile wall and once again I paused. I admired the movement of her buttocks as she ran down the corridor to the one open room—my own. I knew she could not lock that door from the inside, and my step became even more deliberately majestic. I was inevitable.

I found her lying upon my bed, her body huddled into a delightful fetus shape, a pink and shadowed topography of luscious hills and delightful valleys. As I approached she said, "Don't come too close. I'm cool, but I'm not a necrophiliac." (hoo)

Not a necrophiliac? I frowned. She would feel how much heat this body could still generate. Anger added strength to my lust. I spread her flat beneath me and then felt her give up the struggle. She formed a web of her legs for me and her body arched to my own as I took her. One of her hands caressed the back of my neck. Another hand scratched lightly at the small of my back. Another hand began to tickle my right ear. Another hand traced a delicate line down my thigh, while still another hand—

Suddenly a panic so terrible that I could not breathe flooded my chest. I screamed. I struggled to escape. But the soft black spider beneath me held me firm within its brittle claws. "I told you not to come too close," a thin, scraping voice whispered. "I *am* a necrophiliac!"

My shrieks were clogged by something soft and mucous

that filled my mouth. I did not dare to open my eyes.
Then suddenly I fell right through the spider and onto my
bed, flat on my back. I opened my eyes. There was the
white field of sheet spreading away to the foot of my bed.
There beyond it stood Nurse Williams glancing quickly
from me to her wristwatch. And beside her stood Dr.
Stein.

"Terminal erection at seven thirty-eight," Williams
said.

Stein nodded, but his face was a mask of *my* weary
decay. His eyelids drooped, his mouth sagged, his breathing became thin and fluttery. Then his eyes closed . . .

I fell into a blood-red blackness. But was that all? I
have promised to withhold nothing. Yet I might endanger
—mislead you. For I cannot now be certain of everything.
But there is one certainty burned into my memory. As I
fell I was not alone. That tarantula accompanied me all
the way. And all the while it was spinning its web. I
watched it spinning, too fascinated now to be concerned
by the heaviness that was collapsing my chest at these
depths. Then there came the taste of salt water and I
realized that the spider and I were not falling through
empty space but rather through some heavy, sluggish sea.
We were both caught in an undertow that was dragging
us from a forgotten shore to unfathomable deeps. And still
the spider spun unconcernedly. It spun a multicolored
web in which I knew I was destined to remain enmeshed
forevermore—as a spider myself, spinning a web of my
own, the thin strands of it sucked from my own being . . .

That is as much as I can tell you.

And that there was no time during which all this happened. There was not even duration, for that would imply
waiting, a passage. Nor can I recall precisely when I

began to draw new vitality from the web.

Did my life now pass before me in a timeless rush? No. But I did experience final judgment. For only those memories that tortured, humiliated and obsessed me now arose from their hiding places to accuse, judge and punish. Nor were they memories of evil I had done only to others. No. They were each and every one searing glimpses of the evil I had done also to myself. My spider-soul was its own executioner. It arrayed before me every hurt, every humiliation, every pain I had inflicted upon myself from the earliest times, and with a vivid clarity that made their recurrence a hell more terrible than any ever predicted by the most ferocious saint. I will give you but one example.

I have spoken before of what I believe is an innate longing in all of us for pure love. One thinks of the love of brothers, of the love of God, of the ever-present possibility of such love between man and woman. And I have re-ferred also to my instinctual dread of trusting in the purity of something so vital. I am not ashamed to admit that during most of my younger years I remained a bache-lor. I was not without sexual experience, of course. But it had always been haphazard, unimportant—until I met M. And in her, for the first time, I saw, or suspected I saw, the possibility of a pure love as well as sexual attraction.

First of all I ought to describe her. It was essentially in her face that purity resided. She had a very high brow, clear, frank eyes—and she was not what would ordinarily be described as a beautiful woman. Yet with the essential innocence of her face was combined tremendous sug-gestiveness of body. It was somewhat plump—hinted at the luxury of an oriental divan with pillows creased in-vitingly. Her hair was a very dark reddish-mahogany color.

Nor did she dress or comport herself in ways calculated to accentuate her natural gifts. Her mode of dress was usually disorderly, her comportment completely natural. Her physical presence suggested deep somnolence, her attitude was one of modest retirement.

But unfortunately there was more than that to M. There was also the uncanny ability to arouse a man's desires, ensnare him helplessly—there was her primary weapon: Passive Pursuit.

I later tried to explain all this to Learned Counsel in his chambers. But I could tell from the bovine incredulity of his politically handsome face, the leering deprecation with which he heard me out, that I had failed.

"I am not at all sure I know what you mean by Passive Pursuit, Professor Webster," he remarked, in that hearty voice that had long since passed from being an affectation to a definition.

"I mean that she will sit in a chair with her legs properly crossed, her dress properly pulled down to her knees, her hands sitting in her lap, her eyes vacant, and she's unaware of anyone else's presence—and yet she's pursuing them. I mean *pursuing* them! Maybe it's waves or something."

"I would hate to attempt to explain that to a jury, Professor."

"You won't have to. She'll just sit in the witness chair as decorous as you please and every man in the room including the judge will be wondering about her."

Learned Counsel frowned slightly, leaned back in his leather swivel chair, puffed thoughtfully on his cigar and stared wisely at a wallful of law books.

That was only a foretaste of how difficult it was going to be to justify myself to my fellow men.

Q. Now surely, Mrs. Webster, you were not seriously alarmed by your husband's—well, shall we call it a practical joke?

A. I was. I was very definitely at first.

Q. You were angry at him?

A. Yes. But then I felt sorry for him.

Q. Sorry for him? Yet you lied to police officers at the time.

A. I—I thought it would be a good lesson to him.

Of course I knew where this testimony was leading. Learned Counsel had already warned me that police officers had been summoned by M's attorney to testify. But what could their testimony do to mitigate the proven fact of M's malicious lie on that occasion?

For what did not and could not appear from the pallid testimony of the witness stand was the basic inadequacy M made me feel in our relationship. The simple fact of the matter is that I seemed unable to arouse in her that height of sexual passion of which I suspected her capable. There was a languor, a somnolence, in her response that disturbed me. Oh, she was affectionate enough. But it was not affection I was seeking, not merely love I demanded; it was something else besides. Reassurance?

If I came to consider our sexual relationship a continuing challenge, a bitterly fought campaign that I was losing, the fault, I knew, must lie with me. It was a constant, though secret, source of humiliation to me, a bottomless well of agonized calculation. How could I arouse in her more than affectionate warmth? How could I inflame her as I knew she had a right to expect, even if she never mentioned the matter? Nor were more general considerations lacking. I had read psychology. I had absorbed, from the broad hints of national advertising campaigns, the central social dilemma of our times. I knew that American women were dissatisfied with their condition, sublimating passionless sex by exchanging roles with men. I knew the awful statistics of orgasm. And I felt my share of responsibility.

And I wondered too if she would have responded with as much apathy to Tony Buono. Not that he was a part of our life. Only on infrequent forays into the Village did we sometimes catch glimpses of him. In deference to my obvious dislike of him M always treated him quite coolly on these occasions. And this too I found repugnant. It implied that there was another, more natural response to his presence that she might have made without me.

Of course, her attraction to him was childish, I knew. But I felt very strongly that it nevertheless stood between us. And it was purely to exorcise this barrier, to strengthen rather than to weaken our relationship, that I stumbled into disaster.

The inspiration that was to lead to calamity came to me on a raw November night while I was returning late from a meeting of the History Department staff. As I left the subway station and turned onto the slush-filled street that led to our apartment building, I passed two rapists. I knew them by the fact that their overcoats were buttoned up to their necks although they wore no hats. Their coarse and brutal features were composed in a look of dreamy interior lust, while their tiny coal-black eyes examined each woman speculatively as she emerged from the subway station. Finally, as a young girl walked past, they exchanged glances, nodded to each other and followed her off into the night. Here was the type, the true type of Tony Buono, carried to its logical extreme. And how would M react to a real encounter with such a brute?

Perhaps this had been lacking; perhaps a touch of terror, a hint of brute force, would crack open the chrysalis of her indifference. I pondered the matter as I trudged down the street. But now I was standing outside our apartment building. I smiled bitterly to myself as I realized the desperation of my search for some means of combating the shade of Tony Buono. But bitterness turned quickly into resentment. After all, my position was shameful. The degradation of my situation (perhaps underscored by my encounter with the two rapists) presented itself very nakedly to my mind. Who did she think she was, anyhow? What right had she to undermine my confidence?

And it was then, in the desperate bitterness of my soul, that an exciting possibility presented itself to me. And you must understand that my purpose was not only to save my self-respect and hence our marriage, to help M to enjoy sex more completely; it was also social. I would put certain theories to the test on behalf of society as a whole. I would play a joke, a practical joke which, if it did not lead to beneficial stimulation, would at least provide social evidence.

I removed my hat and left it on the polished brass hydrant that emerged from our building. I buttoned my overcoat up to my neck, disheveled my hair and then sneaked around the building toward its rear. I knew I could pass down the narrow delivery passage without being observed. I sidled past rows of garbage cans, careful not to make a sound, until I found myself in the small areaway behind the building. Above me a cat's cradle of fire escape climbed upward, its first stage swung aloft out of reach. I solved that problem neatly by bringing around an empty garbage can to stand on. But as I pulled the fire-escape ladder down, it creaked loudly. I froze, listening intently. No unusual sound disturbed the steady hum of the city's silence; luck was with me. I began to climb. As I progressed slowly and carefully from landing to landing I chuckled softly to myself. I could picture the gratifying terror of M's reaction to what was going to happen. I would do a thorough job of it, overlook no detail. Then I found myself crouching outside the window of our seventh-floor apartment. I took out my pocket handkerchief and fixed it across my face, bandit fashion.

She was sitting in a large easy chair, reading a book and sipping beer from a can. Her position was such that the window was just visible over her right shoulder. Perfect! My plan was to rap once very lightly on the windowpane and then disappear before she turned her head. I would repeat that several times until she grew definitely uneasy. Then I would permit her to catch such a fugitive glance of me as would leave her uncertain as to whether or not anyone was, in fact, on the fire escape. Not until she had risen and shown definite signs of alarm would I show myself completely (I had unzippered my pants for greater effect). Then before she could reach the phone, I would had thrown up the window (the latch of which was broken), torn the handkerchief from my face and been prepared to comfort her. I raised my hand to tap lightly on the glass.

Suddenly the night was turned to brightest, blinding day. Light flooded upon me as from a bursting sun. The very reflection of it on the window blinded me. I reached out, stunned and blinking, to grasp the fire-escape railing, my balance shattered by the great glare that bathed me.

"Make one little move and you're dead!" a hoarse voice called from far below.

When I looked down I could see only the blinding light

of two powerful searchlights directed upward at me. What had happened? I could hear other muffled voices emerging from the blinding light below.

"He's outside seven B," a voice shouted.

"No, no," I protested weakly, "I'm outside seven G."

Then I heard the window behind me open and a voice from within shout, "OK, Jack, get in here quick! Get ready, Mike!"

"I can't move," I explained. "They said I'd be dead if I moved."

"Don't be wise, you bastard!"—the voice from within.

"You got him, Charlie?"—the voice from below.

"You bet we got him!"—the voice from within.

"OK then, take him!"—the voice from below.

I felt huge hands grab my arms and brutally drag me backward through the open window. As I bumped and scraped through, my eyes grew accustomed to normal light. I was lying on the floor at the feet of three burly policemen. Two of them had revolvers drawn. One of them leaned out the window. "OK, we got him. Radio precinct." The lights that inflamed the window were suddenly blackened and I could hear a distant sound of powerful engines starting.

"OK, get up!" A booted foot kicked me in the shoulder. I struggled to my feet, still too stunned to protest at this outrageous treatment in my own home. From somewhere I could hear M sobbing hysterically. I turned to see where she was but could see nothing but blue.

There seemed to be an army of police officers in our living room. From beneath visored caps, faces set in stony contempt stared at me. I knew that my position required an intelligent and understanding face with which to communicate. But as I glanced from one to another I saw only the fixed and savage indifference of triumphant force. I addressed myself to a corporal, hoping that the lines of age around his narrow eyes denoted some experience, some humanity. "This is my own house," I said meekly.

"Frisk him," the corporal said menacingly.

Hands traveled expertly down my body from behind. "He's clean."

"Uh-huh." The corporal turned toward M, who now appeared cowering against a far wall, her hands pressed tightly against her mouth, her eyes still watery. But even in the brief glimpse I recognized something wrong in her posture. When she cried she did not normally bring her hands to her mouth.

"You ever see this guy before, lady?" the corporal demanded.

M's eyes met mine. I then recognized in them a look that boded evil. "No," she said in a stage whisper of calculated drama, "I've never seen him before."

"What are you saying?" I shrieked.

"You shut your filthy mouth!" a harsh voice warned.

"And he was peering into your window, molesting you, correct?" The corporal's tone was precise, indifferently professional.

"Was he? Yes—yes, he was!" M's voice cracked slightly and she stared at me in a way that only I could know was mocking. Suddenly I realized that the reason she kept her hands over her mouth was to keep herself from laughing out loud!

"Corporal, please," I whimpered, "she's my wife. Really—" I cringed as I saw his hand clench.

"You sure you never saw him before?" The corporal did not even glance at me, had not even heard me.

"Never."

"All right, let's take him away." The corporal signaled to one of his men, who produced a pair of handcuffs.

"Wait, wait—I can prove right here and now that I belong here," I protested. "Look—look, I've got identification!" But no one seemed to pay the slightest attention to my remarks. The policemen were reholstering their revolvers while one of them snapped the handcuffs around my wrists. "Let me show you, please!" I begged.

The corporal shrugged. "Take his papers," he ordered.

I felt a thrill of hope. My papers would establish my innocence. A policeman unbuttoned my overcoat. And then everyone seemed to freeze. I realized that the corporal was staring at me as if I were some sort of loathsome snake. His hand, clenched into a fist, was drawing back. In the split second before it crashed into my face and I lost consciousness, I realized that my pants were still unzippered.

Q. And what precinct are you attached to, Sergeant?

A. Tenth Precinct, Counselor.

Q. And when you examined Plaintiff on this peeping-tom-and-exposure charge what defense did he offer?

A. He alluded to the fact that the woman outside of whose window he'd been caught was his wife.

Q. He alluded to that fact?

A. Yes, Counselor, he alluded to it.

Q. I see. And what measures did you take at that time?

A. Well, Counselor, first of all we informed him that it was still an offense even though it was his own wife.

Q. What did Plaintiff say to this?

A. He said it was a sort of a joke and he would definitely not repeat.

Q. I see. Now, in your experience of sexual perverts,
and rapists, Sergeant—

COUNSEL: Objection.

COURT: Sustained. Clerk will strike that last question
from the record.

Q. If the Court so please, it is a question of credibility.

A question of credibility! While on the stand the brutish face of Sergeant McNally peered blandly at the judge
as if it had never smiled savagely down at me from behind
its desk in the 10th Precinct Station House and given vent
to the most threatening and abusive language.

For I recovered consciousness only as I was being
dragged into the precinct station. And there above me sat
McNally (whose name I learned only later, when I attempted to gather evidence of police brutality), his wide,
choleric face staring at me in badly simulated wonder.
"Who brought him in?" he asked in a stage whisper.

"Fifth Squad, Sergeant," the corporal standing next to
me replied.

"Fifth Squad!" McNally's eyes widened and he gasped
in horror. "You're the luckiest man in the city of New
York, Mac," he said wonderingly, shaking his head owl-
ishly from side to side. "Fifth Squad never brings anyone
in alive."

"We looked through his papers while he was in the car,
Sergeant. It looks like he really does live there and is that
lady's husband. She probably won't make any charges."
The corporal spoke very regretfully. But if my hopes rose
suddenly, they were as quickly dashed.

"We don't need any charges from her," McNally said briskly, rubbing his horny hands together over the blotter. "Indecent exposure, trespassing, vagrancy— We could send you up for five to seven years on our own." He frowned thoughtfully for a calculated moment. "What made you do this?"

"I—well—it's a sort of little joke I was playing—"

"A little joke?"

"Well, sort of—yes."

"Like Jack the Ripper?"

"No—it's hard to explain . . ." I could feel the floor slipping from beneath my feet.

"I bet it is," McNally remarked drily. "It's a public menace, too!" he suddenly shouted. "And from what I heard about your wife's reactions I don't think she knew it was a joke! We didn't know it was a joke! Do you think the police have nothing better to do than play jokes?"

"No. I mean, yes—I don't know—"

"Of course," he went on in a suddenly reasonable tone, "it is not our policy to interfere in strictly matrimonial problems. What else have you got to say about all this?"

"I've been hit," I said sullenly.

"Resisting arrest."

"I want to see a lawyer."

"You do?" McNally's voice was definitely menacing now.

"No—no, not really. I mean—"

McNally smiled. "I can see that you're a reasonable man, Mac, in spite of being a nut. Now, it seems you teach at the University. There's no previous record. Tell you what I'll do. Now, if you want to make a federal case out of this, why, there's the telephone, go right ahead. Call anyone you like. We'll send you up for five to seven, take my word for it. And when you get out you're not gonna teach at any university anywhere. On the other hand, your wife phoned us a few minutes ago. That's a loyal little lady you've got there, Mac. A fine woman. In spite of your disgusting behavior, she's willing to take you back. She's willing to let bygones be bygones. Of course you'll have to correct your conduct. Now, I'll be willing to let you go without even entering your name on the blotter— on one condition. That is that I'm putting you in your wife's custody from now on. If she ever makes one complaint against you from here on in, we'll throw the book at you. You got that?"

I felt my head reeling. In M's custody! Her hand only to touch a telephone to have me ruined, imprisoned! A prisoner to her vagaries, her whims! But the alternative was instant disaster. For I had no doubt that McNally's threats were not mere. I nodded dumbly.

"You accept that condition?"

"I accept," I whispered.

"Yep, that's one fine little lady you've got there," McNally said admiringly. "It's not every woman would take back a man and protect him and take responsibility for him after what you've done!"

But what a shadow human justice is! A travesty of the terrible justice of the psyche. For as I sank deeper into unfathomable deeps, I seemed to suffer this black memory in reverse. It was as if a photograph I knew by heart melted into its negative. The aggrieved plaintiff was now the defendant; sharply defined rationalizations disappeared to be replaced by their hollow outlines; blocks of justification became transparent. Was that me, in the negative? Or some hopelessly twisted caricature? An all-engulfing sense of shame was my judgment, my execution,

as my soul became my accuser, as it drew searing strands
of memory more real than existence itself from my falling
being and spun, alongside the spider into which it sometimes merged, a web . . .

I am told that I returned to life on September eighth.
But I have already explained that it could not be truly a
matter of returning to life. Life had now, for me, a new
and dreadful definition. Stein does not know this. Oh, in
his way, in his purely medical terms, he is right. I did
return to life. But now you know what *my* terms are.

The first change was that the web, which had been
grayish, translucent, suddenly acquired color. Now it was
composed of strands of brilliant red, green, blue and
violet. And instead of extending away from me into pure
pattern, instead of drawing from my being, these strands
now seemed to be feeding back strength and consciousness to the center, bit by bit. The spider? It was retreating
now, up those strands of power. It had become, like me,
a witness to the exploding warmth of sentience within my
cells. Can spiders live under water?

For I awoke beneath the sea. The strands of my web
wavered slightly. They existed beyond a film of liquid
light. I was at the core of some deep-sea anemone and my
multicolored tentacles caressed the depths of a milk-white
sea. Nor was this a silent sea. Voices penetrated it. They
were indistinguishable from each other, murmurous, distant, heavy . . .

". . . ay attention to readings."

"One hundred and ten over sixty-seven."

"Glucose three percent."

"Respirator one hundred and one."

"Careful with that tube, if you please!"

One of the red strands wavered abruptly.

"Fifty-four, fifty-three—"

"Oxygen ratio one in two, please."

"Fifty-two, fifty-one, now mark—fifty!"

"CNH off."

"Breathing normal unassisted."

Then silence.

Then—

"You may remove the tent."

The milky-white sea around me crumbled, seemed to tear. Brilliant light streamed down upon me. I was lying naked beneath a sun, a huge and fearful white eye that illuminated every corner of my being.

"Congratulations become meaningless at a moment like this, Doctor Stein."

"They are, in any event, premature. An oscillator reading, please."

A voice said, "Eighty-seven."

Then a fragment of face intruded between me and the sun. It was a narrow rectangle of eyebrows, bridge of nose and wide, staring blue eyes, defined by tight white cloth above and below. The eyes were Stein's. They seemed momentarily frightened and then slowly closed as I fell into a dreamless sleep.

I am told that I slept for two weeks. But I will not bore you with all the details of my recovery. There was a time of tubes when I was aware only of innumerable needles being inserted into and removed from my limbs, of bottles clustered above me. I even had to evacuate through a hose for some time. Then gradually this vital web of plastic was removed, strand by strand. The grayish gruel reappeared on my dinner table. It was brought by Nurse Williams, who now, though she said little, treated me with greater respect. I wondered from time to time if she suspected that I had raped her.

What were my feelings at this time? I had none. I was too exhausted for elation or even for gratitude. Indeed I was unaware that anything more than a severe crisis in my condition had been surmounted. It was true that I felt no pain now; but then, I had expected deterioration. I was afraid to ask questions. But Stein answered them for me anyhow.

Sometime during the third week he visited me. Because of the unpleasant effect his face had upon me, he sat in an armchair facing away from me, staring out the windows that overlooked the park. I could see only the huge bald dome of his head above the brown leather back of the chair. I was still too feeble to fight him.

"You have recovered from a severe crisis," he said.

There was an undertone to his normally shrill voice that disturbed me. But I had determined not to flatter him with questions.

"A very grave crisis," he repeated. He cleared his throat. "In fact, you have been dead," he said slowly, with careful emphasis on each word.

The chill within me now turned to ice, and my determination crumbled. "I have not been dead—"

"Yes, you have. You will have to accept that fact. You must accept it. It is true. You have been dead. You have been dead for six days, twenty-two hours and seventeen minutes. You must understand that this was complete death—there was no attempt to keep you alive artificially in any way. All of your vital organs died with your body. All we did was to reconstitute certain elements—chemical elements of blood and brain fluid—at the proper time.

We have a coroner's certificate of your death dated September first. You were thoroughly, legally and satisfactorily dead. This is a great milestone for science—for the entire human race."

"But I tell you I wasn't . . ." My voice faltered before the stony silence with which Stein greeted my words, before the memory of a web, a spider. I shut my eyes and felt the life in my limbs, my fingers, my lips. My soul would not swallow the lie I was attempting so desperately to feed it. In making his brash statement, Stein had once again judged me correctly. He had allowed me no time to rationalize. Confronted with a bald statement, I was forced to accept the fact of my death and resurrection.

He rose, glanced at me with what was meant as a smile, and left the room.

I did not speak to Nurse Williams that night, nor to anyone for several days and nights thereafter. For if I could encompass the fact of my death rationally, I could not face it emotionally. And like a man in a snake pit I found myself hideously fascinated by the loathsome speculations that now rose from my emotional chaos to strike at me. I could not prevent myself from dwelling upon, even gloating over, morbid details.

It was during this period that Stein took to visiting my room nightly after I'd been fed. He would slump into the armchair at the foot of my bed and stare out the darkening window, observing silence if I did not speak, occasionally proffering unwelcome little monologues on anything in the world that struck his fancy. After several such visits I found myself ready, perhaps even eager, to discuss my experience. But I was shocked to discover that Stein had absolutely no interest whatsoever in listening to me. He evinced no curiosity about what I had known on the

farther shore of death; in fact, I now realize, he never
even permitted me to talk about it. He was a master of the
art of interruption, indirection—of monopolizing conversation. But I should have expected that from such a mon-
umental ego.

One evening, for example, I determined to broach the
subject of the life-in-death I knew awaited us all. Stein
was standing before the window, staring out into the vivid
evening sky. "Have you ever thought of death as a giant
tarantula, Doctor?" I asked. "A spider with hairy legs
that—"

"The swine! The unutterable swine!" he interrupted,
shaking his fist angrily at the view.

"The clouds anger you?" I asked, disconcerted.

"No. That great pile of concrete—those distant spires of
thievery anger me. Oh, the unutterable swine!"

"Who?"

"The Institute, of course!" He shook his head and
slumped wearily into the armchair. "We caught another
of their spies today."

"Spies?"

"Yes, spies," he said impatiently. "I assume you are
aware of the tremendous amount of espionage that goes
on between and among these foundations. Some of them
will stoop to anything. This is the second Institute spy
we've captured within the week. It's really getting to be
too much!"

"What do they want?"

"Who?"

"These spies."

"Research secrets of course! They try to steal our secret
research information for their own ends."

"Money?"

"No!" Stein slammed his hand down on the arm of the chair. "Not only money. Prestige! It's the prestige they're after! They want to be able to announce every great life-saving drug, every new physical insight, every discovery, as their own!"

"Well, aside from the money, does it really matter?"

"Does it really matter?" he mimicked me, and I was grateful he was not looking at me. "Of course it matters! How would you like the National Tuberculosis Association to announce a cure for—for cancer? What would have happened if the American Heart Association had announced the Salk antipolio vaccine? Suppose the polio foundation had announced the discovery of penicillin? In fact, what if *we* rather than the Rockefellers had announced the discovery of insulin? The greatest confusion would have resulted."

"But humanity would still have gained—"

"That's not the point! I'm afraid you simply refuse to understand. Why not allow the American Cancer Society to discover a cure for heart disease?" he demanded with bitter irony.

"It would still be a great boon to humanity, wouldn't it?" I asked.

"No, it would not! Not under those circumstances!" He breathed deeply, obviously trying to control himself. "There has been a leak somewhere," he whispered. "They know we are on to something big with you. The spies we have so far captured are small fry. Someone here is a traitor. But we'll find him one day, and then . . ." His voice died ominously.

"What do you do with spies?"

He laughed harshly. "We treat them. We treat them to a little electro-shock therapy to cleanse their foul minds and, incidentally, erase their memories. That's what we do to them. And then we send them back to The Institute swine or the cancer people or the tuberculosis thugs—or to whoever sent them—as examples. Personally I think we've been too damned decent about it all."

"And what about your own spies?"

Stein shrugged, but I could tell I'd struck home. "We maintain only a counterespionage service," he replied evasively. "We've had a few casualties over the years—martyrs to science."

He lapsed into silence. I tried to return to the subject. "Dying is a strange sensation," I remarked.

"No doubt, no doubt," he muttered. He glanced at his wristwatch, glared once again at the distant towers of The Institute and bade me good night.

I soon realized that Stein was not a normal man. This was proved by the fact that he had no desire to discuss my case with me in any of its aspects. When I brought it up—even in simple medical terms—he simply waved his hand deprecatingly and muttered that I could not be expected to understand the intricacies of it.

Instead, Stein amazed me by speaking about himself, with the utmost frankness, in the most intimate detail and about matters I had never expected to hear any man confess. I soon judged that he was mentally ill.

For instance, he had been married in the remote past and divorced. Only a completely masochistic woman could ever have lived with him. It was not that he loathed women; he simply could not resist abusing them. He admitted very freely that he had made a thorough study of his wife's predilections for the sole purpose of frustrating them. According to his analyses his wife could experience pleasure only orally. He described in clinical and unabashed detail how she used her mouth to chew, to sip, to form words, to breathe. And he told me too how once a month he would carefully plan an evening designed to insinuate oral pleasure—how he would watch her lips swell, grow moist, fairly drool with anticipation, and then, when her lust had reached hysterical proportions, this fiend would offer her only his large toe. And the poor creature in her humiliating greed would even accept, devour it. But that was many years ago. He was a disgusting man. He now used prostitutes in this same manner. I felt sure he was a secret masturbator.

It was only after a series of such revelations that it dawned on me that Stein might be practicing a little rough-and-ready psychology on me. Had he not recalled me from the dead physically? And by emphasizing himself as a hate-object perhaps he thought he was reactivating my mind, or leading it into experimentally acceptable channels. And yet I am certain he spoke only the truth. In any event, he was naturally hateful and had no need to emphasize it artificially.

I am not a patriot. In fact, the first published disclosure of certain aspects of the Theory of Place and Decay earned me a severe reprimand disguised as a solicitous inquiry from several of the University Trustees. No, I am not a patriot. And yet, I confess to a great feeling of relief when I learned that Stein was not a native-born American. He was a Hungarian, although he'd been naturalized forty years before. I realize that you, my fellow countrymen, make much of his citizenship because of the glory of his medical achievements. But you do not know the true Stein. Could a native-born American have tortured his wife in the ways he related? Brutality, vice, perversion— all these may be admitted to be part of our national character. But they rarely accompany an intelligence insidious enough to make them effective. No, Stein's aberrations smacked of an older and even more degenerate society than our own.

It seemed impossible to discuss my case, even in its nonemotive aspects, with him. As the drugs were slowly withdrawn, as I felt strength returning to my limbs and purpose to my will, I naturally tried to find out my exact medical condition. But Stein would hear nothing along those lines. To illustrate the absurd lengths of evasiveness to which he was willing to go to avoid my questions, I give but one example. Nurse Williams had just left the room and Stein had entered.

Determined not to give him any opportunity to bring up some irrelevant subject, I spat out my question even before the door shut. "Doctor Stein, I would like to know just exactly what my physical condition now is." He did not answer, but slumped into the armchair. "I am asking you officially and formally for a statement—"

"Shhh!" His finger went to his lips and his face assumed an air of cautious insinuation. Then he frowned thoughtfully.

I was so taken aback by this response that I simply stared at him dumbly.

"Professor," he said softly, his eyes intent with meaning, "do you know why we have not discussed your case openly?"

I shook my head, unconsciously drawn into his conspirative manner.

"Because we are never alone in this room—or anywhere in The Foundation."

"If you are referring to these imaginary spies—"

He waved his hand impatiently. "No. You refuse to understand. I suppose you think I am a fool. Your cynicism amazes me. I do not expect you to believe in the powers of good—that is now unfashionable. But I am surprised you have no faith in the powers of evil. You obviously do not believe in heaven. Do you also disbelieve in the Syndicate —in the Mafia, for example?"

"What? Uh—" I stuttered in open amazement. Was there no limit to this man's paranoia?

Stein studied me thoughtfully for a moment. "One hardly knows where to begin with you, Professor. Do you realize, for instance, that most of the great hotels in this city are owned and operated by the Mafia?"

"I hadn't thought about it."

"It is unquestionably true."

"Why?"

"But surely you must see. First of all, the entire bookie industry is absolutely controlled by the Mafia. You must acknowledge that."

"Perhaps."

"And what do bookies require more than anything else? What is the one implement that is essential to their trade? The telephone!" His voice rang with triumph. "And where can thousands of telephones be more effectively disguised and distributed than in a large hotel?"

It was, as always, very logical, if unreasonable.

"And of course they've taken over the commercial laundry business."

"To supply the hotels?"

"Exactly!"

"And the staffs of these hotels are all criminal then, in the employ of the Mafia?"

"Have you never stayed at one of our larger hostelries? Have you never noticed the indifference and inefficiency with which they treat their guests? Of course, there's service enough to keep a dull nose off the scent. But to a man used to experimentation, to miscroscopic observation, to logical analyses—to a scientist, in short—it is all transparent. These people are not primarily concerned with innkeeping but with some criminal operation of their own."

"Have you ever discussed these suspicions with the FBI?" I asked drily.

He snorted. "I want to live."

"Perhaps," I suggested in sudden inspiration, "they've even infiltrated The Foundation?"

He nodded vehemently, glanced around uncomfortably and said in a slightly raised voice, as if he were making a sworn statement, "I know that. *I have no objections.*" He smiled. "They may even have planted radio microphones throughout the building. *But I don't mind that, either.*"

It was difficult to imagine Stein as a child. If asked, I would have unhesitatingly sworn that he'd emerged fully grown from the thigh of some Hungarian vampire. And yet he'd had something vaguely similar to a childhood. He spoke nostalgically at times of the streets of Budapest, of the baronial estates and manors he'd known as a youth. He claimed that his first ambition had been to be a playwright and that this talent had been thwarted purely by chance. He had written a play based on the legend of Leda and the Swan, which was performed at his parents' country estate near Plith. He was fourteen years old at the time and, as he himself admits, completely and irrevocably spoiled. From his earliest recollections his parents had indulged his every whim. Until early manhood he was accustomed to throwing tantrums if his wishes were not immediately granted.

He'd been given a swan for his birthday that year (if one knew why Stein had wanted or his parents had chosen to give him a swan for his birthday, I suspect one would be much closer to an understanding of his basic character). In any event, the bird inspired him with the ambition to make a play out of the ancient legend. The cast included himself, the swan and one of the younger housemaids on the estate. This girl submitted to his direction with the ancient resignation of a class for centuries accustomed to the whims and debaucheries of the rich. But Stein was not, I fear, very frank with the poor girl. He was even then a perfectionist and, above all, a realist. The climax of the play was not rehearsed; it was left for the first actual performance, which took place in the evening on the shores of the lake behind the chateau. The audience consisted of Stein's parents and several house guests. That they made no objection to any of the proceedings and in fact expressed disappointment at the outcome may very well serve as a capsule explanation of the revolution and subsequent stormy history of their country. But you will already have guessed what Stein had arranged. You will already have seen how he suddenly and unexpectedly bound the poor housemaid and propped her over a bench in the third act, hailing the swan for his realistic denouement. The girl was saved only by the fact that the swan was in fact not a swan but a pen—which may have been due to Stein's parents' foresight.

There is no doubt that Stein was a very great doctor. His synthesis of CNH, the so-called instruction gene, has unlocked the final mystery of life and death—as my own case so vividly proves. But he is one of the few medical researchers I have ever heard of without any sense of modesty. One day as I was staring at the globe of his head rising beyond the back of the armchair, I decided to prod him on this.

"Of course," I said, "your own work rests upon many generations of research—"

He waved his fat hand deprecatingly. "My own work has been along lines previously unexplored. That is why they spy on me incessantly."

"Have you caught your master spy yet?"

"No. But we will, we will."

"No doubt your own staff has contributed greatly to—"

"Only when they thought I was watching. My staff is a collection of mental laggards, scientific main-chancers and institutional remittance men. What I have achieved I have achieved alone and in spite of their so-called co-operation. And I will achieve more."

This last remark chilled me. He intended to go further? The experiment was not complete? This decided me. I could no longer risk remaining in his hands. He might decide to kill me over and over again by way of experimental confirmation. It would be prudent, I decided, to discover what my legal status now was.

"As I understand it, our legal contract is now terminated," I said, with an indifference calculated to reassure him.

"That is correct. The person Paul Webster no longer legally exists. Legally he is dead. All his contracts and obligations have terminated."

I was unprepared for this reasonable admission. I became suspicious. "In that case," I said slowly, "if I decided to leave, you would have no legal means of preventing me. Not that I would dream of leaving while undergoing treatment."

"Of course that would be very foolish of you," he agreed pleasantly. "But your previous conclusion is somewhat faulty." He turned to face me suddenly, and his expression predicted the deep suspicion my own face masked.

"You promised not to face me," I said reproachfully.

"But I must, to make myself perfectly clear." His eyes widened with fear a split second before mine did. "As I say, Paul Webster is dead. He no longer legally exists. Who then are you? You are something created by myself and The Foundation. You belong to us in somewhat the same sense as our jars of reanimated livers, kidneys and hearts and dog brains in the vaults."

I could not bear the prediction of my rising hysteria on his face, and shut my eyes.

"Or if you prefer a different analogy, you have in a sense been born to The Foundation. You are our legal ward. We, of course, must see to your proper maintenance. After all, even foster parents have their obligations and res—"

"Stop!" I cried. "You're mad! My name is Paul Webster. I'm a free man! Stop looking like me!"

"I'm sorry," he said quietly, and purposely turned his face away as he walked to the door. "You must realize that you are the freest man who has ever lived—while you are here. There are very good reasons why you cannot be permitted to leave. But take comfort from the thought that in all the long passion of mankind you are at the very pinnacle, as it were. You are, I repeat, the freest man who has ever lived. Good night." He left the room in his light, floating balloon manner.

I puzzled over his last remark. Free? Did he mean free from the fear of death? Did he mean that having experienced death I was now free of the fear of it? If so, he was hugely mistaken. But I doubted he referred to that. Stein was not a psychologist, not a spiritualist. His references were always concrete, specific. As at so many other times in my relations with him I regretted once again that my studies had not included the physical sciences, especially anthropology. For the burden of his remarks seemed to have some anthropological basis. Suddenly one of Suskind's *bon mots* came to my mind—something he had said long ago. "Humanity," he had once lisped, "velly much like kosher pickles. Must lemain many years in bline ballel of life until explode to leleax soul."

It surprises you to learn that Suskind was something of a philosopher? He was more committed than that. He was a lay social-psychologist. Who else could conceive of human beings as potentially explosive green cucumbers bobbing and sinking in a highly spiced social brine? But this aspect of Suskind, this dedicated ruthlessness hidden behind his impassive Oriental façade, was revealed to me only after Harry's death.

For in the days immediately following Harry's electrocution and burial I experienced what was for me an uncommon emotion. By now you will have realized that I have been essentially alone most of my life, with the single exception of my relationship to M. Professional contacts I had aplenty at the University, but they did not ripen. I had never had the fortune to make friends easily. So I was unprepared for the feelings I experienced after Harry's passing. There was the chill I could not banish from my stomach every time I walked down the dim passageway to my room. There was the twinge in my bowels whenever I passed the now sadly overflowing garbage cans. To use the bathroom (from which I had removed the lethal electric heater) brought a lump to my throat.

And I found myself almost unconsciously listening in the small hours of the night for the shuffle of Harry's feet, the deep tubercular cough, the gently inquiring rap on my door. Nor was mine a morbid fancy. I had no desire to visit Harry's grave in the basement, even with Suskind riding shotgun on the rats. I had no desire to possess any mementos of his existence; I do not enjoy funeral meats. No, I was suffering from pure and unalloyed loneliness caused by the death of the man who had been my only friend.

It was largely to exorcise this feeling that I struck up a closer acquaintance with Suskind. After all, we were now the sole inhabitants of that ancient building. And, of course, we shared a guilty knowledge. Loneliness, conspiracy, propinquity—and simple neighborly courtesy—drew us together. It was I who made the first move.

I'd been taking notes that night on Prescott's *Conquest of Mexico* (so rich in examples of the influence of place on decay), and as usual I'd given myself up wholly to the author. I was accoutered in sacrificial feathers, being led by hideously masked priests up the thousands of steps of the great pyramid. The night was illuminated by fiery torches and the great drum of Moctezuma reverberated with chilling horror in my bosom. Slowly, slowly, the procession climbed to the very top of the pyramid. There was the insinuatingly stained sacrificial stone, the high priests clutching obsidian blades in their talon hands. Suddenly I was seized, dragged to the block, stretched across it, as nightmare figures swooped down to tear the living heart from my chest. The great drum boomed twice in quick succession and I jumped up, upsetting the table, spilling books, lamp, notes, cigarettes and coffee cup onto the floor. For a fraction of a second I stood there feeling my chest for a hole where the obsidian blades had penetrated—until I realized that Suskind had pulled off a double-header in the basement below.

My first reaction was, I confess, bitter. As I carefully righted the table and gathered up my scattered notes I reflected that if our basement was the bowels of the earth, then Suskind and his shotgun were surely a sort of purge. It was not a pretty image, but my feelings were upset. I heard his heavy tread upon the stairs and down the corridor to the closing of a distant door as I prepared myself another pot of coffee. But after all, his was a necessary function. I wondered idly what would happen if he abandoned his Horatio-like post in the basement. Certainly the rats would soon take over the entire building, perhaps then spread to neighboring buildings, perhaps conquer the entire city? These fancies were abbreviated by my sudden realization that I was out of sugar. I cannot drink unsugared coffee.

As you know, I have strong feelings about privacy, and even stronger feelings about household thrift. But it was two in the morning, my nerves were taut, my work for the night was completed and—let me be completely truthful —this was Harry's hour. This was the time when we would have shared a strong pot of coffee and exchanged gossip and news of the day. But Harry slept below and the echoes of Moctezuma's drum still sounded in my soul. I picked up a cup and walked down the corridor to Suskind's door, at which I tapped politely.

"Who?" Suskind growled from within.

"It's me," I called softly, reflecting that it could be no one else.

The door opened and Suskind's pendulous body filled it. His bald head dully reflected the light behind him and his slanted eyes peered at me suspiciously.

"I was just wondering if I could borrow a cup of sugar," I said. "I'll give it back to you tomorrow . . ." My voice faltered before that inscrutable stare.

"Sure, sure," Suskind said, with a bargaining smile. "You give it back teacup and a half alla same?"

"Yes," I agreed. But I was no longer looking at him. My attention had been distracted by the scene that his body partly blocked. It was unbelievable. The room behind him was a veritable warehouse of junk: towering piles of objects, of things—things like car seats, refrigerator doors, tools, broken toilet seats, bundles of newspapers, bits of furniture; things made out of metal, wood, plastic, that I could no longer identify, since they'd been broken out of their normal context. It was a vast museum of the fragments and discards of our material civilization, staggering in its complexity. Cartons and boxes lined every wall, rising to the ceiling, and these bore labels, some of which I could make out in the dim light: BOLTS, MILK CARTONS, CIGARETTE WRAPPERS, BULLETS—a complete list would be as long and heavy as a small-town telephone directory.

A few bare areas of floor space contained Suskind's filthy, rumpled bedstead, a small gas stove and—final surprise—a desk covered with papers and notes. Before this scene of dedicated acquisitiveness my natural discretion vanished. "You collect things?" I asked stupidly.

"You think alla Chinee lun hand laundry, *weisenheimer?*" Suskind demanded. But he backed away from the door and bowed me in courteously.

My awe in the presence of such a Himalaya of junk caused me to overlook the implications of his last remark.

"I get sugar," he muttered as he disappeared down an aisle between the mountains of trash.

I took the occasion of his absence to study the papers

on his desk. But I could make nothing of them. They were covered with delicate brush strokes but were not Chinese. No doubt lists—a catalogue, perhaps. When I looked up I saw him watching me with a thin smile, my teacup filled with sugar in his hand.

"You not lecognize Heblew Chinee?" he asked with a chuckle. "No one steal my notes."

"A very secure system," I admitted. Then I could resist no longer. "What is your field?" I demanded baldly.

Suskind shrugged. "I am lay sosher-psychologist."

"Lay social-psychologist?" I repeated, savoring the madness of the thought even as my lips expressed it. Had he claimed to be a lay Martian he could not have amazed me more. Then a wave of shame reddened my cheeks. After all, why should I be surprised? Because Suskind was poverty-stricken? So was I. Because he lived in this improbable tenement? I lived here also. Because he was a Chinese? So was Confucius. Because he was a Jew? So was Freud. Here, in fact, was an intriguing line of speculation. Social interrelations has always been a study dominated by Chinese scholarship. And psychology has ever been a subject at which Jews have excelled. Who could have been better qualified to be a social-psychologist than Suskind? As for his being a lay practitioner, that meant only that he had escaped the ennervating embrace of a formal degree. And was I not also a refugee from that same detestable academic world? I suddenly felt extremely close to Suskind. I felt that I understood that man in whom East and West had met at last to flower into scholarship. "I am a scholar, too," I said warmly.

"I know," Suskind replied, setting the teacup down on the table. I noticed that the top of it had been scraped across carefully with a knife so that it was a level rather than a heaping teacup of sugar. "I observe you closely."

I nodded sympathetically. "Are you working on something in particular?"

Suskind hesitated. His eyes flickered over me, over the table, toward the open door. Then he indicated a wooden stool. "You sit down," he muttered, as he carefully locked the door. When he was certain of privacy he seated himself on the edge of his desk and said softly, "Levolution Against the Industlial Levolution." Then, as he correctly interpreted the look of wonder on my face, he continued, "I makee study alla symptoms of levolt of the masses against mechanical age."

"Revolution against the industrial revolution?" My mind reeled before the awesome concepts that title evoked.

He nodded vigorously. "Velly much connected with consumer-oriented society. Many sosher-psychologists study flom opposite point of view. They study alla symptoms of buying things—alla things—alla manufactured things—as ploof mankind's plogless or ploof mankind's leglession. Leglession most fashionable nowadays. Evlybody velly busy buying evlything because evlybody velly sick, velly nervous, velly dissatisfied, velly alienated. More they buy more nervous they get—become victims of buying things, become victims of things, become more and more disoliented. You know alla 'bout theories like that."

Of course I did. My own work was not too far afield from that very area.

"But me study flom opposite angle. Me study to ploove mankind determined to destloy evlything manufactured. Not thlow away evlything because they want to buy new things alla time. Thlow away evlything because they hate it. Thlow it away so they can buy more things to thlow

away—because they hate alla things. Thlow away more
and more because they hope one day they thlow away
evlything and not be wollied any more. Mankind still
fighting back against matelial downpour. Mankind not
give up the fight. But no longer lecognize why they do it.
I ploove to them why they do it and give them coulage to
do more, thlow away more things, maybe even begin
thlow away factolies that make things." He paused. "Alla
this"—he waved a proprietary hand around—"evidence.
Alla things mankind thlow away. I gather things—study,
classify them, observe patterns of disposal, gather facts—
study much, work much. One day my Theoly of Levolution complete, I give to mankind flee gift!" There was no
mistaking the dedication of his tone.

Of course I comprehended at once. And I was terribly
excited at what was, to me, a completely revolutionary
view of the consumer society, not to mention the industrial revolution. By studying the trash habits of our society, Suskind planned to develop a theory which would
establish that far from succumbing to the industrial revolution, mankind was actively fighting against it in the only
way it knew how—by buying as much as possible in order
to destroy it as quickly as possible. Simple? All strokes of
genius are apparently simple.

"Velly dangelous business," Suskind sighed.

"Dangerous? But how?"

"'Gainst the law. 'Gainst the law to glab things flom
tlash ballels, 'gainst the law to pick up things ahead of
Department of Sanitation. They catch me I go pay big
fine or maybe to jail. Alla this 'gainst the law too—illegal
to have mountains of tlash in tenement building. All
illegal." He shrugged, and sighed thoughtfully again.

Of course he was right. I hadn't thought much about it.

But it certainly was against very many ordinances, statutes and laws to constitute oneself a one-man, private, unlicensed trash-disposal unit. And the storage of unhygienic, combustible trash in living areas was a grave offense. Suskind, I now realized, took very real and large risks for his scholarship.

"How do you do it?" I asked.

Suskind stared at me gravely for fully two minutes. He seemed to be weighing something in his mind. His eyes appraised not only my face but also every inch of my body. Then he closed his eyes and pondered for a while. Finally he said, "I got schedules of when evly stleet in Manhattan permitted to thlow away big articles furniture and stuff—Department of Sanitation tlucks do some stleets evly night. I get there ahead of them. You likee see how? You got plenty *chutzpah?* You wanna come tonight?"

I confess that at the moment he made this offer I felt a slight twinge of fright. Of course, even if we were apprehended, any charge brought against me would be a minor one, involving only a small fine for—perhaps for trespassing, or loitering, or discarding—or whatever. But I had encountered the police once before and found them less than understanding. "Where do you go?" I asked cautiously.

"Tonight is night for West One Hundled and Tenth Stleet by Liverside Dlive," he said. "Tlucks come along at two A.M. sharp. People mostly off stleets by one A.M. We get there then."

After all, the primary risk was his. And was I not also a scholar? I did not want to appear any less dedicated than Suskind. "Very well," I said with a dry mouth, "I'll be delighted to go along."

"Velly good!" Suskind jumped up and shook my hand with sincere appreciation. "You got *chutzpah!*" he announced. He rushed into a dark corner behind a mountain of newspapers. I heard rustlings and grunts, and then he returned with two light-green uniforms. "One of these maybe fit you," he declared, offering me trousers and jacket.

Now I appreciated Suskind's cunning. The uniforms were, of course, those of the Department of Sanitation. He had stolen them long before. As I pulled on my uniform (it fit surprisingly well) he explained that they were only for the deception of passers-by. In case some building superintendent, for example, became suspicious of our activities. He also supplied a plastic raincoat, which he advised me to keep buttoned up to my neck. Impersonating a city employee could be a serious offense. But this combination of disguises afforded a very flexible means of response to several types of danger.

As we waited for the hour of departure Suskind outlined his objectives for the night. First we would scavenge down the streets for discarded ice trays. These, he explained carefully, were usually but not always to be found in thrown-out refrigerators. He figured we could expect an average of five doorless (it is against the law to place a refrigerator in the street for collection with its door attached) discarded refrigerators per street. A few of them would still have their ice trays. But, on the other hand, it was not very unusual to find ice trays amid general litter and rubbish. It was Suskind's view that the percentage of ice trays discovered, when calculated against the percentage of refrigerators, would help him in his statistical analyses of hard-goods disposal.

Upon the approach of the Department of Sanitation

trucks we would turn from ice trays to automobile cigarette lighters. The method was simply to walk down the
darkened streets, peering into parked cars, keeping count
of those that had lighters and those that did not. Samples
were to be collected also. The purpose was interesting.
According to Suskind, people were eager to dispose of
their cars, perhaps even more eager than they were to
destroy other hard goods. And they invariably started
with the cigarette lighters. They "lost" them. Actually, it
was his view that the high incidence of loss afforded clear
proof that this smallest and most easily disposable part of
a car was being intentionally discarded, even though most
people were not psychologically prepared to admit it. Although I had not the means to dispute this theory, I was
willing to maintain an open mind about it.

When our hour struck, Suskind put on his own shape-
less but very large dark-blue plastic raincoat, and I was
gratified to see how effectively it disguised our disguises.

We arrived by subway at 110th Street exactly on the
stroke of one A.M. It has since occurred to me that Suskind
must also have mastered the subway schedules to time
things so nicely. But at the moment we stepped from the
station I did not think about that. Instead I stood in
stunned silence staring at the darkened buildings of the
University. In all the talk of social behavior, all the
meticulous explanation and planning that had consumed
my mind for the past two hours, I had never stopped
to consider that Suskind's target for the night was the
scene of my own past mistakes, humiliations, griefs. It
came over me in a rush.

There, towering darkly across the street, was the very
building that housed the very lecture hall in which my
ultimate confrontation with M had taken place. Nearby,

with one faint light showing on the fourth floor, stood the Faculty Club, where my disgrace had been made apparent and where misfortune had lead me into academic disaster. And on the other side of the street—dared I look? Yes—there was the very apartment building that had witnessed the tragedy of my failed marriage. I felt a lump rising in my throat. My eyes were misty, and my mind raced and careened down lanes of bitter memory. Suskind tried to shake me out of it. "Let's go!" he whispered hoarsely. "Let's get moving!"

I nodded dumbly, but could not move. I felt like a man who had stumbled into the scene of what he had always imagined to be a nightmare. Was that why I had been so frightened of tonight's adventure? My subconscious had rung alarm bells when Suskind mentioned the neighborhood, and even though I had not consciously recognized the address he'd given, those bells had clamored somewhere deep within me. I knew I could not go on.

"I—I can't do it!" I muttered shakily.

Suskind stepped around in front of me and peered quietly into my eyes. "No," he murmered finally, satisfied by whatever he saw there, "you not do it." He frowned.

"I'm sorry—"

"Not important." He fumbled into his pockets and brought forth a small police-type whistle. "You stay here," he said. "When see Department of Sanitation tluck or police car, you blow thlee times on this. You understand?"

I nodded and accepted the whistle from him.

Still walking in what seemed like some sinister trance, I followed him across the avenue and took up my station in the shadowed doorway of a delicatessen. Suskind looked at me thoughtfully once more, seemed about to speak, but then shrugged his shoulders and walked quickly off down the side street, his canvas bag slung carelessly over one arm.

I hardly noticed his parting. I was desperately fighting against the nightmare. As I stood there in the night, within a block of the scenes of my defeat—of my crimes, if you like—I could think of only one word, which I muttered over and over to myself as a sort of incantation, a magical charm to ward off the evil memories that flooded in upon me. The word was "justification."

Q. Now, Mrs. Webster, would you please tell this Court in your own words what happened when Mr. Webster was removed in police custody that night?
A. Well, first of all, as soon as the police left I realized that maybe I'd gone a little too far, even as a joke. I mean I became frightened. So I called up the only person I could think of who might be able to help me.
Q. And that person was?
A. Mr. Anthony Buono. He was an old friend who ran a bar down in the Village. I knew he'd had contact with police officials from time to time. I mean, I knew he would know what I ought to do about it all. So I called him. And he came over. It was very kind of him.
Q. And did Mr. Buono give you advice?
A. Yes, he did. He advised me to call the sergeant right away to make sure that Paul—Mr. Webster— wasn't charged.
Q. You made the call?
A. Yes, just as Sergeant McNally described it.
Q. What did you do then?
A. Well, we just sat there and waited for Paul to come home.

Q. That is all you did?

A. Oh, I see. No. Actually we played through a score by Bach. You see, when I called Mr. Buono he was already on his way out to a rehearsal of a string group he plays with down in the Village, so he had his cello with him.

Q. And would you kindly describe what happened when Mr. Webster returned?

The voices, the murmurous voices, jumbled and confused; aggrieved voices, accusing voices, insinuating something about myself I desperately refused to face. As I dissolved into those voices I struggled hopelessly against the nightmarish inevitability of events. Justification.

Even as I walked home that night from the police station, taking a roundabout way along Riverside Drive, I knew that my life had reached some sort of watershed. I even recall how clean the solitary night air seemed against my face, how terribly clearly my problem presented itself.

On the one hand was this relationship that threatened to destroy me. How terribly complicated and *involved* my life appeared to me. It even showed in my work.

Just what had I accomplished during my two years, nine months and three weeks of marriage? A large section of analyses—of other people's ideas; a large amount of compilation—of previous work. Where had my intellectual vigor gone? Of course, I was thinking about my *Theory of Place and Decay.* My daily routine at the University had long since lost all but passing interest for me. But even in that I could detect a loss of energy.

And for what had I exchanged freedom, challenge, the cleanliness of solitude? For confinement within an endless round of daily minutiae, for an endless battle to preserve my own identity, for the continuously frustrating struggle of sexual assertion.

These reflections floated like seaweed on the still surface of my disgust. But what prowled about in the darkest deeps of that disgust I could not name.

On the other hand, how dry and dreary my life appeared without M in it. It was this very disorder that nourished my spirit against the dull oppression of the world. And of course the day would come when this little contretemps with the police would appear in its true ridiculous perspective. And it was M, after all, who had called McNally. Perhaps after all my little scheme had accomplished something! She had not remained indifferent in a crisis, had responded. And perhaps it was not beyond hope that the evening's farce might even have awakened that extra dimension of response within her for which I longed. By the time I'd reached our apartment door I was almost thankful for the night's events, thankful they'd led to this spirit of reconciliation within my breast.

I was still fishing in my pocket for the key when I heard them. The soft pliancy of a violin and the demanding, full-throated boom of a cello.

I will not try to explain what happened next. At that instant something froze solid in my chest and my hands began to tremble. If I hadn't kept my teeth clenched they would have chattered. Of course it was all clear to me. Tony Buono was in there! In a moment of crisis she'd instinctively turned to him, to his strength! And far from being involved in my little drama, as I'd fondly imagined, she remained coolly detached. Calmly playing duets with Buono while I grappled with demons! Perhaps they'd even enjoyed a mild laugh at my expense! My mind sank beneath a weight of bitter outrage. I turned the key hastily in the door, flung it open.

There they were! She was standing behind him, leaning over his shoulder to read a score propped on the table before them, as she played. His huge bulk squatted on a chair, his hairy hands gripping the cello bow as if it were a toothpick. So intent were they on their *shared* activity that they hadn't even noticed my entrance.

Words spilled through my mind. Phrases of all sorts rose to my lips. But I rejected all of them. Nothing could possibly express my indignation at this open scene of betrayal. "That's it!" I cried. "That does it!"

M stopped playing instantly, detecting no doubt the cold finality in my tone, while Buono played on stupidly for at least two bars. Her eyes widened with alarm as she read the meaning in my face. "Paul," she said weakly, "Tony was the one who advised me to call the station— he's the one who got you out—really—"

"Hi, Paul," Buono started jovially.

But I was already rushing him. I flailed out blindly, savagely—and felt myself picked up casually and thrown to the floor. "Now look, Paul," he said, "after what you've done tonight, you better think twice about who you try to hit—" He straightened his tie. From somewhere, M's voice was still rushing on, indistinctly. But behind Buono's gruff manner I could detect the triumph. It was not merely the fact that I was presumably in the wrong in attacking him. It was the glint of contempt in his eye that underlined the humiliation of my physical weakness. I'd been tossed aside as if I were a child—degraded in my own home—in front of M. The whole situation had crystallized into a nightmare of hysterical rage in my mind.

I got up, my lips tight, my eyes smarting. I could afford no more of this, of any of this.

I heard M's voice as from a distance as I walked swiftly into our bedroom, gathered my things together and threw them into a suitcase. No doubt she was trying to explain, no doubt she may even have pleaded with me, no doubt that Buono creature even attempted to justify himself in one way or another. I heard none of this. Something deeper even than shame or jealousy or rage had been stirred within me. Through my mind in agonizing repetition passed a single word against which all other words were powerless. The word was "dirty."

Q. And after your husband moved to the Faculty Club did you try to contact him?
A. I sent him letters.
Q. We will now offer into evidence for this Court defense documents numbered four to thirty-six, which constitute a series of letters sent by Defendant to Plaintiff during the period in question.
COURT: Clerk will receive this evidence.

How did I supply evidence to be used against me? Simply by not opening any of these letters. They were all returned to sender. For the truth of the matter was that I almost instantly achieved a deep peace of mind on returning to bachelorhood. Now, of course, I realize why. But at the time it was as if a great weight had been removed from my shoulder. I felt like Sisyphus liberated. And my work showed it.

I had for some months been preparing an outline, gathering notes, checking references, on what later became my chapters regarding the breakdown of human personality under the impact of the Great Plains. Now, in solitude, the work lifted itself from this essential drudgery. Once again I found my imagination, relieved of impingements, making those bold leaps upon which so much of my theory is based. I was able, for instance, at this very period to conceive of "Kansas Man," an inspiration that enabled me to solve the problem of suppression of genius on the Middle Western steppes. This conception—the imaginary influence of an imaginary prehistoric "Kansas Man" on the pacification of the Great Plains, as compared, say, to Piltdown Man's civilizing influence on prehistoric Europe (chapters 27 to 35, vol. III)—is, you say, an obvious idea? But all inspirations appear obvious after the fact. The usefulness of considering what the lack of "Kansas Man" in the prehistory of our continent has meant— the lack of his subjection of the land, his pacifying of its spiritual-psychological chaos—is indisputable. By conceiving of his tasks as having been left for the present inhabitants, among whom "Kansas Man" has finally emerged, the apparent barbarism of a vast section of our society is understandable. Justification.

A nightmare from which I could not escape invaded my consciousness. Nothing of it was to be spared me.

Q. And when you received these letters returned unopened, did you make any other attempt to contact Defendant?
A. Yes, I did. I went to the Faculty Club. But they wouldn't admit me. They said they had orders from him. So, the only place I was sure of seeing him was his classes. I went to one.

Can you understand what this meant to me? Understanding is the beginning of charity.

Once a week I gave what were known as "open" lectures. That is, they were general lectures on the subject of American history, which any member of the University could attend. Some drew course credit from these lectures, while some merely audited them. They were of a very general nature, suitable to the audience, and did not, of course, reflect my own very particular opinions which emerged in my private work. You can imagine my shock upon entering the lecture hall to discover M seated demurely in the very first row, notebook in hand, wearing a tight-fitting green sheath with a suggestively deep cleavage, exuding what can only be described as studious Passive Pursuit. I determined to take no notice of her whatsoever. Her presence was a blackmail that could be resisted only by indifference.

It was my habit to speak from notes that were no more than subject headings and outlines. My subject for the series was "The Influence of Puritan Ideals upon American Modes of Thought," a very safe guided tour of very well explored terrain. And as soon as quiet was established in the hall I launched into it, barely needing recourse to my notes, so familiar was the topic to me.

I don't know exactly what I expected M to do. I had imagined everything from some hysterical outburst to cold denunciation. But she sat in respectful silence, paying very close attention to what I said and even making notes from time to time. I began to gather confidence, and soon found myself forgetting her presence as I warmed to my subject. But as a driver's attention is attracted by the slightest sound of disharmony in his engine when he is driving a long and boring road, and as his fascination grows with the disturbance and he conjectures about valves and pistons and cooling systems all the while proceeding on his route, and as a subconscious wish grows for the expected breakdown to at least put an end to speculative suspense, so I found myself glancing from time to time in a rhythm of mounting momentum toward

M. From glance to glance her skirt seemed to be rising above her knees, revealing more and more mesh-stockinged thigh. And her expression of rapt attention became more and more obviously a thin veneer covering a foundation of deep contempt. As my nerves tautened I lost all doubts; she had come here to publicly disrupt my lecture. And as she made no overt commotion my forebodings simply increased. What was she planning?

I found myself referring oftener to my notes as I wandered from the track of my discourse. I found my glances in her direction becoming compulsive. Was her skirt not now dangerously high? Were her eyes not now expressing open defiance? Was her mouth not now trembling on the very brink of a grin of contempt? Was her skirt not now pulled higher still? Suddenly, in cold clarity, I foresaw the outlines of her plan; it should have been obvious from the beginning. There was always a question-and-answer period following each lecture. That would be her opportunity. No doubt she intended to either ask some question or make some public declaration that would shatter my image before the class, would perhaps open our private affairs to ridicule, might even blow my position at the University sky-high! I found myself mopping a sweaty brow with my handkerchief as the lecture approached its conclusion. Then, suddenly, it was over. I felt an icy chill in my breast as I saw M's hand rise with several others for permission to ask a question.

I resolutely ignored her. I accepted questions from every other direction but did not so much as glance at her. If only I could prolong my answers the bell would ring, the period end, and I could escape the public confrontation. But my nerves were so tense that my speech became rapid, abbreviated, my answers increasing in momentum until they had rolled over every question and only M's hand remained raised. Still I refused to look toward her. But years of lecturing make any man sensitive to the attitudes of his audience. I was already aware that many students had noticed. There were whispers, puzzled glances; a definite current of hostility against which I could hold out no longer was being created by my obduracy.

"Yes?" I demanded harshly, compressing my lips into a line of threat I hoped she would understand.

"Why?" she asked in a pleasant, relaxed voice.

Of course I knew to what she referred. But I determined to treat the question as a continuation of my previous answers. "Because, as I have endeavored to explain, so many of the descendants of the founders of the Massachusetts Bay Colony later rose to important administrative, educational and political-military leadership during and after the Revolution—" I was aware that my voice was uneven.

"No," she interrupted, "not that. Why—"

"Because"—I almost shouted the interruption to drown the question that could lead only to catastrophe—"of their intellectual accomplishments and discipline, that very discipline that we today associate with the repressive aspects—" My voice sounded to me like the rattling of dry bones in a cardboard box.

"No," she interrupted yet again. "What I wanted to know is why—"

There was no avoiding it, then? Then I would meet it head on, by God! "You know why!" I cried out. "You know goddamned well why!"

"I do?" she asked, in a controlled, puzzled tone which infuriated me still more.

"Yes, you do!" I shouted, pointing an accusing finger at her, oblivious now of lecture hall, audience, everything, except her intention of bringing our private quarrel under public scrutiny. "You started it all yourself, with the cops! There's no one to blame but you! Now you want to make me ridiculous, but it won't work. You'll never get me!" I paused for three reasons: first, because I was out of breath; second, because the bell had just rung; third, because I had suddenly become aware of a profound and terrified stillness in the auditorium. I glanced around wildly to see the entire audience staring at me with that apprehensive loathing that the sight of a madman generally arouses. My very fear of disaster had led me into it. I tasted for what seemed an interminable moment the bitter humiliation of what I had myself wrought.

"What I wanted to know," she said in her infuriatingly plausible voice, "was simply why you consider that the Puritan Ethic died with Hemingway?"

All was now lost. "To hell with you!" I screamed, rushing from the lecture room and leaving behind me a stunned student body, an irreparably damaged academic career—and M, stunned at this public humiliation. Well, hadn't I been humiliated too? Justification.

I had been conscious of some slight but growing disturbance throughout the latter part of that dreadful reverie. At its moment of bitterest despair—when I rushed from the lecture hall screaming—I slowly came back to a recognition of my surroundings, and of the disturbance itself. Once again I was standing in the darkness of the delicatessen doorway, a whistle in my hand, and there was a grinding, low-pitched roaring noise very close at hand. It was familiar somehow. Of course! A Department of Sanitation truck! Instantly I placed the whistle to my lips and blew on it—three long blasts. I prayed I was not too late. The truck was not in sight. Perhaps it was even now far along the street, perhaps even now catching up with Suskind.

I waited tensely, eager to hear the quick shuffle of feet, the heavy breath that would indicate Suskind's approach. Had any other trucks gone by during my nightmarish disconnection from reality? Had I already betrayed my trust? The seconds passed. They lengthened into minutes. Should I blow again? But that might indicate something else to Suskind, if he could still hear it. Cautiously I left my hiding place, cautiously I turned the corner into the street down which Suskind had departed. And immediately I froze in my tracks.

For there, more than halfway down the block, stood a parked police car. In the steadily revolving light on its roof, illuminated as in the sweep of a lighthouse beacon, I made out two officers interrogating a large bald figure who carried a heavy canvas sack in his right hand. With relief I saw that Suskind's raincoat was still buttoned to his neck. Further down the block the lumbering Sanitation Department truck continued placidly on its rounds— a huge mechanical cow, ruminating its cud of civilization's refuse. I had failed. Even in the simple duty imposed upon me I had failed. In the bitterness of that knowledge desperation was born. It was my fault that Suskind was now in custody. Within minutes he would be bundled into the police car and hastened off into the grip of that very organization whose cruelty I had once experienced myself. Action was called for.

I turned quickly and cautiously back the way I'd come, confident that I'd been unobserved by the police. Once again I stood outside the delicatessen window. Of course I knew what I had to do. Whatever charges the police might see fit to bring against Suskind could be only minor ones. Rifling the city's trash was an offense, but surely no more than a misdemeanor. On the other hand, if Suskind was made to open his raincoat—well, impersonating a city employee would be serious. So far, with the proper diversion, the officers might be persuaded to discount Suskind as simply another of the curious specimens thrown up nightly upon the shores of the city's desperation. I searched about frantically. Nowhere could I find a single stone, brick, bit of loose concrete, so thoroughly had that mechanical cow already browsed this area. I finally had to settle for the heavy metal trash basket on the corner. Using all my strength—for it was uncommonly heavy—I lugged it over to the delicatessen, slowly and painfully raised it above my head and then, with savage exertion, sent it crashing through the window.

Instantly the night was made hideous by the clanging of the burglar alarm. Now I brought out my whistle and blew it continuously, shrilly and, as I hoped, hysterically, all the while running down the street. When I reached the corner I tossed the whistle aside and started shouting, "Help! Help! Help! Help!" I was gratified to see that the two officers had already started running, with drawn revolvers, in my direction. I ran on toward them. "Around the corner!" I cried. "There's a holdup!"

The police paused as they reached me—undecided, I'm sure, about whether to take me along on suspicion. But I quickly threw open my raincoat. "I'm on my way to work," I said breathlessly, "and I see this guy holding up a delly—right around the corner—there was some sort of fight—he broke the window—you better hurry!" The sight of my uniform was evidently sufficient for them. They hurried on, rushed around the corner and out of sight.

"That velly good," Suskind whispered in my ear, his hand gripping my arm urgently. "Now lun like hell!" I had not heard him approach, but my admiration for the silence of his movements was only momentary.

We ran like hell. Down the street, around the corner of Riverside Drive, for three blocks downtown, then up another street, to throw ourselves breathlessly but safely into the grateful anonymity of a subway station.

You can imagine how I felt about all this. Not only had I ruined Suskind's carefully planned campaign for that particular evening, I had jeopardized his entire project. He would not be able to operate openly again for days, weeks, perhaps months. And even then, he would probably have to either assume a different disguise or conduct his field research in distant areas of Brooklyn. Once again my mere presence, the slightest touch of my personality, had been enough to endanger another person's entire life's work, perhaps even his existence. I reproached myself endlessly, bitterly.

Suskind? You cannot conceive of the magnaminity of the man. Never once, in all our future contacts, which were as frequent as I desired, did he so much as hint about or in any way allude to this night's disaster. He bore himself with Spartan fortitude and with unfailing courtesy and delicacy of feeling toward me.

Oh, how I wished Suskind were with me now! To see that massive bald head appear at the door, to look once again into those slanted eyes. Suskind would know how to deal with The Foundation. I must copy his bravery, his determination and above all his inscrutable Oriental wisdom if I was to escape. For I had decided to escape. And if I was to succeed, then my personal feelings of rage, terror and claustrophobia must in no wise be taken into account. I must view myself and my surroundings unemotionally.

But, it may be objected, what right had I to escape? Stein was right. I legally belonged to The Foundation as either their possession or their ward. It could be pointed out that if one of the re-created livers in their research vaults could by any means make its escape, then The Foundation would have every right to expect society's fullest co-operation in reclaiming the errant organ. Likewise a ward, if maintained under reasonably humane conditions, will certainly be returned to his guardians if he attempts to run away.

I may reply that the Fourteenth Amendment to the Constitution of the United States prohibits the holding of property in human beings.

But it was also true that, except as a ward of The Foundation, I had no legal existence as a human being. And it may be added that the Supreme Court has never reversed itself in the Dred Scott decision, by which it clearly ruled that nonhuman beings can claim no rights before the law.

This view cannot lightly be brushed aside, *except through an appeal to history*. And I was, after all, a historian.

But simply because I had no legal identity does not mean that I had no individuality. That is the fine point of reason on which I built my case.

Now, The Foundation, as an eleemosynary institution chartered under the laws of the State of New York, was certainly a part and an extension of society.

Proceeding: it must be granted, then, that my relation to The Foundation was that of an individual to society. I received my food, lodging, et cetera, from society. In return I had to fulfill my function. If I failed to do so, then society might withdraw its benefits. This is known as the Social Contract. It assumes that we have, each of us, signed a contract with Society to observe Its laws, customs, regulations, prejudices, etc., and to fulfill our functions within It, in return for room and board. If either Party to this Contract fails to fulfill his part, then the other Party is free to demand redress of grievances.

Example: A man commits murder, thereby breaking the terms of his Contract with Society. Society is now free to re-establish relations with that man on totally different terms.

Example: Society fails to provide sustenance to individuals. They are now free to overthrow It (viz, the French, Chinese and October revolutions).

N.B. It is not to be supposed that the above examples imply morality. Morality is the rationalization of past events by those who survive them and the restriction of the future by those who fear it. We are speaking here of practical historical right, not of cowardice.

Now then, allowing these precedents, a revolt against The Foundation (and escape is viewed herein as revolt) was justified because The Foundation had neglected my spiritual sustenance. It had launched an attack against both my soul and my psyche. It had submitted me to endless boredom and to fear, two most destructive emotions.

But, it may be replied, I was provided with everything I might reasonably desire. My physical needs were continually granted. Accepted. Let me argue once *ad-hominem*. Take yourself as example. You find yourself with more food than you can eat, more entertainment than your nerves can stand, more leisure time than you know what to do with, more comfort than you can profitably enjoy. In return for all this only the simplest demands are made upon you: that you appear to agree with the basic tenets of Society, that you engage in profitable labor, that you do not incite to the rupture of The Social Contract. If such were your case would you not be overwhelmingly *bored?* Would you not fear for the extinction of your very soul? Now to this boredom you must add an imagined state of fear. By stretching your imaginative faculties, you must try to put yourself in the position of someone living in a profound and *continuing* dread of sudden physical catastrophe that Society may at any moment inflict.

If the above were your case, would you not hold yourself justified either to escape from Society's clutches or to go about Its subversion and destruction by any means whatsoever? Q.E.D.

That very night I took stock. My normal strength and vigor had returned to me during these weeks of recuperation. Of course, they had been slight enough to begin with, but medically, I judged, I had completed treatment because I was no longer subjected to any type of medication save only my daily vitamin injections. Physically, then, I was independent, though not very strong. As always, my wits would have to be my sole support. Now, as I conceived of the situation, my first move must be to adopt a disguise for my intentions. What attitude would be most calculated to allay The Foundation's suspicions? Not one of passive compliance. That would be suspect. No, they would expect a certain measure of resistance. I would have to keep up a running sore of complaint, a continuous and picayune argument with them—like a liberal, for example. They were prepared to cope with that. They could argue, assuage, ameliorate and postpone indefinitely. Such an attitude on my part would assure them of my basic supineness. And behind such a mask I could watch and wait.

To essentials, then. How did one enter or leave The Foundation? I had entered through the reception hall but clearly could not leave that way. The windows were walls, and any other exits would be, of course, well guarded. There was the possibility of physical disguise —but The Foundation Security Forces would certainly be alert to this most venerable of all escape methods. Besides, to get hold of a disguise I would have to overpower someone and it was highly problematical that I could overpower even a nurse in open combat. What of the other patients? They went out past the reception desk if cured, no doubt. And if not cured? I felt a thrill of inspiration.

The one certain way out of The Foundation was to die.

Over my evening gruel I questioned Nurse Williams carefully. When she bent over to arrange my plates on the wheeled table I found that I no longer cared whether or not she wore a brassiere. My rape had satisfied me.

"Who are we eating tonight, Williams?" (I had long ago decided to accede in the matter of pronouns; it made for simpler communication.)

"I beg your pardon?" (hoo)

"I say who is this mush we're eating?"

"That's high-calorie, protein-available, Instant Diet." (hoo)

"Mmm. It tastes like some dead patient."

"Now, Professor, let's not be morbid."

"We're not being morbid. We believe we grind up the bodies of dead patients for this gruel."

"Certainly not!"

"Well then, what do we do with them?"

"Why, we send them to the mortuary of their choice." (hoo)

"Very democratic of us. And if they've made no choice?"

"Why then their families decide, of course." (hoo)

"And if they are completely alone in this world?"

"Then their remains are respectfully cremated in The Foundation's Integrated Interdenominational Chapel at no cost to them." (hoo)

"Mmm. Then perhaps their ashes find their way to the kitchen."

Nurse Williams compressed her full lips in what was intended to be a look of grim reproval but what necessarily became, on her face, an inviting bow. As she cleared away the dishes she favored me with a smile and said, "We really mustn't let ourselves become morbid or we may find ourselves down in Psy some day." (hoo)

I said no more, feeling that I had perhaps already evinced too much interest in the matter. But I pondered long and deeply her parting remark. Sent down to Psy? That would mean leaving my room, being led through corridors. I might at least have a chance to orient myself. Perhaps with shrewdness or luck I might even learn more about the disposal of the dead. And it was through a long night of pondering this very subject that a convenient role suggested itself to me. When Stein appeared in my room the following morning, I was ready.

"How do you feel today?" he asked, with his usual complete lack of interest. He walked over to the windows and stared down at Central Park. "It is a fine autumn day," he muttered. He glanced at me and then looked back out the window.

I was staring fixedly at the lighting fixture above my head. I kept my face lax but immobile.

"Have you ever," he asked, "thought of these buildings that surround the park as sentinels? I've been watching them for years. Early in the evening their windows catch the sunset. They seem to be signaling to each other. Of course, The Foundation never signals. We are all gray glass and anodized aluminum. We are the gravestone at the head of the park and all those other buildings are the guard of honor at some giant military funeral."

The image of The Foundation as a headstone was the very thing that had unnerved me when I first entered the place. It troubled me that he should see it the same way. Any such evidence of human solidarity in Stein was troublesome to me. It would be unbearable to think of him as normal. I did not respond.

He turned to glance at me again. The slightly worried expression on his face gave way to a reflection of my own rigid composure. My effect must have been good.

"You know, Webster," he said, "I don't mind admitting that when we gathered together your papers and brought them here I took the occasion to glance through some of your notes on *The Theory of Place and Decay.* I was very much impressed. You could continue your work here under The Foundation's auspices."

Oh, he was clever! He was reaching out now to touch my most vulnerable point. The outrageous effrontery with which he admitted spying, prying and thrusting his huge nose into my private papers was well calculated to arouse my anger, while his offer of Foundation aid was designed to stimulate my greed as well as to drive home to me the helplessness of my situation. I did not miss the note of irony in this offer. For here indeed would be the ultimate condition of a Foundation scholar—not only supported but actually physically owned by it.

Suddenly I felt not a pain but a violent wrenching movement in my large right toe. But as I had been prepared for exactly that sort of thing from Stein, my attention remained immovably on the lighting fixture, and my face retained its icy composure.

"Catatonic," he muttered regretfully. Then he pressed the call button next to the door. He stared at me while he waited, his face alternating between reflections of my own rigid composure and flashes of subjective annoyance. To him, my critical mental condition was evidently only another device of fate to frustrate his plans. When Nurse Williams appeared he nodded toward me and said, "Send Doctor Ritchie up here immediately. Tell him Webster's in what appears to be a catatonic trance."

Williams glanced at me and shook her head slowly. "I suppose I should have alerted you last night, Doctor. He thought he was eating dead patients!" (hoo)

Stein frowned. "Indeed you should have!" he snapped. "Now get Ritchie." As she left he sighed wearily and slumped down into the armchair.

My real test was now approaching. The simulation of a catatonic trance was not so difficult beneath the scrutiny of someone untrained in psychiatry, and I had correctly guessed that Stein's background would not have included more than a cursory study of that subject. But this Ritchie was sure to be an expert. Fooling him would require all my concentration. And if he gave me an injection of some sort? How would I be expected to react?

The door opened and Williams entered accompanied by a short, stocky individual with black curly hair, an aggressively square jaw, a large nose, puffy cheeks and an unlit pipe clenched between his teeth. He was dressed in a white T-shirt and rumpled white-duck pants. It was evident that he had just been roused from sleep. He carried a small black bag in his right hand. The instant he entered my room I felt a twinge of recognition. That face—like some familiar shadow flitting across my mental landscape, indefinable, yet naggingly familiar. He nodded curtly to Stein and walked directly over to me. He bent close to my face and I suffered an overpowering odor of garlic. He placed his left hand on my forehead, pried my eyelids farther apart and stared into my eyes.

I did not, of course, know what he was expecting to see. I could only pray that in his still somnolent condition he would imagine he saw it. I stared past him at the lighting fixture.

He nodded slowly, removed his hand and stepped back. He placed his little black bag on the bed table, opened it and drew forth a hypodermic syringe. "Well, you can't say I didn't warn you about this, Stein!" His voice was hard, belligerent and tinged by a strange accent vaguely English and vaguely Western. His entire being exuded belligerence. The way his jaw clamped down on that old brier pipe, the pugnacious manner with which he tossed his black bag onto the foot of my bed, the hard glare of his blue eyes—all these details bespoke a man whose basic attitude to the world had become one of simple defiance. Did that defiance extend to The Foundation as a whole?

". . . but you just couldn't bring yourself to listen to me, could you, Stein?" he was saying in his harsh tones. "Well, you're up the baobob tree now!" His voice held bitter satisfaction.

The baobob tree? Suddenly I recognized the accent. Ritchie was Australian. That explained in part his belligerence. It was defensive. It was the aggressiveness of the man whose natural feelings of inferiority had been multiplied by the unfortunate accident of his birth in a barbarous wasteland and compounded by his immersion in a field of science utterly foreign to his nationality. Added to this was the humiliation of constant intercourse with sophisticated technicians and representatives of a vastly superior culture. He must have felt somewhat as an educated Vandal would have felt working in Rome.

"But he seemed to be making progress," Stein said, in a voice that held a faint but unmistakable note of pleading.

I felt a thrill of hope. Could it be that the omnipotent Stein had anything to fear from a mere psychiatrist? Were there powers of appeal, then? Was Stein answerable to someone somewhere?

"Are you sure he's not faking?" Stein asked.

"What's the difference?" Ritchie demanded impatiently, as he drew a pale liquid into his syringe from a glass vial. "If this man's so far gone that he's willing to fake something like this, he's in a bad shape anyhow. Bad shape. There'll be bloody hell about this."

"Well, what do you propose to do about it?" Stein asked savagely.

"Don't shout at me, Stein! This never would have happened if you'd let me at him in the first place. But what I have to say isn't important, is it? And now I have to clean up your mess. What made you think you could face a man with his own resurrection and not have him go off his feed? There's been a definite lack of teamwork around here. A definite lack."

"All right, all right. But will you kindly deign to tell me what you propose to do?"

"I'm going to shoot a little Torpomine into him. That affects the central nervous system. It's a tranquilizing stimulant that'll relax him. He'll babble for a while and we may get some idea of what's bothering him. Then he'll sleep. By the time he wakes up we'll have his theater ready for role therapy."

"Role therapy?" Stein cried. "But that takes weeks— months . . ."

"You can't buck The Foundation, Stein. Should've thought of all this when you decided to freeze me out in the first place. Now, this man will be out of his catatonic condition by morning. But the mental condition that brought it on—who knows?" Ritchie held the syringe to the light and squinted at it.

"You realize that The Foundation has called a press conference for next Friday? We had intended to make the demonstration then."

"Well, postpone it. Or go ahead. Go on and freeze me out again. Go ahead and make a demonstration. People ought to be happy as wallabies when they find out that resurrection makes a man insane. Oh, very happy!" He chuckled. Then he nodded to Williams, who approached, lifted my arm and held it as he plunged the needle in.

I felt nothing and for the first time *realized* that I felt nothing. I mean by that, I felt no pain. I did feel, for a fleeting instant, the point of the needle against my skin, I felt Williams's hand on my arm, but I felt no pain as the needle broke the flesh. I have already mentioned my immunity to pain; this was the first time I was aware of it. And then I remembered that when Stein twisted my toe I'd felt the wrench of it, but no pain. But these speculations were brief. What was the theater? What was "role therapy"? What was a wallaby? But of primary and vital urgency—this injection was expected to make me babble. I had only a few seconds in which to find something suitable to babble about. It would have to be convincing, appropriate and something with which I was so familiar —a flash of true inspiration seized me and I was ready. After a few seconds I composed my face into an expression of contemptuous hauteur, and mumbled, "Why do our priests fail to touch our mouth with the instrument *urhekau*?"

Ritchie's eyes narrowed and he stared at me belligerently. He waved Stein and Williams back, and said, "Take it easy, Professor."

"We are impatient for the ceremonies to begin," I muttered.

Ritchie took his pipe from his mouth, started stuffing it from a leather pouch he drew from his pants pocket, and asked in as casual a voice as his natural tension permitted him, "Just what ceremonies would you have in mind, Professor?"

"'My mouth and nostrils are opened in Busiris, and I have my place of peace in Memphis which is my house.'"

"I see, I see. Well, I've been to Memphis but not to Busiris. Where's that? Way out in the outback?"

I realized suddenly that this improbable Australian might not recognize my role. Perhaps something more obvious—

"'I embrace the great throne which is in Memphis and I keep watch over the egg of the great cackler. I germinate as it germinates, I live as it lives, and my breath is its breath.'"

"Kept hens out there in Busiris, did you?"

Williams was staring at me in open wonder. But Stein's eyes were intent. They were the last thing I saw as the drug took effect and I lost consciousness.

Ritchie had described the drug as a "tranquilizing stimulant," which seemed a contradiction. But as I fell into oblivion I understood what he meant. For if the drug erased present consciousness and put me to sleep, it simultaneously stimulated those deep subconscious regions from which dreams arise and which are the refuge of every distasteful experience of our lives. It must have been a powerful drug, for it liberated in my dream-consciousness a memory so awful, so humiliating and so deeply buried that not even my journey into the realms of death had jarred it to the surface. And now it unfolded before me and within me with a torturing vividness, with a clarity too insistent to be suppressed. For not only was this memory humiliating in itself, not only was it the very watershed of my existence (dividing as it did my University life from all that followed), but also it was involved with the first failure of my body, the first large-scale warning that my system had gone awry.

My illness was a subtle and, at first, a hesitant enemy. Headaches, biliousness and a general enervation came and went with no regularity. Its onset coincided with my final separation from M, and so I attributed many of these symptoms to nervous prostration. Later I tried various patent remedies, which momentarily assuaged the surface signs of my dissolution. My enemy was sly. It gave no serious warning of what was afoot until remedy was too late. Even the disaster that overtook me at that final faculty reception was of so common a nature as to be attributable to simpler, more prosaic and less threatening ills.

Generally, I never attended faculty receptions. I detested everything about them, but above all the exaggerated air of intimate understanding that prevailed. All ears were inevitably tuned to catch every allusion, no matter how obscure, and then there followed on every face that intolerable half-smile of recognition that passes for a badge of membership in the intellectual community. Then, too, there is always a suffocating air of importance that smothers every breath of wit—the importance of simply being present. And the gabble of the women only underlines the somber and ponderous atmosphere. The faculty wives seem to have very long necks at faculty receptions, and their voices speed recklessly down half-paved intellectual side roads, skidding with laughter over their well-informed ignorance. Their husbands generally huddle near the buffet, in small groups arranged by department and rank, their heads bowed, their hands weighted with sandwiches and punch glasses, taking turns lecturing one another on such indifferent topics as the decline of scholarship, the lack of recreational facilities and the parsimony of the trustees.

My illness would have been excuse enough to avoid this particular reception. I had been overcome by a bilious attack just the day before, and felt generally weakened. But my attendance had been commanded by Dean Halvorsen. For the affair was being given in honor of Sir P. V. M. Basehart, who was then making a lecture tour through a few of our Ivy League colleges. You are probably familiar with Basehart's work—at least the condensation of his thirty-five-volume history of the world that was a best-seller for over two years. No English historian since Gibbon has undertaken so huge, so weighty and so scholarly an assault upon the human myth we call history. And although I was only an assistant professor in the History Department, I had written a long, thorough and highly critical analysis of Basehart's views, which ran in several succeeding issues of *The American Historical Review*. My critique had itself been subsequently attacked (among others by the head of our own History Department), but its very appearance had, I was certain, guaranteed me a full professorship for the coming semester. In those days I little understood the administrative mentality. When Basehart's work first appeared (of course, I refer always to the complete Oxford edition and not to any subsequent abridgements) I immediately smelled an opportunity. It was his insular view of American history that particularly irritated me. Only a historian whose methods were completely uninformed by any spiritual intuition could have been so optimistic about us.

I came to the reception late and feeling definitely weak. Already, little groups of my colleagues were gathered like solar systems around the central constellation that consisted of Dean Halvorsen, several heads of departments, wives and Sir P. V. M. Basehart himself. He was identifiable by the twin vents in his tweed jacket and the massive bush of white hair that crowned his long, aquiline head. I slipped past the buffet unnoticed and made my way to an unoccupied corner of the room. But there I was soon trapped by the wife of one of my assistant lecturers. She was not an unattractive woman, and she dressed so as to reveal as much of herself as faculty decorum permitted. But the essential banality of her face was only emphasized by the gold-flecked horn-rimmed glasses that decorated it.

"Oh, Professor Webster," she said eagerly, "have you

met Sir P. V. M. Basehart yet?" Her intonation revealed that Basehart's recent knighting was, for her at least, his most important aspect.

"No, I haven't had that pleasure."

"I simply can't wait to hear the two of you talk together," she said breathlessly. "John says you're the only historian on this side of the Atlantic who's stood up to him."

John was, of course, her husband. No doubt he was ambitious for my place. No doubt he had explained to her just how quickly Basehart would demolish my critique once we met face to face. I admired her ambition but resented her use of flattery as an offensive weapon.

"I wouldn't put it exactly that way," I said.

"Wouldn't you?" Her voice was gathering momentum now. "But you absolutely demolished his Theory of Cyclical Renewal in your articles."

"I wouldn't say that either."

"But it's directly contrary to your own theory, isn't it? I mean the one about our big death wish and about the uh—effect of the western prairies and deserts and all that?" Something in my eyes made her titter nervously.

The fact that I was becoming used to hearing my theories misrepresented, mocked and degraded by simplification did not lessen my irritation at that moment. I wondered what she would do if I reached out my hand and gave her a long, inquisitive goose. I was almost certain I would blunt my finger against a girdle. It even occurred to me that such women should wear mental girdles to protect themselves against the infamous mental goosing they receive daily. And then I felt the first warning sign that my illness was returning: a sense of weakness in my bowels. Gas pressure was building up within me, and though I might not be able to prevent its release, I felt reasonably sure of controlling it.

"Now, you're simply being modest, Professor. We all know how you are."

I was concentrating too intently upon the growing agony and weakness within me to even acknowledge this false flirtation. It had suddenly become urgent that this woman quit my immediate vicinity. "I wonder if you could bring me a glass of punch?" I asked.

"Why certainly, Professor. And I'm going to tell Dean Halvorsen that you're hiding over here in the corner. I saw you slip past them. I know you'll never do it yourself and—"

"The punch, please."

She had gone but a few paces toward the buffet when I felt the gas leaving me. And I was congratulating myself upon my discreet control of my sphincter muscles when a totally unprovoked, unforeseen and useless outrage occurred. Absolutely unpredictably, uncontrollably and irrevocably, I found I had defecated in my trousers!

My first reaction was one of helpless, frozen panic and horror. But mingled with these feelings was a deep resentment. The body in which I had always placed such unthinking confidence had betrayed me in a churlish and atavistic manner. That I was ill, had been ill for months, did not then seem a sufficient excuse to offer either to the company or to myself. I felt my forehead bead with cold sweat. My breath became shallow and an icy emptiness invaded the pit of my stomach. I glanced around furtively to make certain that no one had noticed. Then my gaze fell upon John's wife. She was speaking to Dean Halvorsen and pointing discreetly in my direction. The dean, a tall and angular New Englander whose sharp nose had hooked many an errant instructor and student, smiled benignly at her, glanced at me inquiringly and then turned to say something to Sir P. V. M. Basehart. That dirty little bitch had made my presence known! I ground my teeth together in misery. Escape was now my only logical course.

I backed slowly along the wall, side-stepping very carefully, my progress as slow and yet as skitterish as that of an aged crab. I was unreasonably, overwhelmingly, almost tearfully grateful now that I wore jockey-style shorts. My destination was, of course, the door. To reach it I had to pass the buffet table, which was beseiged by hungry assistant lecturers in front and served by two students behind. Clearly, I could not make my way through the lecturers. I would have to squeeze between the student servers and the wall. As I shouldered past the students, who were ladling out punch, they turned to stare in resentment and surprise. But there was that in my face that must have frightened them, for they quickly dropped their ladles and slid along the wall to let me pass. Only a few feet to the door now.

And then I saw Dean Halvorsen turn away from Basehart and glance searchingly around the crowded room. His cold blue eyes picked me out, his thin lips compressed slightly and he started to walk toward me. I felt my gorge rise in pure terror. Pretending not to notice his approach, I had just reached the door when he called out, "Hello there, Webster. Come over and let me introduce you to Sir P. V. M. Basehart. He's quite eager to talk to you."

"I can't," I blurted out urgently, in a tone I realized too late sounded like sullen defiance.

Dean Halvorsen cocked his head to one side, his expres-

sion one of plain annoyance. His nose seemed sharper
than ever. I suddenly had a vision of it hooking into my
spine, raising me dripping from my limpid pool, tossing
me triumphantly at Basehart's feet. "Oh, come now, Webster. No need to be shy. Basehart's read your critique of
his work. He's a very pleasant old fellow, really."

"I'm not feeling very well at the moment," I pleaded.

Dean Halvorsen's face cleared. This was an excuse acceptable to his sense of his own importance. "Really? Anything serious? Can I have something brought for you?
You do look a bit pale."

"No, no, nothing really. I just need a breath of fresh air.
I'll be back in a minute." I forced a smile and then backed
out the door, leaving Halvorsen staring after me with a
speculative look on his sharp face.

Why did I lie to Halvorsen then? Why did I not tell
him of my illness? Simply because something deep within
my psyche forbade me to acknowledge the seriousness of
my condition even to myself. If I looked upon my present
mishap as simply an accident due to some upset of my
digestive tract, I could comfortably hide the seriousness
of my illness from my own consciousness. If this is cowardice it is universal.

The corridor was empty. I continued to sidle along the
wall toward the toilet, only a few doors down. With continuing care and good luck I was reasonably sure of making it. To me it was now a transcendental goal. I
understood in those painful moments something of the
determination of Columbus, the dedication of Cortés, the
desperation of Saint Augustine. That toilet had become my
New World, my Eldorado, my City of God. And the corridor itself had become an interminable desert. Perhaps
the toilet was only a mirage? Was it really on this floor?

Could I safely descend a flight of stairs?

Then I was standing before the pebbled-glass door, my eyes wet with relief as they devoured the large word MEN engraved upon it. I glanced once up and down the deserted corridor and entered. How cool and refreshing the white tile seemed, how secure and inviting the row of cabinets!

"Evening, Professor."

I stiffened and felt my cheeks burn as if they had just been slapped. Of course—Henry, the attendant. He was leaning against the far wall next to the last wash basin, studying the sports section of the evening newspaper. He did not look at me.

"Good evening, Henry," I said, and then quickly entered one of the cabinets, locking the door behind me with trembling fingers. Safe at last! But with the flood of relief and triumph, a flotsam of bitter outrage surged into my soul. I reflected on the stupid uncontrollability of titanic forces. As I slipped off my trousers I thought of the constant humiliation of Man before the majesty of nature. Earthquakes, volcanic eruptions, tidal waves, meteors— what were these but constant reminders of the futility of Man's hope? And the body of Man—what was it but a charnel house for other species and a humiliation to the mind it served?

For you must not suppose that I am recounting this bitter episode only to explain a personal transaction, to record the decay of my own body beneath the onset of natural decay, to justify my subsequent attitude toward the University. I believe there is something universal in this experience. Have we not all been betrayed, humiliated, brought low in helpless rage, by our bodies at one time or another? If there be any who have not, then this experience should prove an exemplary and moral lesson to them.

I had cleansed myself and was about to dispose of my underwear when it suddenly occurred to me that I was faced with a problem. If I risked flushing the offending garment down the toilet it would undoubtedly stuff up the drain. The bowl would overflow. Henry would come to investigate. I could picture his investigation and the look on his face as he turned toward me.

There was no window in the wall behind the cabinet. Nor could I safely toss my underwear over the partition wall into the next cabinet. My name was printed on it. I would be discovered, prosecuted—

I submitted to necessity. I cleansed my underwear as best I could, wrapped it in toilet paper, stuffed it into the right-hand pocket of my jacket and emerged from the cabinet.

"You been down to the reception, Professor?" Henry inquired without turning from the newspaper.

"Yes, I have," I said as I washed and dried my hands.

"When do you figure they'll break up?"

"Oh, I should think in about another hour or so. Good night."

Henry sighed wearily. "Night, Professor."

A delicate problem now presented itself. Should I return to the reception, my jacket pocket malodorous, or should I risk the disrespect I would incur by fleeing the building?

The decision was not mine to make. Dean Halvorsen awaited me in the corridor. His eyes gleamed with determination. There was clearly no hope of escape. "Feeling better now?" he asked perfunctorily. "Well, come along then, and meet Sir P. V. M. Basehart." He slipped his arm through mine and led me fraternally back to the crowded reception room, brushing past groups of babbling lecturers, until we had reached the nerve center of the evening and Basehart himself stood before us. His thin, ancient face, his short, stubby red nose, the wild bush of white hair—all these reeled before me as I tried to keep my free arm pressed against my jacket pocket even while shaking hands with him.

"Webster!" Basehart spat the word out, sniffed at it. "Delighted, delighted!"

"How do you do?" I muttered.

"Well, actually"—he pronounced it "ekchully"—"I thought I was doing rather well, don't you know, until I ran into that very amusing review of yours. Tell me, Webster, do you really fancy that America is the home of some sort of demon of death and decay?"

"You may put it that way," I replied warily.

"Mmm. I thought belief in witchcraft over here died out with Cotton Mather." He smiled to acknowledge the barely audible titter that rose from the throats of the faculty wives within earshot.

"Only the European variety. European varieties of many things have a way of dying out in this climate." I was aware of an odor rising from my jacket pocket, though it seemed to have escaped everyone else. But I was determined to stand for no nonsense from Basehart.

"I hope I shall survive," Basehart responded jovially. "But come now, Webster, everywhere I've been in your remarkable country I've found a tremendous vitality—a tremendous surge of civic interest, for example, of determination to improve things. It bears out very obviously my theory of Cyclical Renewal. But you understand all this perfectly well. I don't really see why you dispute it."

"I did not dispute it. I called it irrelevant. All these cyclical waves of civic virtue or what you will are surface ripples on an ocean of death and decay." I regretted the dramatic phrasing as I noticed Dean Halvorsen's eyes narrow in annoyance. But I could not afford lengthy explanations. I had to escape before my personal odor of decay became too apparent. "I mean," I added hastily, "an American might take an entirely different view of America."

"There seems to be a fairly international understanding of the facts," Basehart replied coolly.

"Yes, yes, of course. But you interpret them wrong."

"Oh?" His glittering eyes warned me that he was merely reeling out enough line for me to hook myself on properly.

"You see American history as a triumphal progression—excuse me if I simplify, but that is the way you see it in the large view. To you it is evidently a cyclical thing. 'Cycles of progress' you've called them—toward human freedom, or understanding, or oneness with God or what you will. I'm not implying that you overlook the retrogressions either. But to you it is a matter of two steps forward, one step back. Progress does inevitably take place."

"You can hardly deny that."

"I simply interpret these facts differently." I noticed Dean Halvorsen sniffing furtively and glancing around with a puzzled frown. I moved sideways, away from the dean. "I see our history as basically one of continuing defeat. We are being defeated by the continent—by the very land itself. Every square mile of concrete that we lay is another badge of defeat, every megalopolis that spreads over the countryside is a testament to loneliness and despair. This continent is simply not yet fit for human habitation. Not enough generations of humans have lived and died in it. We lack a prehistory. You can read it in the face of the land—what land is left. The Indians knew it. They tried to make themselves like the land, and they succeeded briefly. We've tried to make the land like us, and we've failed."

"But you can't present the slightest evidence for such a romantic theory." Basehart smiled indulgently at me and followed me as I slowly retreated.

"There is more incipient violence on any American street, in any saloon, in any tenement, in any country club, than in all of Europe put together. I don't mean cruelty or yet hatred. I mean simple, barbaric violence. Culture doesn't tame it, politics doesn't touch it. It's a natural response to the savagery of the continent. And we haven't time—that's the main thing—we haven't much time left to alter it. The only Englishman who ever understood America was D. H. Lawrence. He said that a tremendous death-happening was awaiting the human race here."

"Lawrence? D. H. Lawrence? Extraordinary!" Basehart's eyes widened in mock surprise. "But I must insist on something more than mere intuition."

Dean Halvorsen was no longer glancing around. His gaze was fixed in steady speculation upon me. I felt sweat gathering on my forehead. I had to get out. The odor seemed all-pervasive and unmistakable to me. "Intuition is a more valuable guide to the human condition than mountains of statistics," I said recklessly, reaching for my handkerchief.

"Spoken like a fan of D. H. Lawrence, Webster, but hardly like a historian. You cannot disregard the tools of sociology, archaeology and political science, and still profess to be a historian." Basehart smiled thinly.

"Spoken like a politician," I retorted savagely.

"I didn't mean to question your bona fides, Webster."

"You'll have a chance to tear me to shreds when my own theories are published," I said sullenly.

"Well, I'm sure I didn't mean—" Basehart's voice stopped in midpassage. His eyes widened. He was staring at my forehead. His thin jaw dropped open to expose a row of gold fillings. He stepped back quickly as if he'd almost fallen into a pile of refuse.

I glanced around wonderingly. Dean Halvorsen's face was a deep scarlet, his lips tight in compressed rage. The other members of our constellation were staring at me in pure horror. It was only then—after that moment of empty dread, a moment disassociated from time and suspended in the arid wastes of eternity like a sword over my head—that I realized I had, in my panic, my near-hysteria, used my underwear instead of my handkerchief to mop my sweaty brow.

I glanced down at the offensive garment clutched in my right hand. No amount of will power could banish it, no intensity of death wish could terminate my existence on the spot. I felt my psyche retreating before these people. I was receding, diminishing, flying off into a cold and outer void. In their eyes I had almost disappeared. And at that moment my despair turned to anger. "Yes, Basehart," I cried, brandishing my underwear at him, "decay—decay everywhere. Every American is marked with it! On me it's just become obvious, that's all! Decay! Decay!" I kept crying the word as I pushed past Dean Halvorsen and fled the room. I ran blindly down the corridor, down the stairs, out into the cold night. And when I reached my apartment I found I was still clutching my soiled underwear.

The very next day I received my notice of dismissal

from Dean Halvorsen personally. I did not attempt to justify or defend myself at the interview. I could not admit to myself that I was the victim of a fatal disease. And to take advantage of an illness seemed to be avoiding the main point, which was that by seizing upon my temporary weakness as an excuse to cast aside my theories, they were putting themselves historically in the wrong. I only regretted that I had not soiled Basehart and Halvorsen with a little of the decay that had so hypocritically horrified them.

Have you the power to will yourself out of a dream and into consciousness? I do not think this is very uncommon; at least, I have always been able to do so. When the footing on the high suspension bridge becomes too uncertain, when the pinnacle is about to collapse, when the fearful fiend doth too close behind me tread, then I am able to force my subconscious to relax its grip. Or perhaps it is not a matter of will, but of fright or humiliation so deep that my conscious mind interposes to preserve its dignity —that is to say, its sanity. Of course, the implicit assumption on which the mind operates here is that consciousness, no matter how unpleasant, must always be less frightening than the nightmare. Were it not so, we would dream endlessly.

You will understand, then, that I had begun to will myself awake as I was walking back toward the faculty reception room in Dean Halvorsen's grip—for that which frightens me most is not private disaster but public exposure. But as is usual with that particular reverie (which recurs fairly often, being both recent and pungent), I was unable to shake the horror of it until its very end—was forced to drink my subconscious draught to the last drop before consciousness intervened.

But when I awoke I found myself deep in a wide-awake nightmare. I was no longer within The Foundation. Where was the gray window-wall? It had been replaced by solid slabs of granite, closely fitted, each with a ten-foot-square face, some decorated with a sort of chicken-scratching. Where was the armchair? It had been replaced by a strange sort of sloped half-couch made of wood and rattan, gilded and carved with lion's paws for feet. Where was the bedside table? It had vanished completely. Only the indirect lighting was familiar—a soft, shadowless light suffused the place. The door was no longer visible, being sunk back into granite walls five feet thick. My first feeling of dismay grew gradually into panic as I saw that *all* the walls were made of these granite slabs. And my bed? That was the most frightening discovery of all. For it was not truly a bed. It had a prow that curved up above my feet to point back at me. Its sides rose up a few inches above my body and described a vaguely oval shape indicating that the bed came to another point behind my head. But if this discovery was an assault on my sanity, it was also the first clue to my condition. For my bed was a boat. And so quickly does one's mind leap to a logical explanation, no matter how improbable, simply to avoid the chaos of madness, that I instantly understood all. My bed was indeed a boat, a *solar* boat, and those chicken-scratchings on the walls were hieroglyphs. My room was in fact an Egyptian Dynastic tomb. Perhaps you will understand how close to the edge of sanity those surroundings had driven me when I tell you that I wept for joy—literally wept for joy—when I recognized my room for what it was: a skillful re-creation of a Pharaoh's tomb.

Reason immediately replaced panic. After all, I had

assumed the role of Pharaoh. This, then, must be what Ritchie had meant when he referred to "role therapy." Praying, I raised myself slowly, cautiously got out of bed, tentatively reached out a hand to touch the wall—and felt a great wave of relief sweep over me as my finger tips identified the "granite" as some sort of composition board. This was indeed a set designed to aid me in my "role." But my investigations were cut short by the sound of someone fumbling with the latch of the door. I scrambled back into my solar boat, pulled up the blankets (which I now noticed were a heavy brocade embroidered with the crook and flail emblems of the Pharaohs) to my chin and stared stonily at the ceiling, as Ritchie entered.

And it was then that I experienced my second shock. For Ritchie was dressed in a pale-blue uniform that made his figure somehow familiar. I had seen that man, dressed like that, somewhere before. His pipe was still aggressively clenched between his teeth. He glanced at me and then bent over and picked up the clip board that hung at the foot of my boat. Suddenly I remembered. Of course—my dream figure! This was the shadowy vision who'd entered my room late at night on more than one occasion before I died. Then he was not a dream, but real. Yet he had remonstrated with Stein for not having been allowed to see me before. Who was this Ritchie, anyhow?

He was evidently The Foundation's head psychiatrist. Yet he wore The Foundation uniform as if he were simply another technician. Did he wear it for economy, or—more probably—as an exterior badge of identification and *loyalty*? He was also a man who had sneaked into my room before I died and taken notes. He was a man whose activities, disguised by an unnecessary belligerence, were, when viewed objectively, *surreptitious*. I could almost hear

Stein's voice as he spat out savagely, "There's a traitor here!" And as a logical solution emerged through my identification of Ritchie, I felt a thrill of hope. But I would have to act quickly and bravely. I decided on a desperate gamble.

"We've met before, Doctor Ritchie," I said, in as insinuating a tone as I could muster.

He straightened abruptly and dropped the clip board; his hard blue eyes narrowed appraisingly at me. I saw the lines of muscle in his jaw tauten as he clamped down harder on his pipe. "Can't say that we have, old boy," he said with a jocularity that barely concealed his tension. I'd struck home. "I'm glad to see that you've dropped the Egyptian pose, though. There *is* such a thing as a catatonic condition. But your symptoms, although imaginative, were not exactly convincing, mate."

"No more convincing than—"

"Perhaps you're wondering about all this." He waved his hand around as he casually but determinedly interrupted me. "Had it done overnight. This is the sort of thing that makes Administration howl! Costs a fortune. But it's generally worth it. You understand the theory of role therapy, of course."

"I'm not interested in that at the—"

"But you should be, old boy, you should be! After all, you're in it, aren't you? It's simply a logical extension of behaviorist theory—still experimental, but our results have been very positive so far. You see"—he jutted out his jaw aggressively—"the idea is that some patients, especially in the schizophrenic group—I won't corner you with details—spend entirely too much energy creating a dream world for themselves. It's not a dream world, of course; it's their alternative real world, one in which they feel comfy. Now, by helping them along, by making that world as real as possible for them, we relieve a terrific strain on their superegos. Leaves them more energy to devote to treatment, relaxes them to the point where they're more willing to accept treatment. Gives them confidence that they're not completely nuts. I mean, we start right off by accepting their fantasies as real and then lead *them* to eventually tell *us* that they're not real. It's quite complicated, but that's the gist. Of course, the important thing is to identify the patient's fantasy world correctly. We've had some lulus in here, let me tell you! Once had one of these Black Muslims in here who thought he was a Ku Klux Klansman. Used to go around in a sheet and pillow case, and all just because his name was Bino. That was the root of it all—I mean, his parents had thoughtlessly named him Albert. Imagine growing up in Harlem with a name like Al Bino."

I was determined to press on. "Yes, we have met," I insisted. "Or perhaps I should say I recognized you when you sneaked into my room a few weeks ago to steal information from the clip board. You broke in several times. I remember you perfectly well. You thought I was asleep, but I wasn't. I *know* you." My voice gained speed and assurance as I saw my remarks hitting home. Ritchie stood rigidly at the foot of my bed, his hands clenching and unclenching, his face a study in repressed panic. I pressed my advantage ruthlessly.

"You're a spy, Ritchie! A spy! What Foundation do you work for? Do you know what they do to spies around here?"

"Why, you—you—" He jerked the pipe from between his teeth. "You swine!" he hissed. "You dare to call me a spy! You're insane, really insane! Why, I'd sooner give my own mother shock therapy than—than spy!" He spat out the word as if it were something tangibly distasteful. But the twitching of his throat muscles betrayed him.

'They'll get it out of you when I tell them," I whispered. "You can lie to me but not to Stein!"

The mention of Stein's name had a totally unexpected effect. Ritchie's lips curled back in a sneer and he jutted his jaw so far out that I thought he would dislocate it. But at the same time his hands began to tremble and his voice quavered beneath its pugnacity. "Stein? Stein? He—Why, he wouldn't listen to such nonsense! He'd laugh you right out of court." He paused and his eyes did not meet mine.

I felt a thrill of fear. Perhaps I'd gone too far. Behind those eyes Ritchie might even now be contemplating my murder. "I won't tell anyone," I said hurriedly. "I wouldn't want to get you into trouble."

Ritchie's eyes still smoldered with suspicion and fear. "How can you get me into trouble? You are insane, remember?"

"I'll say nothing if you help me get out of here."

His mouth compressed into a grim smile. "They'd kill me if I tried anything like that." He paused thoughtfully. "And of course, if you started to imagine things like that, I'd have to give you shock therapy—a little insulin, old boy, a little insulin."

"Well, then we'd both get it—" I shut up as I heard the door open.

Stein walked in, followed by Nurse Williams. He nodded at Ritchie and then stared at me. His face instantly assumed my own mask of stony indifference. "How do you feel this morning?" he asked.

" 'The perfume of Arabia has been brought to me to make perfect my smell through the scent of the god. Here are brought to me liquids which have come forth from the god Ra to make perfect'—"

"Very good, Professor," Stein said, in a voice that was under desperate control. "An excellent rendition of the Book of the Dead. But I very much fear you have picked a paranoid fantasy a little too obvious. I would have expected Lazarus from another patient, but Cheops will do, I dare say, for a historian."

If Ritchie was innocent or if he intended to outbluff me, now was the time for him to speak. But he kept his silence, his eyes intent upon Stein. And his stillness bespoke my victory. I racked my memory for more lines.

"'Our members shall become young in Arabia,'" I continued, "'and our soul shall appear over our body in Taneter.'"

Stein sighed and removed his spectacles, which he polished with the lapel of his white jacket. "Professor Webster, please," he said wearily, "let's try to be sensible for just one minute." He replaced his spectacles and turned to Ritchie. "Has he been babbling like this all the time?"

"Yes, he has," Ritchie said without hesitation.

"Webster"—Stein turned again with a pleading note in his voice—"is it nothing to you that I saved your life? Is it nothing to you that your name will go down in history for all time as the first man to return from death? You are a historian. I appeal to your sense of history, to your sense of the continuity of human progress. I appeal to you in the name of all mankind."

"'We journey on our legs to the immortal abode. Our hands are carried into the House of Eternity.'"

"Stop it!" Stein shouted, his face alternating between my own stony indifference and his open irritation. He lit a cigarette. "Do you realize what you are doing? If you insist on playing this farce you'll be kept down here in role therapy indefinitely—until you decide to give up. But in the meantime humanity awaits a deliverance which only—" He paused thoughtfully. "Let me explain as simply as I know how. My discovery is so revolutionary, deals so intimately with mankind's basic fears and hopes, that only actual demonstration will ever convince humanity of its validity. And so delicate is the balance of acceptance and rejection in a matter such as this that any aberration on your part will absolutely ruin it. For example, mankind has read for two thousand years of Jesus raising the dead. Some have believed, some have not, in all ages. Today, hardly anyone believes. Why? Is that not the hope of the world? Does a man not *want* to believe he may live again? Indeed he does. But it takes a mighty faith to believe in resurrection. If all the organized religions of Christendom, if centuries of teaching and preaching, if ages of lying, conniving and terrorizing, if regiments, armies of priests and battalions of popes and millions of Bibles cannot convince man of his potential immortality, what chance have I of gaining acceptance for my discoveries? Only one. That one must be clear, visual and tangible. It must be an unimpeachable demonstration conducted under strictly controlled scientific conditions. The slightest sign of aberration, as I say—the faintest suspicion of either manipulation or lack of integrity—will ruin everything. Man will not seize upon a hope so deep if he even faintly suspects it may be a fraud. Your play-acting would cast a pall of improbability over the entire proceedings. I appeal to you in the name of the countless thousands who statistically face death every day!"

" 'We journey on our legs to the immortal abode. Our hands are carried into the House of Eternity.' "

"You've already used that line!" Stein shouted. He commenced to float back and forth at the foot of my boat, his huge head bowed in thought, the cigarette dangling from his lips. "What are you after, Professor?" he asked himself more than me. "I can understand a psychic shock involved in returning from death. But this fantasy—absurd—too complicated—painfully ornate—"

"The dead suffer no pain," I intoned.

Stein stopped pacing and stared at me speculatively. "You do," he said.

"Our members are perfect and feel no pain in Osiris."

I saw the suppressed excitement in Stein's eyes. At last I had offered him something tangible to work on. He could now force a physical manifestation of my duplicity. "And if the dead *did* feel pain they would not be dead, would they?" he asked reasonably.

"Pain does not dwell in Ra," I said contemptuously.

He pulled up the embroidered blanket to expose my right foot, removed the cigarette from between his lips and brought it suggestively close to the sole of my foot. I saw Nurse Williams make an instinctive but quickly suppressed gesture toward him. I saw Ritchie's eyes widen and his jaw muscles work painfully.

"Very well, Webster," Stein said. "I am about to burn a hole in your foot, to see if pain dwells in Ra. If it does, you will admit this fantasy to be sheer fakery?"

"Our solar boat awaits."

I felt the touch of the cigarette against my sole, saw smoke rising, smelled singed flesh. But of course I felt no pain at all. "We shall go to the place of Ra in everlasting glory," I commented.

Stein's face paled. He stepped back, staring first at my foot and then at my immobile face.

"Gorblimey!" Ritchie exclaimed. "Did you ever see the like?"

"Doctor Stein!" Nurse Williams said, in a hushed but shocked voice.

"Deep in the Land of Egypt," Stein said in reflective despair. "And the work—a lifetime's work—" He turned away with a heavy sigh.

At that moment I felt a very real wave of sympathy for Stein. His eloquence had not left me completely untouched. I was not unmoved by his appeal to history, to humanity, to God. I have thought long and deeply about these matters. And I suppose that, like most people, I would be willing to sacrifice my own life for the survival of the race. I would perhaps accept a crown of martyrdom once for the sake of mankind's life everlasting. But to accept such a crown time and again (for I had no doubt that Stein would have to "demonstrate" many times) was beyond my courage and my faith. But on a more personal level, too, I felt for Stein. I confess that were not my very existence to be at stake over and over again, I would willingly have revealed my fakery to assuage the sorrow that shook his huge body. But my sterner nature conquered. "Our solar boat shall float in the majesty of Ra forevermore," I intoned relentlessly.

"Oh God!" Stein cried. Then, bringing himself under control, he said, "Bandage that foot, Williams. I have to think about this." And he left the room without glancing at me again.

Ritchie and I exchanged meaningful glances. But his had in it an element of calculation as well as conspiracy.

Williams produced gauze, iodine and tape, and bent over my foot. I felt instinctively that time was now of the essence. I had to talk to Ritchie alone, somehow get rid of Williams.

"We find thee sumptuous, daughter of Set," I said.

"I *am* putting on a little weight" (hoo), she muttered absently as she started to wind gauze around my foot.

"Thy breasts are choice plums. Permit us to savor their flavor, O child of delight."

She blushed slightly, made an irrelevant move to button the top of her uniform, but continued winding. "Really, Professor!" (hoo) she said.

Was there no embarrassing her?

"Thy limbs are pillars of alabaster which guard the temple of heat. Permit us to enter the temple, O goddess, and worship therein."

She compressed her lips grimly and began to tape the gauze.

"Lie down beside us, daughter of the Nile, and we will disport ourselves between thy legs."

She glared at me, finished bandaging the foot and then stood back, contemplating her handiwork.

I glanced at Ritchie. He was chomping nervously on his pipe. Did he understand?

"Shall we not enjoy this daughter of Set together, O priest of Ra? Is her body not delectable?"

Ritchie's eyes widened in sudden comprehension. Nurse Williams glanced at him uncertainly. He removed his pipe from his mouth and leered at her.

"Come now, captain of a thousand chariots. Pharaoh grants you permission to sate your lust upon this temple prostitute. We shall enjoy her together, seeking admission through every portal—"

"Really!" Williams said. "That's too much!"

Ritchie edged toward her.

"What the hell is this?" she demanded.

"Better play along with his fantasy," Ritchie whispered insinuatingly.

"Oh yeah?" Williams backed to the door. "Well, you can play along with it, not me. That guy's nuts!" She left the room, slamming the door behind her.

Ritchie chuckled and started to stuff his pipe from a tobacco pouch. "Now then, what's on your mind?" he asked casually.

"Get me out of The Foundation!" I whispered.

"Why should I? Risk's too great. They'll never believe anything you say about me now. You've convinced them you're crackers, old boy, crackers."

"But I'm worth something to the people you work for," I pleaded.

"How?"

"Stein brought me back from the dead."

"We've already got all that data, old boy." Ritchie puffed serenely on his pipe.

"But—I can't feel pain. You saw just now that I couldn't feel the pain. That ought to be worth something."

Ritchie walked thoughtfully back and forth before my boat. "You may have something there." He was bargaining with me, but two could haggle.

"Who are your friends?" I demanded.

"What's the difference, old boy?"

"I don't intend to go through all this again. I might as well stay here in The Foundation. I'm not jumping from one frying pan to another—or into the fire, for all I know."

"I can assure you—" Ritchie began.

"You can't assure me of anything!" I snapped. "Unless you're willing to reveal who you work for, I'm not moving."

He shrugged. "Well, why not, then? I work for The Institute. Now, they're fine people—not like this lot—and they would treat you with every consideration. Good conditions there."

I did not believe Ritchie. His eyes were entirely too frank and open as he spoke, his voice too calm and measured. But one possibility swayed me: to escape if I could during my transfer from one place to another. The chances were, I realized, slight. But they were infinitely greater than any prospects I could have entertained of slipping out of The Foundation. Ritchie was, of course, perfectly well aware that I must be intending such a move, and he would take all precautions to prevent it. But at least I would be in motion, at least in a position to measure my wits and determination against new surroundings. "All right," I said, "I'll go."

"Good!" Ritchie instantly dropped his indifferent pose, and jutting his chin out aggressively, he rubbed his hands together in satisfaction. "This'll pay old Stein back!" he muttered. Then he glanced at his wristwatch. "Be ready any time from now on."

"What are you planning?" I asked.

"I can't tell you that at the moment—"

"I'm afraid you'll have—"

"Don't worry, old boy!" He cut my objections short. "I can't tell you at the moment because I'm not sure how we're going to manage this. But be ready for anything. The code word will be 'Nelson.'"

"'Nelson'?"

"That's right. Anyone coming to you with that word will be one of ours. The counter word will be 'John D.' You will use that unless you have some reason to think things are going wrong. That's your way of letting us know everything's all right. Got it?"

I nodded. "I've got it. But I'd still like to know—"

"No more time for chit-chat!" Ritchie cried, and he stalked from the room, favoring me with a curt nod as he left.

And now that I was fully committed, I suffered misgivings. I will not hide the fact that these misgivings were emotional as well as logical. I have not denied I felt a certain tie to Stein, a certain relationship developing with him. This was now to be severed, and very frankly, I found myself disturbed by the prospect. Not only Stein but also The Foundation itself had insensibly developed within me a kind of comfortable recognition, a certain relaxed intimacy in its association. If I found myself within the walls of The Institute, would I develop the same homey understanding of my surroundings? Clearly, for very many reasons, I had to concentrate all my energies on escaping before arrival.

A desperate venture? Yes. And there were psychological dangers of which Ritchie could not have been aware. For this was not my first encounter with simulated madness, not the first fight I'd waged against mental submersion. I still bore the scars of a Pyrrhic victory I had won years before.

You cannot imagine me in the Army? I met a corporal once, at Fort Dix, with a wooden leg and a glass eye. It is true he was in limited service, but I mention him so you will believe me when I tell you that the sinister buffoons who composed my local Selective Service Board did not hesitate to draft me during the manpower famine of the forties. The weakness of my physique, my astigmatic eyes, my manifest fear—none of these factors weighed with the servants of Moloch. But this tragi-farce has been celebrated too many times for me to repeat it here. I was assigned (in the face of my scholastic accomplishments and the improbability of my survival) to an infantry rifle company. I made the usual progress through the various anterooms of hell (induction centers, troop trains, et al), and eventually found myself in Fort McClellan, Alabama ("the Home of the Infantry," as it was called by those who had indeed found it a natural residence). I realized from my very first whiff of the place that it had been perfectly designed to torture me into that state of insensible, cringing depravity from which all military virtue arises. But I did not comprehend how desperately *unsafe* this place could be until, early in the second week of training, I was brought to bay at the Obstacle Course.

It was an afternoon late in August, oppressively sultry, overcast and threatening, when we were marched up to this death trap. I had already suffered every humiliation that individual sadism could suggest to my fellow trainees —a group of huge and hairy ruffians who enacted roles gleaned from attendance at patriotic Grade B films. But only this first glimpse of the Obstacle Course clearly revealed to me that I was the dupe of a *planned and organized* conspiracy of my fellow citizens.

We were required to go through the course with thirty-pound field packs on our backs, gas masks on our hips and rifles in our hands. The first obstacle was a wall that one was to vault. After all the other men in my company had surmounted it I was still hurling myself in despairing frenzy against it and bouncing back with the punctuality of a rubber ball. Finally I was permitted to go around it. This I did, weak with relief and gratitude. But what was my horror to discover beyond it a swamp filled with ingenious devices for the entrapment, debasement and liquidation of the unfortunate? Here was the rope stretched high above a muddy stream, to be negotiated hand-over-hand (I waded across); there was the great net like a veil against the side of a cliff, upon which one was to crawl spider-fashion (I found a trail sneaking around the side of the cliff); beyond were the cunningly devised cactus mazes, the dummies that popped out to affright the unwary, the deadly pits, the cruel barbed-wire entanglements and finally what can only be described as an Obstacle to Life Itself. This was a smooth-faced wooden tower thirty feet high that offered neither hand nor foot holds. Near its summit was a large square hole. We triumphed over this through teamwork. Without having time to reflect upon the daring idiocy of what I was doing, I found myself clambering up the backs of a human pyramid, being pulled, pushed and dragged through the hole and into a shadowy room ten feet square. The square hole opposite was meant to suggest the next step—egress by the same method.

I think I had already decided upon my course of action when first I entered that elevated room. But I cannot pretend to have planned a campaign, to have coolly and objectively assessed the situation and devised a means of surviving it. No, my first decision was dictated by exhaustion, disgust and, above all, fright. A deep instinct of self-preservation whispered beseechingly to my psyche, advising me to remain exactly where I was, to press my luck no further, to accept this habitable box as my final resting place. So while my comrades made their way up to, through and then down from that eagle's nest, I huddled in a dark corner, invisible to their sweaty, exalted eyes. When the last of them had passed through, when their animal howls of triumph faded in the distance, I emerged.

The room, though small, was airy. It commanded, through each "window," a fine view of the forests and

swamps around it. If determinedly defended, it would be
secure enough. I gratefully removed my field pack, my
gas mask, my helmet, and set to work. My field jacket
attached to the stock of my rifle made an effective broom,
with which I tidied up the place as best I could. Then I
brought forth my small stock of photos from home and
stuck them on splinters as décor. Finally, I did not neglect
to provide privacy by curtaining the windows with my
shirt and undershirt. Next I examined my resources. I had
four packages of K rations and a canteen full of water. But
I did not calculate the days and hours of potential survival. I was too relieved at having escaped more immediate dangers. Let tomorrow provide for itself, I thought
light-heartedly; today, I was snug and safe from all
alarm.

But the outer world soon intruded in the guise of our
platoon sergeant, who bawled up at me, "Awright, Webster, git yo ass outa theyah!"

For a moment I debated whether or not to reply. But of
course my rude curtains revealed my presence. "I'm fine
up here, Sarge," I called down.

"Ah sayed git yo ass down an' make it gawdamned
quick!" he shouted.

"I can't!" I cried desperately. "It's not safe!"

"Jes crawl outa thet window, hang on like at the edge
an' then let go."

"I mean it's not safe *down there*," I explained.

"Gawdammit, Webster, if yore not down outa theyah in
two minutes Ahm gonna have yo coat-mahsheld when we
git back!"

"I'm not going back," I said, and understood suddenly
that it was true: I would in no wise return to Moloch.

"What jest do you mean, yore not goin' back? Yore a
deserter!"

"No, I'm not. I've resigned," I explained.

"Whah yo misrahble sonofabitchin' bastahd, Ah'll come on up theyah an' throw yoo out!"

I reached for my rifle and extended its snout a few inches out the window. "No, you won't, Sarge," I chuckled.

There was a momentary silence during which I could hear the metallic whine of the swamp insects. Then the sergeant spoke in the tone of assuaging simplicity suitable for children and maniacs. "Well, well. Awright, Webster. No call to git het up. Ah'll tell yoo what—you jes stay raht up theyah. Yes, sir. Yoo rest easy up theyah for a bit an' Ah'll uh—Ah'll git the chaplain to talk things ovah with yoo." His voice revealed his palpable relief as this solution occurred to him. "Doan go 'way naow," he called as he trotted off.

I had no intention of going away. But now, with the first opposition to my solution overcome, I began to consider my action. I could not, of course, hold out longer than my food and water lasted—perhaps a week with abstemious rationing. And, of course, they could easily devise some brusque and unpleasant means of removing me from my perch. I would have to exercise profound cunning, great caution and never-sleeping alertness to achieve the goal that now presented itself to my mind in vivid simplicity.

I ate a quarter of a bar of chocolate, stretched out on the floor and waited. Within the hour a voice hailed me from below.

"Private Webster! Oh, Private Webster! Are you up there?" The voice was gentle, patient, even genial.

I looked down to see the battalion's chaplain standing below. He smiled at me and waved.

"I'm here, Chaplain."

"Well, well. That *is* good." He paused thoughtfully. "You're OK up there, eh?"

"Just fine, Chaplain."

"Well, we were all just wondering when you planned to come down."

"I'm not coming down, Chaplain," I replied regretfully.

"Is something bothering you, Webster? If it is, you can feel free to confide in me. I always hold everything in strict confidence. That's my job, you know—to help fellows when they go uh—when they feel depressed. Maybe some trouble at home?" he asked hopefully.

"No, nothing like that, Chaplain."

"Nothing wrong at home?" He digested this information sorrowfully.

"Well then, maybe it's girl trouble? I mean, a lot of the boys bring me those kinds of problems. Believe me, if you're in some sort of trouble with a girl, you'll find we're all on your side—all in it together, so to speak."

"No, Chaplain, I don't have a girl."

"You don't?" He paused and cleared his throat. "Now look, Webster, I'm used to dealing with sexual problems of *all kinds*. I understand. Sometimes, what with all the pressure out here and surrounded by thousands and thousands of men and all—well, sometimes a man gets some funny ideas or maybe goes a little off the beam and—what I'm trying to say—well, I'll be glad to talk over *any kind* of sexual problem you might have, you understand?" The glad repugnance in his voice annoyed me.

"I have no problems of any kind," I said coldly.

After another long pause the chaplain spoke in a voice tinged with awe and reverence. "Webster—you there, Webster? Webster, do you believe in God?"

"I don't think so," I replied.

"Haven't you ever longed, Webster, for the comfort a

man can find in religion? Now, I don't want to pry into your private beliefs, but whatever your religious affiliations may be, I think you'll find that I'm pretty inter-denominational. Don't you believe anything, Webster?"

"Yes, I do," I answered thoughtfully.

"Swell! Swell!" His happy excitement moved me to pity.

"I believe this is a very unsafe place," I said, in as hollow a voice as I could muster.

"Well then, come on down."

"No, I mean down there. I mean the whole Army. I feel unsafe."

"Why, this is just training, Webster. They're not trying to hurt you. They're trying to train you to protect yourself and even save your life when you get into combat. They're trying to save you, you understand?" A note of exasperation had crept into his voice.

"You mean they're going to send me somewhere even worse. Sorry, Chaplain, it doesn't seem safe."

"Webster," he called after a pause, "have you ever undergone any sort of psychotherapy? I mean, have you ever had funny feelings maybe, and gone to some doctor about them? Or anything like that?"

"I don't trust doctors," I replied. "I don't feel safe with them."

"I see, I see," he ruminated. "Well, I'm no doctor, Webster. I'm a friend. I might be able to help you with those funny feelings. Why not come on down and we'll have a nice comfy talk about it, all?"

"Chaplain," I called down wearily, "do you believe in God?"

"Of course I do!"

"Pray for me, Chaplain. Pray for me!"

"Now look, Webster," he cried in sudden alarm, "don't

do anything hasty! I mean, there's plenty of time to think things out. It's a crime against the United States Army to commit suicide—"

"It's not that, Chaplain," I said sorrowfully. "But if I have to stay up here any length of time I'll probably start abusing myself, and that's a sin, isn't it? Pray for me."

"Why, you lousy goddamned bastard, get down from there!" he shouted.

"That's blasphemy, Chaplain!"

"I don't give a damn what it is! You had your chance! Now we'll just see what Captain King has to say about all this!"

I saw what Captain King had to say the following morning. I had just wakened from a deep and dreamless sleep. The dawn was flooding the woods and swamp with delicately hued shadows, the forest birds were busily gossiping and I was breakfasting on a can of corned beef when a thin but peremptory voice hailed me from below.

"Webster! This is Captain King speaking!" His brusque tone spoiled my idyl.

"Good morning, Captain," I called courteously.

"Webster, you've got until nine o'clock this morning to get down out of there. If you're not down by then, we'll come and get you."

"You're going to kill me?" I asked.

"Not unless we absolutely have to, Webster. But we're not going to stand for any more nonsense!"

"I knew this wasn't a safe place!" I cried. "Well, go ahead, Captain, get a machine gun and riddle me! Bring up a howitzer and blow one of your own men to bits! Why not use poison gas? You'll be able to explain it all at the court-martial."

"Webster, whether you know it or not, you're a deserter, and deserters have no place in this man's army!"

'That's what I've been trying to tell everyone, Captain. You're the first person who's understood."

"Don't try any of that wise-guy stuff on me, Webster. You've got until nine o'clock. Think it over." And he marched stiffly away.

There was nothing to think over. Either they would succeed in removing me or they would not. I had no intention of being killed. I would resist only to the limits of their temper, no further. I was anxious to learn just what those limits were.

Punctually at nine o'clock the platoon sergeant and a squad of M.P. riflemen arrived. They had brought a ladder with them. Paying no attention to my shouted warnings, they placed the ladder against the side of my tower and started to climb. I waited until they were about ten feet off the ground and then, using my rifle as a lever, toppled the ladder over backward. It was too simple. I realized that there was something almost ritualistic about it. It was as if they had to rehearse some well-prepared preliminaries in order to get on with the main rite.

"Awright, Webster," the sergeant bawled, "yoo have shoan an' demonstrated physical resistance to lawful effoats of the Yenited States Ahmy to reclaim yoo foah active duty. Squawd, fall in!"

Of course, I knew what their next move must be. This was the moment of truth. I hunched up in a corner.

"Squawd, tenshun! Load!"

I heard the bolts snap home.

"Webster, this is yo last chance. Now, are yoo comin down?"

I did not reply.

"Aim!"

My mouth was open, my lungs full, the words of surrender on my lips. But just as I was about to utter them the sergeant made a fatal error. He gave me yet another "last chance," thereby revealing the emptiness of his threats.

"Noaw weh gonna shoot, Webster, 'less yoo agree to git down!" he called.

Not only the words but also the note of supplication in his tone reassured me. I did not answer.

"Sheet! Squawd, order ahms—at ease," he sighed. Then, "Aw, come on down, Webster, like a reglah fellah. Yoo had yo joke, naow come on down. Po Captin King's jes the laughin' stahk of the regiment. He's a combat vetran, Webster. Thet man's got a wahf an' too kids. Yo killin' his cahreer, Webster."

"I don't feel safe down there!" I cried.

"Sheet!" The sergeant spat and marched his men away.

I was left in peace for the next two days and nights. This was, of course, psychological warfare. Left strictly alone, they hoped, I would fall prey to imagined terrors; and they could always simply outwait my small stock of food and drink. But I kept myself busy by doing housework, by mastering tic-tac-toe and by singing. I sang every song I could remember and then sang them over again. I was singing "The Long, Long Trail" one evening by moonlight when a new and unfamiliar figure appeared, a tall, thin man with a scar running down his right cheek. He wore the gold oak leaf of a major. The moonlight glinted from the rims of his steel spectacles. He stood patiently, his hands clasped behind him, staring up at me impassively, waiting for me to finish the song.

"Where the nightingales are singing
And a white moon beams—"

I faltered and then stopped. There was something patiently sinister about this presence.

"Blease—" he called up in a cordially guttural voice. "Blease do continue. It iss charming, charming!"

It was not simply the fact that this was the first field-grade officer who had ever addressed himself to me. There was more to it than that. There was something about his manner—something about the whiff of accent in his speech that expunged my self-confidence almost immediately. But I determined not to show it, and continued in a slightly quavering voice,

"There's a long, long night of waiting—"

Suddenly I stopped. A major with a patient manner, a slight but unmistakably Teutonic accent—

"Charming!" he called out. "You're endire bervormance iss charming!"

"Good evening, Doctor," I said.

"Good efening, good efening!" He rocked back and forth on the balls of his feet, his face wreathed in smiles. "You are in good voice donight!"

"I'm afraid I haven't got much range—"

"But chust enough so that we hear you, no?"

"No—I mean—"

"Nefer mind, Private Webster. With me it iss not necessary to carry on the charade. I belief you. Oh yes, yes, I belief you!" He laughed suddenly.

"What do you mean, you believe me?" In spite of his cordial manner I could not suppress a mounting tremor of uneasiness.

"Why, I belief you are zick. Yes, zick! You can come down now."

"I don't know what came over me," I muttered. "It's— all this—the whole thing—it makes me nervous—very nervous—it's all so unsafe!" I spoke brokenly. This was the moment I had been working toward for the past days. I must not cheat myself of the fruits of victory by any untimely admissions. I threw myself into my role. "I can't go back down there," I sobbed. "They want to kill me down there!"

"Vor you, Private Webster, it iss not safe anywhere, no? We agree with you."

"What do you mean by that?"

"You are zo charming! Thiss—it is all fery charming. A marvelous bervormance—unique in my exberience. Your suberego iss to be congraduladed! Over the chablain's eyes you haff bulled the wool— Even over your own. You would make a suberb case hisdory."

"You think— You don't believe me?"

"But I do, I do! I belief you more than you belief yourzelf." Suddenly his smile vanished, his body tensed and his voice became savagely aggressive. "You are a fery zick man, Private Webster! Fery, fery zick! You are not berhaps aware of this fact. You think you are fooling us. You are nod. You are fooling yourzelf! I do nod for one moment belief this charade—not for one moment!"

His sudden attack caught me completely off balance. I had recourse to mere sullenness. "Well, I'm not coming down."

"Haff you conzidered, Private Webster, how deeply disturbed you must be to make zuch a bervormance? Haff you conzidered how zick you must be, how mentally disturbed, to go to these lengths to secure a discharge? Oh yes, I belief you are zick all right! You should never haff been drafted in the virst place!"

I swallowed these insults, determined not to be side-tracked. "Then—"

"Yess, yess"—he waved his hand impatiently—"you will be discharged under Segtion Eight. You are not mendally combetent to bear armss."

"Are you sure of that, Major?" My voice trembled with excitement. It took great effort to erase any faint note of triumph in it.

"Private Webster," he said quietly, "I am efen more sure of that than you are."

"You want me to come down now?" I asked tentatively.

"Oh no, no, Private Webster. We do nod want you to come down now. There iss Captain King to conzider. Yess, your calculations haff been accurate, most accurate. You realize, of course, that Captain King will be judged on his ability to remove you *without* bodily harm. You were quite corregt. You haff become a broblem in strategy and tagtics. We must nod undermine Captain King's solution, must we? Cleffer. Schizophrenics are sometimes cleffer. Rarely as cleffer as you."

I ignored his insinuations. "What am I supposed to do?"

"Wait. You haff only to wait. Someding iss being ar-ranged. You will be removed domorrow morning and will be brought to me diregtly. I haff already made out the nezessary pabers. I will be able to regommend a good man in New York for you to zee. Unfortunately, we haff no vacilities here for comblicated cases such as yours. Good night, Private Webster." He wheeled abruptly and disap-peared into the shadows of the forest.

I could not sleep that night. Nor was my wakefulness inspired by the excitement of triumph. For I had won my victory, hadn't I? I had deliberately set out to prove my-self insane and succeeded. But there was that in the major's manner that had implanted a worm of doubt in my soul. Something offhand, careless, professionally certain, about his conduct—as if he had reached an unshakable conclusion on a relatively simple matter. But was this not what I had desired? Yes, except for one thing. *I did not feel that I could fool the major.* His bearing, his speech, his accent—all these bespoke a long, perhaps even distinguished career in psychology. I could not possibly have fooled him. In the final analysis one cannot fool such professionals. So then—so then his diagnosis of my condition was based on objective factors? Impossible! I was perfectly sane. And yet I could not sleep. I heard the forest owls calling to each other until dawn while, slightly amused by the irony, I arranged the arguments I would use to prove my sanity.

With sunrise I made myself ready for departure. I returned my photos to my wallet, packed away the remains of my K rations, swept the place for the last time, removed the curtains from my windows and dressed myself for my last military maneuver. I had no idea what the captain had arranged, but I was confident. And I will not hide the fact that as I surveyed my little nest I felt a twinge of regret at leaving. This aerie had a certain lived-in hominess about it now. How perfect these moments might have been if the worm of discontent planted by the major had not still been coiling within me. But I had little time for reflection.

The sound was unidentifiable at first—a distant, stuttering, metallic noise combined with a crashing sound—the uproar one would expect from a giant mechanical dinosaur plodding through the forest. As it drew nearer I discerned the sound of a powerful engine, the crunching of treads, the crackling and toppling of trees. Instantly my hopes vanished. I had been sold out, betrayed. They were bringing up a tank. They were going to blast me out, after all—or perhaps more likely, smash down the tower with me in it. I cursed my former optimism, my blind faith. And in that moment of despair I resolved to perish rather than surrender. I would show them how a soldier could die at his post!

But I might have spared myself these exalted sentiments. For as the racket grew to deafening proportions I saw coming through the trees a large steam shovel. In the scoop of the shovel itself I could see four helmets and they were—yes! I shouted for joy—they were medics' helmets, with a large red cross emblazoned on a white field.

The rest was easy. The shovel rose to the level of my window, its iron lip lowered to form a ramp, and the medics, finding me co-operative, carried me gently into the gaping maw of the shovel. Within the hour I found myself seated across from the major at a large, glass-topped desk. In his hands he held official-looking papers.

"Private Webster," he said briskly, "these are your orders. They azign you on my endorsement to Fort Dix, New Jersey. There you will rezeive your discharge. You will leaf on the next medical drain. In the meantime you will be kebt here in hosbital for your own protegtion." He sighed, removed his spectacles and stared at me somberly. "I regret that we haff no means here of helbing you. You will see that I have regommended you to Doctor Hofstatter in New York. A fery good man. I worked together with him in the old days. If you zeek treatment immediately you may avoid commitment."

"What makes you so certain that—" I started to protest and then stopped. How could I possibly argue my sanity with him? And yet, I was curious. "I suppose you see very many malingerers pass through here," I said casually.

"Nefer one," he replied, replacing his spectacles and studying me.

"Never one?"

"Nefer one. Many bass through my hands who imagine they are malingerers, but they are all basigally zick."

"But surely there must have been some who faked the thing. I mean, some who were so clever they might have fooled you?"

"Nefer one. They vool only themselves, no?"

"But back there in the forest you said I was—acting a charade."

"Yes. A charade invented by your suberego to shelter you from something in your id too awful to face. You were not really vooling anyone."

"How can you be so certain?" My voice had risen now. I saw my hands shake slightly and placed them on my lap.

"I can be zertain."

"What would you say if I told you everything I've done is a fake?" In one split moment it suddenly became more important to me to penetrate the smug assurance on that scarred face than to escape the Army.

"I would egsbegt you to say that. But you would be wrong."

"Well, suppose I say I was faking and I'm not wrong!" I shouted.

"Blease, Private Webster, blease control yourself. You are nod fit to be in the Army—"

"Yes, I am! I'm as fit as you are! I'm perfectly fit!" I had

risen from my seat and was leaning over the desk, my face
very close to the major's. I saw his eyes narrow thoughtfully, saw his right hand press a button on the call box
next to him.

"I am fery sorry for you, Webster, you must belief
that. But unfordunately, I can do nothing. Here we haff
nothing—nothing! I am resbonsible for the mental health
of twenty thousand men. I cannot take time off to dreat
any man in debth."

"I'm not asking for treatment!" I cried. "I'm telling
you—" Suddenly I felt heavy hands on my shoulders, my
arms. I was being dragged backward. My last glimpse of
the major was his impassive face slowly shaking back and
forth while he made a soft clucking sound in his mouth.

Of course, I later understood everything. But I will not
pretend I did not suffer months of anguish after my discharge. I even came close to visiting Doctor Hofstatter.
For the one conviction I could never erase from my mind
was, *you can't fool them—not really*. It was only with the
most extreme effort of mental discipline that I was able to
think things through rationally. I will not bore you with
details. My conclusions, painfully arrived at but secure at
last, were simply that I *had* indeed fooled them—they
were not used to dealing with intellectuals—and my outburst in the major's office had been the final clincher, the
final bit of emotional proof he'd been seeking. Though
scarred, I was, in fact, victorious.

Oh, I have thought about this frequently since those
days. I sometimes wonder, sometimes find myself recon-
structing the long chain of logic that ends inevitably with
my own verdict of sanity. But this is a small price to pay
for survival.

So it was not without some experience, some confidence

in my wits, that I considered my coming attempt to escape.

Of one thing I was determined. I would never again go unarmed into these situations. I glanced quickly around my room, looking for something even faintly useful as a weapon to be concealed upon my person. My eye came to rest finally upon the gilded crook, the shepherd's-crook scepter of the Pharaohs of Egypt that lay upon my curved stool. I slipped out of bed, walked over to it, studied it carefully, lifted it. My heart leaped with excited joy when I realized that it must weigh fully ten pounds. It was evidently a piece of lead pipe that had been decorated for its purpose. I enjoyed the heft of it in my hand, and re- flected on how handily it would hook into my belt *be- neath* my smock. I was about to try it on, when I heard footsteps at my door. I leaped back into bed still gripping the crook, which I now hastily secreted beneath the sheets.

My door was opened by the leading edge of a wheeled bed-table. Behind it walked a white-smocked attendant. His face was coarse and unfamiliar, his figure imposing, his manner casually confident. He wheeled the table over to the side of my boat, waited for a second and then coughed.

"Well?" he asked irritably. "What're ya waiting for?" Then he frowned. "Oh, I forgot. *Nelson*," he whispered heavily.

I felt my heart leap. "John D.," I replied.

"Yeah, yeah, get on board." He pointed to the table.

Suppose something had gone wrong? Suppose this was some complicated scheme of Stein's—or Ritchie's, for that matter? "Where are we going?" I asked.

"Mortuary," he replied impatiently.

"Mortuary?" I could not suppress a quaver in my voice.

"Yeah. Come on, get aboard and lay like you're dead, see?"

"What happens at the mortuary?"

"I don't know. None of my business. Now, are you coming or aren't you?"

No time. No time to think, no time to plan, no time to regret or to evade. I crawled carefully from my boat, my right elbow pressed against the shepherd's crook beneath my smock.

"What's wrong?" the attendant asked impatiently, staring at my arm.

"Kidneys," I muttered as I crawled onto the bed-table.

"Yeah, well, keep it quiet," he snapped. Then he drew the sheet up and over my head. "Make like dead." he whispered.

I held myself rigidly beneath the sheet, my hands crossed upon my chest, my chin jutting out. And I held my breath as much as possible.

I felt myself wheeled out of my tomb and down a long corridor. The table paused twice as doors were unlocked. There was an elevator ride down, down, then more doors and corridors, until finally the table came to rest. But since I could not be certain I was safe I continued my interpretation of a corpse.

"Here he is," I heard the attendant say, his voice ringing as if in some hollow vault. "Where's the dough?"

"You needn't shout!" It was Ritchie's voice, and angry. "One, two, three, four, five," he counted quickly. "Five hundred, as we agreed."

"I been thinking it over," the attendant replied slowly. "I took a hell of a chance. I think it's worth a grand."

"Get out of here!" Ritchie snarled.

"I said one grand, Doc."

I heard a metallic clicking sound.

"Now wait a minute, Doc! I didn't mean anything by that. I was just —you know— Hey! Look!"

"Shut up and turn around!"

"All right, all right. Now look, Doc—"

His voice died abruptly as the sound of a bone-cracking thud came to my ears. I pushed the sheets from my face just in time to see the attendant slump to the floor. Ritchie was holding a pistol by the muzzle. "I reckon that'll keep him quiet until we're out of here," he said. Then he stooped over the body and took back the five one-hundred-dollar bills that were scattered on the floor.

I had never before realized just how dangerous a game this was. But I saw now that I had to deal with truly desperate men. It was with some relief then that I saw Ritchie slip the pistol back into his uniform pocket.

"What's going to happen?" I asked.

"Why, we're getting out. In a hearse." He smiled coldly.

"A hearse?"

"A disguised Institute ambulance, old boy. Nothing to worry about." He jutted out his chin confidently.

"Are you coming, too?"

"Can't stick around here. This is too big a haul. This is my last job here, old boy." He rubbed his hands together. "They'll give me the Winthrop Medal for this. You'll see." He drew his pipe from his pocket and clenched it unlit between his teeth. "Now we simply wait. Hearse'll be here in about five minutes. Just lie still there and pretend you're dead, old boy, dead." He laughed soundlessly.

I glanced around the dimly lit vault. There were several other wheeled tables lined up along a wall. The room was concrete, and from the chill I assumed it was below street level. A glass case containing a fire extinguisher decorated another wall, while directly before me was a large double door made of steel. I knew instinctively that it must lead to the outer world—to freedom! I was within a few feet of freedom at this very moment, and I had less than five minutes to act.

"My foot hurts!" I said suddenly.

"I thought you said you couldn't feel pain," Ritchie replied suspiciously.

"It doesn't exactly hurt," I said hastily, "but it feels as if it's been wrenched—out of place—maybe a bone's broken —something's happened down there—" I gritted my teeth and tried to assume an expression of fright.

Ritchie frowned, shrugged and bent over my foot. As he pulled the sheet back to examine it I brought the heavy shepherd's crook down on the small of his skull with all my might. He slid senseless to the floor.

I was acting purely by instinct now. I did not even glance at the prostrate figure as I jumped from the table and rushed to the steel doors. I would be free!

They were locked. They were immovably, irrevocably and completely locked. And there was neither latch nor keyhole on this side of them. Obviously, they could only be opened from the outside. I felt my eyes watering. But instinct came to my rescue again.

I quickly shed my smock and tore the uniform from Ritchie's inert body. As I put it on I realized that it was ridiculously small for me. But no matter. It was my only chance. I picked Ritchie up and laid him on the wheeled table, covering him completely with the sheet. Then I dragged the attendant over to another table and deposited him beneath a sheet, too. It was then that I heard the squealing of brakes and the idling of a powerful engine beyond the steel doors. A car door opened. There was a padding of feet. Something metallic scraped the steel doors. And then they opened wide.

I felt the chill night air on my face, saw a burly figure outlined against powerful headlights. Behind him was a ramp, mostly filled by a large black hearse. But above it I could just make out a star twinkling in the night sky. Blessed star! Blessed night! Blessed freedom!

The burly figure approached and whispered, "Radio City."

A new code word! How stupid of me not to have anticipated that. I would try. "John D.," I replied.

"Hey, what is this? Where's Ritchie?" The figure stepped back suddenly. But it was too late. I had already whipped out Ritchie's pistol. "Don't move!" I hissed. Then, imitating the only example I knew, I said, "Turn around, quick!"

The figure turned around obediently. "Look," it whimpered, "look, I mean—" I brought the handle of the pistol down hard against his head, and he crumpled to the floor. And at that moment the alarms went off.

They began with a distant and persistent throbbing of bells. Then a siren commenced to wail somewhere deep within the building, and the clang of the bells grew closer. The siren screamed.

I pocketed my gun and ran for the doors. But they were *automatically closing!* I squeezed through them just in time. They clanged shut and drowned out the bells and siren as well as trapping Ritchie and his friends forever within the walls of The Foundation.

I raced past the hearse and up the ramp to the street above. For a full minute I was completely overwhelmed and disoriented. I was an alien from a distant galaxy thrown suddenly into the city. A maze of winking lights, of buildings, of automobiles—and sounds. After the silence of The Foundation, sound poured in upon me.

Before me spread the wild reaches of Central Park. With the sure instincts of a hunted animal I darted into the street toward an opening in the park wall.

I do not remember now whether I heard the horn, the shrieking tires, or even my own scream. One moment I was racing for freedom and the next I was struck down by something huge and metallic. I felt myself thrown violently, saw the world teetering crazily around me, saw the black pavement rushing toward my face, tried to ward it off and then fell into a darkness even blacker than the pavement.

Despite our deepest yearnings, time does not have an end—not even a beginning. It is a mere adjunct, a function of space. And space is only a projection of the infinite deeps of our subjective will. The material globe, the very universe through which it wanders, all tangible reality, is nothing more than energy willed into certain forms, by us, by others, by the entire sentient creation together. And that vast collective desire is an ocean in which our human will is a small and very muddy drop. There is that in the mind that requires, conceives, creates and remembers time. But that is only because the mind cannot imagine space without time. And if space itself is but the projection of unfulfilled desire, of inchoate will, then time can be no more than a prop to reason, a hastily constructed barricade against self-knowledge. Time is, in fact, no more than a symptom of the human condition.

But just as I pretend to understand myself no better than any fellow human understands himself, so I do not pretend to comprehend this symptom. Therefore I cannot truthfully claim that from *this* time to *that* time certain events occurred. I cannot even report that *during* a particular time my own condition was such and such. What I can say is that when the part of my condition reported to me by my senses was as described, then the time symptom existed in a certain way. But I am not trying to bore you with egotistical speculations—only attempting to explain why I cannot tell you how long I lay on the street between The Foundation and the park.

At one moment I felt an impact (not a severe one) on my left thigh, the next moment I was flying across a tilting night to a cold, harsh landing on black asphalt that merged immediately with darkness. And at that same moment I was scrambling to my feet, crawling from the blackness into the starlit illumination of the night, running again toward the deep foliage of the park, dimly aware that some element of my consciousness either was not functioning properly or was lagging somewhat.

I do not know whether the vehicle that struck me stopped or fled the scene of the accident. I did not wait to investigate. After leaping the low wall that separates the park from the sidewalk, I blundered desperately through bushes, past clumps of trees, over grassy hillocks, keeping always away from the cement paths, the open patches of moonlight, hugging shadow and foliage, racing on in a crouch, incurious about what lay behind me, avid for what lay before. And during this escape I was aware of only one immediate fear. Since I could feel no pain, I could not judge the effects of the accident. Perhaps I had broken a bone or two; perhaps I had suffered internal injuries. I might be crippling myself permanently in the very act of flight. But I did not halt or even pause until my breath tasted like salt in my mouth and my legs simply collapsed beneath me. Then I crawled behind a clump of bushes, and while recovering my strength, I assessed my situation.

I was deep in the park. Judging by the encircling buildings and by the distant bulk of The Foundation, I had run well over a mile. Of course, this was a matter of small satisfaction; the park itself was but a rectangular trap, easy to block, easy to sweep. I was near the eastern edge of it, and the lights of cars speeding by on Fifth Avenue flashed across my eyes. From the paucity of traffic I judged it to be well after midnight. While getting my breath I determined to examine my body for injuries. I took off Ritchie's uniform jacket, satisfied myself in the flashing light that I was unbruised above the waist, then put it back on and removed my pants. It was at that moment, when the full helplessness of my plight was underscored by nakedness, that my nerves were shattered by a long, deep, awful roar, a savage and bloody bass-throated growl that echoed from every direction but was certainly nearby. It was followed by a wild chattering and a staccato screaming of monkeys and birds.

The open cage, the easy leap over barriers, the hot breath of hunger and the lust of the hunt—did the lion even now scent his prey, even now stare with blank and avid eyes to judge his leap while the monkeys and birds cried out in delight? Something large and powerful and exultant was prowling through the park, the torn, terrified face of its keeper upturned in a mangled body upon the cement behind, while new prey huddled in the bushes ahead— It roared again—no closer—and again—no closer —until in my shrieking mind there was distilled the realization that the beast was simply pacing its cage. For behind me, not more than fifty yards away through shrubbery, rose the buildings of the Central Park Zoo. I understood then how terror can obliterate not only reason but even sensuous judgment. I had run not one but at least three miles. I felt blood trickle down my chin from the tooth marks in my lower lip.

The lowered trousers revealed a huge black-and-blue mark, a spidery splotch on my right thigh. But careful probing disclosed no broken bones. At the moment of the impact the vehicle must have been going very slowly. No doubt my flight through the air was at least partly due to my own motion and to my being thrown off balance. No longer able to trust the signals of my own body, I examined myself very closely in the flashing light. Finally I replaced my pants and was congratulating myself on my good fortune, when my blood froze.

I do not know whether the constancy of the flashing light finally penetrated my dulled wits before I heard the voice or at the same moment. I think somewhere deep within, I had pictured myself as a castaway on some lonely shore beneath the steadily revolving sweep of a lighthouse beacon—that is to say, I was on the track of reality, even if I had not caught up with it.

Not ten feet away, beyond the tangle of bush and bramble, the voice whispered harshly, "He's in there somewhere. Hear anything?"

And another voice whispered, "No. And I'm not going in after him. He might be just a nut or he might be something else. I say we wait right here until the cars arrive."

By this time I had already raised myself onto my knees and could see through the obscuring foliage two uniformed policemen from whose drawn revolvers the constantly flashing light glinted. The light itself was, of course, the slowly spinning searchlight atop their patrol car, which was parked in a moonlit patch of open ground behind them.

"Well, he can't get out this way, and if he beats the cars to the street it's not our fault," the second voice muttered. "I'm not going in there."

I admit that at this moment I briefly considered the possibility of throwing myself upon the mercy of the police. Why not simply give myself up to them, confess everything, demand their protection against Stein? Of course, they would not believe me at first. They would toss me into a cell and then investigate. It was the very thought of that cozy cell, secure and prosaic, that urged this course upon me. The police inquiries would speedily prove the truth of my story. Which was? Well, stripped of mere assertion, that I had been a patient in the psychiatric ward of The Foundation, had slugged (and perhaps killed with my amateurish blows) a doctor and an attendant and made my escape. Any claims I might make beyond this were debatable. Against my already suspect word would be marshaled all of Stein's persuasiveness, all of The Foundation's authority. In all likelihood I would either be returned to them for further treatment as an escaped maniac, or be tried for the murder of two of their staff. The mere possession of Ritchie's gun was a grave offense. The very most I could hope for would be an exchange of prisons: The Foundation for Bellevue. I determined to make no such choice.

I edged carefully and slowly backward through the bushes, crawling commando-style on my belly, and as I crawled, for the first time in my life a fugitive from society, I knew what my eventual destination must be.

It took the vast reaches of space, the incalculable light-years that measure distance as a function of probability, for me to cover the fifty yards of stony, cold ground and wet grass that separated me from the first building. Then my cheek scraped against concrete, my nostrils filled with the fetid odor of latrines and animals, and I was among the outdoor cages, railings and ancient brick buildings of the zoo. The hideous clamor of monkeys told me I was huddled within the shadow of the primate building. I scrambled to my feet and listened intently. To my muddled senses the deep-throated darkness around me was a jumble of sound. The screaming of birds, the chattering of monkeys, the occasional cough and deep grumble of the insomniac lion, the traffic noise on nearby Fifth Avenue were now underlined by the low wail of a distant siren. But there was no need to assume that this barely perceptible note was the horn of my hunters. They would have no reason to announce their approach, to start their quarry. I pictured police cars by the score gliding silently up to the Fifth Avenue entrance to the zoo, disgorging hundreds of tight-lipped, efficient, determined officers. I was a gasping, squirming animal within their tightening net. The congestion (which any normal man would have felt as pain) in my chest as I gulped air, the frigid tightness of my stomach, the weak trembling of my exhausted limbs—all these were due not only to the great physical exertion of my escape but also to the panic of flight itself. For the advent of the police had objectified my fear.

What are the limits of reality? They dissolve, redissolve and are finally distilled within the individual psyche. They recoil endlessly upon themselves, needing to be symbolized to become objectively acceptable. How long did I crouch against the wall? I have told you; there was only duration. I was a naked thing wound into a tight coil of sensuous and even titillating terror, alone on a moonlit savanna of tall grass, my pursuers in sight now, circling the horizon, drawing closer, their weapons glinting in the mist. Then the net was tossed. It sailed high and lazily past the stars, too wide to dodge. Even if I started to run I would never reach its edge before it settled upon me. So I waited, in passive compliance with fate. I would be snared, bound, transported—an indifferent object for display behind the bars of force, beyond the bars of communication:

HOMO SAPIENS

Habitat: Elsewhere

DO NOT FEED

I sat in sullen subjection to a naked body and a mind that had only itself to feed upon, while the little children tossed peanuts to me and at me and pestered their parents in an unknown tongue.

"Hey, lookit—why does it just sit there like that, hey? Hey?"

"Can I feed it a peanut too, can I, hey? Can I, can I, can I? Hey?"

"Don't get too close. Get down off those bars right this minute before an attendant sees you! Just throw them in from back here. That's the way. See, it isn't hungry now. Come along and we'll see the other animals. I said not too close! It might be dangerous."

"Hey, lookit—what's it doin' now, hey?"

"Come along!"

"But what's it doin'?"

"It's not a nice animal. Nice animals don't do that."

"Is it because it itches?"

"Never mind! Just come along. I've a good mind to write a letter to the Park Department. They shouldn't let them do that in public. It isn't decent. Now, if you don't come along this very minute you're going to get a good smack!"

"Aw, but what's it doin', hey?"

The low insistence of the sirens was louder now. The hunters had not scrupled to sound their horns after all. Did that mean they were confident I could not escape in any case, or did it signify a certain fearful hope on their part that I *would* escape? Potentially dangerous game lurking in their particular patch of jungle? I recalled a trick that had worked once.

I straightened, brushed at my jacket and pants, ran my fingers through my hair, wiped the sweat from my face. I had only one chance. Lights were flashing now against the walls of nearby buildings, footsteps rang urgently on the paved walks. I walked quickly toward the broad flight of steps that led up to the main entrance. My plan was simple; it would either work completely or not at all. It depended on the fact that one unfamiliar uniform is much like any other in the dark. Mine was that of The Foundation, but under stress and in shadow it might as well be that of some obscure branch of the Park Department. I started to trot briskly toward a group of shadows at the foot of the stairs.

There were perhaps a dozen of them, some holding flashlights, others with drawn revolvers, clustered around a sergeant who dispatched them with whispered instructions down various paths into the zoo. Above him, at the head of the stairs, several squad cars were parked on the avenue. "Sergeant!" I called out breathlessly as I ran up to them. "Sergeant! He's back there by the reptile house!"

"Shut up!" A square and angry face peered at me from shadows while flashlights blinded me. "You saw him?"

"Yeah. I was making rounds and I saw this guy. Back there by the reptile house. Scared the shit out of me. I'm glad you guys are here. We're not armed, you know."

"Was he armed? Did he threaten you?"

"I didn't wait to find out. He had a gun and he looked tough. I just ran. I've gotta call our own security."

"OK. Murphy, you and Klein take area A. I'll go with the others. Now, I don't want any of you guys taking chances. We may be dealing with a desperate case. If it comes right down to it, shoot to kill. And for Christ's sake, don't shoot each other! Now, let's go—quietly!"

I watched them slink off into the shadows between the buildings, and then skipped up the steps to the avenue, passed two officers who had been left behind near the patrol cars, crossed Fifth Avenue and turned into a side street. I rummaged through the pockets of my uniform as I half walked, half trotted east. I found only about one dollar in change, not enough for a taxi, and the five one-hundred-dollar bills, each too large to be changed by a cabby. But now I was standing outside a subway entrance. I composed myself as best I could, and clambered down the steps.

As the express roared past me on the deserted platform I picked an empty car, ran along with it for a few yards and entered it when the train stopped. I quickly picked out a corner seat and crumpled into it, burying my face behind a discarded newspaper. I began to breathe again when the train started.

The steady rumble with its cavernous echo, the high-pitched whine of the wheels, the singing rails, the air rushing past an open window—all of this soothed my nerves as only the best-remembered lullaby could have done. For the first time in many months I was back in my familiar world. The sour, sickly-sweet odor of dust, dried vomit, sweat and electricity was perfume to my nostrils. The flashing lights of local stations whirling by, the sudden encounter with an express heading south (two glowingly vivid earthworms racing easily past each other with their cargoes of undigested life)—this subterranean welter of precise, scheduled yet mysterious activity exhilarated me, touched me with a light-headed gaiety I had almost forgotten. At immense speed, growling along beneath the world of search and harry, safe from seizure, I was hurrying away from The Foundation, from the police. North, ever north, toward the Bronx, toward home and, above all, toward Suskind and his ingenious abilities. I was content.

The drunk boarded at 86th Street. His clothes were of fairly decent quality but in disarray. His jacket was incorrectly buttoned, his pants incompletely zippered and in need of pressing, his shoes stained, his hair disordered. He kept fumbling with his loosened tie as if trying to find the knot. His face was pallid and thin, the flesh of it flabby, the eyes watery, the expression one of vague anguish. I knew with sudden and sinking certainty that he would head straight for me. I pretended to be deeply engrossed in my newspaper, not even turning my head when he tapped me on the shoulder.

"Beg your pardon," he mumbled thickly.

I had the feeling that if I rose and changed cars he would undoubtedly follow me. If I was rude to him he would make a scene, attract some conductor's attention. I decided to humor him. "Yes?" I replied noncommittally, still staring at my paper.

"You got the time?" he demanded.

"I'm sorry, I don't have a watch."

"I got a watch," he said with a giggle that almost drowned me in the fetid odor of stale teeth and alcohol. "I got a watch but it's half an hour slow, see?"

I nodded and continued reading an advertisement for liver pills, which I had by then almost memorized.

"So why don't I just correct my watch, eh? It's not as simple as that." He paused. "You think I'm drunk," he complained. "You're right. I been drunk for two months now. That's right—two months. I think it's two months now. Know why?"

I shrugged.

"Hey, you some sort of cop or something? What's that uniform all about? I never seen a uniform like that."

"Department of Hospitals," I said quickly.

"Yeah? That's where I belong. Hospital. Treat you good there. Listen, I know all about the sacrifices you guys make—lousy hours, no pay—just to take care of people— it's goddamned decent of you." The sob in his voice sounded sincere. "Me. I need help, too. I'm sick. Been sick for two months. Two whole months. But I wouldn't let you guys get hold of me! Fat chance! Steal all a man's money and then kill him with an injection—you guys are nothing more than murderers!" I could feel the glare in his face as it pressed aggressively close to my cheek. "You know why I've been sick for two whole lousy months?" he moaned.

"Tell me," I replied, trying to keep my voice noncommittal.

"Because of this watch, that's why!" he cried. "It's late —it's half an hour behind."

There was so much despair in his voice that I turned to glance at him and was shocked to see tears in his eyes.

"I used to be all right, see?" he snuffled. "I had a wife and two kids and a good job. Wanta see a picture of them? I mean of the kids? I have one here somewheres— hell, I don't know where. Just two months ago I was all right. You understand—*all right.*"

I nodded sympathetically.

"But my watch. It went half an hour slow, see? Let me just ask you a simple question, just one very simple question. Have you ever fallen half an hour off schedule in this town? You can tell me, I won't tell anyone else."

I found myself considering the question seriously and was mildly surprised to discover I could truthfully answer, "No, no, I don't believe I ever have."

"Boy, you're lucky! Lucky! That's what happened to me, see? I fell half an hour off schedule. And I never climbed back on. Listen, this is serious. Take you for instance. Do you know me? Do I know you? No. Neither of us know each other, do we? Of course not. I haven't met anyone I know for two months. Listen to me. Just listen. Man like you probably wouldn't think anything of it, would you? You're one of the lucky ones. Pretty cozy all wrapped up in your time zone, aren't you? In fact, pretty damned smug, eh? No offense, if you know what I mean. But you've got it made, haven't you? Don't get me wrong. You're a nice guy. I can tell because you're willing to talk to me. I like to talk to people. Where was I? Oh yeah— the time thing. That's the thing, see? You wouldn't believe it, would you? Would you believe it?"

His hand suddenly fastened onto my arm with a cruelly urgent grip. His eyes were wide and desperate behind their tears. Suddenly I was afraid. Perhaps he was mad.

"You've got to believe it," he whispered. "I've fallen half an hour out of time. And it piles up. I mean when I got home there was nobody there. I never caught up with them. Maybe they think I'm dead. Maybe I am. I'm half an hour out, see? I'm outside everything. All I ever see are strangers like you. And what do you care? You don't give a damn. I can go straight to hell, can't I? Well, just suppose—now, just suppose I was to hold you like this!" Now he grabbed me with both hands, one on the wrist, the other at my throat. My lips trembled as I realized I was truly in the clutch of a maniac. I dared not move, barely dared return his fevered stare.

"—And not let you go for half an hour. I mean, you must be going someplace. No one rides the subway for fun, do they? No. You're heading somewhere maybe, to see someone or get to work or something. And here I am holding you. I could hang on to you for half an hour and not let you go. Then you'd fall half an hour off schedule like me. I'd have a friend. You don't know how lonely I've been— I'm very lonely, very lonely." He released me, buried his face in his hands and began to weep uncontrollably just as the express pulled into a station.

I waited, then quickly jumped up, ran for the door, which was already closing, and squeezed through it onto the station platform. The behind-time man stared at me through the dirt-streaked windows of the car, his face a mask of anguish and accusation. His eyes burned into my mind like stigmata as he was borne swiftly away into the dark bowels of the city, a man betrayed.

For some reason, my encounter had completely unnerved me. Suddenly the subway was no longer a friendly refuge but a place of menace, a closing box of darkness and odor from which I had to escape. All my old panic returned, heightened now by claustrophobia. I ran through the turnstiles, down a passageway, up a flight of stairs and out onto the street. And so blinded was I by terror that as I stood on the corner breathing deeply I did not at first recognize my surroundings.

But when my fear subsided it was replaced by a growing exultation. Above me, the street sign; behind me, the darkened newstand; and on down the street, the kosher butcher, the dry cleaners—of course! Fate, the gods, luck —or my own subconscious had delivered me precisely to my old neighborhood in the Bronx! Everything was dearly familiar: the empty lot littered with debris, the rows of boarded-up tenements. Even a newspaper blowing down the gutter and a black delivery truck parked nearby seemed so utterly familiar as to be permanent features of this landscape. Then my own street, my own building were just around the next corner! I hurried down the avenue on feet that would have danced all the way had they known how, rapture swelling my chest, tears of gratitude watering my eyes. A few more yards, a few more hasty steps— I turned the corner—

And stopped short as if I'd walked into a glass wall. For fully five minutes I must have stood in stunned and disbelieving contemplation of the scene before me, panic growing once again in my bowels. For in place of the cozy filthiness, the familiar tumble-down warmth of my street, of my neighborhood, there now stretched level and bare acres of land, from which spidery traceries of steel rose against the night sky. Derrick booms, Quonset huts, dump trucks, wooden fences, littered the silent area. A large sign nearby proclaimed that this housing project was being constructed under the authority of the Borough President of the Bronx. *Look on my works, ye Mighty, and despair!*

So great was the shock, so bitter the disappointment, that at first I simply refused to believe my eyes. I studied

the street signs, glanced back down the avenue, searching
hopelessly for some indication that I'd been mistaken. Of
course there was none. Still, perhaps behind the fences,
perhaps lurking amid the huge steel skeletons of these yet
unclothed structures, perhaps somehow, improbably, my
own building had survived—

I walked down the street cautiously, like a man entering a lunar landscape. There were no points of reference,
no recognizable features. Halfway down the block—my
own building had been about halfway down the block
from the avenue—I peered through a hole in the wooden
wall, and looked out on a gigantic excavation. "Oh, no," I
mumbled, "no, please—" Suddenly I felt very weak, very
tired. I sat down on the pavement, leaning against the
fence, and wept.

For what did I cry? Partly of course for Suskind—that
strong, poetic, inscrutable personality was gone, vanished.
I had no hope at all of finding him now. Had he been able
to salvage any of his museum of junk? Was he even now
indomitably carrying on in some remote and still-decayed
area of the city? Who would now ride shotgun on the
rats? Of course there would be no rats left on this
seared landscape. But mainly I bewailed the obliteration of my own past. Here on this very spot I had fash-
ioned a small corner of the world into a home. Into it I had
placed not only photos, papers, books, sticks of furniture,
but also memories, feelings, faint scrawlings of my individual personality. Society had sought out my tiny world
and so obliterated it that not even a smell remained. Now
I was a man without a tangible past. My entire previous
life now existed only within my own frail mind. And with
the passage of time, memory would dim; it had already
faded. I was a reservoir from which more of my own past

relentlessly evaporated with every passing minute.

Some may think such an obliteration of the past a cause for rejoicing rather than for distress. But this is not so. For the weight of memory always remains somewhere within —even when specific circumstances have been forgotten. The man without memories remains bowed down like a broken, aged weight lifter, walking stooped toward his grave. No more terrible argument can be adduced against the desirability of reincarnation.

I found myself desperately scavenging my mind as if I might lose bits of my life if I did not recall them *now*, *immediately*. And in my panic I could barely tell myth from reality, as I purposely conjured up the past.

For instance, there was my father's warning, administered one evening while he was hosing our tiny, fenced-in bit of front lawn. I remember that the sky was heavy with midsummer heat, smog and that ponderous, beery, varnished-linoleum oppressiveness that gives Chicago its individuality. I was seated on the lowest of five wooden steps that led up to our front porch, gazing idly at the gray stains that spread over the glittering concrete sidewalk where the hose splashed it. I was twelve years old. My father stood with one hand on his hip, his large stomach swelling his T-shirt, his face a mask of bovine complacency, while with his other hand he directed the nozzle of the hose as if he were urinating. He did not water the lawn in an orderly fashion but splashed first one area and then another like a dog rushing from spot to spot to lift a proprietary leg over the frontiers of its holdings. A few cars passed slowly along the street, a few housewives wheeled metal shopping carts along the sidewalks. I disrobed the younger of these as they passed, exploring their bodies with a lazy curiosity that soon developed into

urgency. I was just about to get up and go to my bedroom
when my father said, "Your mother tells me you've been
staining your sheets."

My stomach suddenly became a cold and hollow cavity.
I felt myself blushing, glanced hurriedly around to see if
anyone had heard this statement, tried to form words on
my trembling lips.

"That's a nice thing for your mother to find, isn't it?" he
demanded, still intent upon the jet of water that streamed
out before him, never turning his face toward me. I was
certain that his voice could be heard for many miles.

I found nothing to say. A sudden image of my mother
lifting the corners of one of my sheets between the tips of
her fingers, a look of sad but complete revulsion on her
face as she noticed the gray stains, burned words into
ashes in my mouth.

"Well, is that or isn't it a nice thing for your mother to
find?" he demanded relentlessly.

"No," I said. It was not an answer to his question. It was
a supplication to God, to Fate, to distant powers, to
obliterate the word, the evening, the world—to completely erase this event from time at any cost.

"You've been abusing yourself, haven't you?"

One of the passing housewives glanced at me. I was
certain she'd heard. "No," I pleaded.

"Yes, you have. Those stains weren't from wet dreams,
either. Too widely spaced." He glanced at me then and
shook his head slowly while the hose gouged a hole in the
turf before him. "That'll drive you nuts. You understand
that? It'll make you insane. Not only that, but you'll never
be able to have any kids of your own." The look on my
face must have satisfied him, because he nodded and
turned to direct the nozzle of the hose to another random

patch of grass. "I want you to promise me you'll stop abusing yourself," he said over his shoulder. "It's for your own good. Remember, it'll drive you nuts. You'll wind up like your Uncle Jake. Promise."

I had been biting my lower lip and now became aware of the salt taste of blood in my mouth. "I promise," I blurted out as I ran into the house.

Then there was Uncle Jake. He was the standard of evil against which all sin was measured by my father. Jake was his younger brother and had been accidentally gassed in training in Louisiana during the First World War. His lungs supported him for the rest of his life, assuring him a pension that needed little supplement in those Depression years. He was tall, thin, affected a tragic cough and parted his hair in the middle. He also drank. He passed his days and evenings in a select series of bars on Belmont Avenue amongst a group of derelicts he had organized into an army to help Chiang Kai-shek drive the Japanese from Manchuria. He led this army on parade down Belmont Avenue from time to time, and on those occasions my father locked all the doors and windows of our house, drawing the shades and sitting in mortified silence as Uncle Jake's voice bawled up the street, "About face! Forward march! To hell with the fucking Japs! Who wants to join up? Hooray for Chanky Check! Hey, Webster, we wanna hold a meeting! We know you're there, Webster! My own fucking brother and he won't let me hold a meeting!" From this sample diatribe I have omitted the drunken pauses, the insinuating belches, the garbled cries and curses of his followers; nor can the peculiar stridency of his voice, like a man playing a clarinet with a mouth full of water, be accurately conveyed.

Actually, his accusations against his brother were not

entirely justified. My father never failed to give him twenty-five or fifty cents for a decent meal as the price of peace, and my mother allowed him to sleep in the basement coal bin for two dollars a week. But this generosity seemed not to touch his sensibilities.

"My brother's a tightwad," he'd grumble at me when I visited him in the coal bin. "He wouldn't even let me take back the Coke bottles." Uncle Jake had fixed up the coal bin by pinning old obscene calendars on the lath walls and installing a folding army cot and a crate, upon which he sat and stared morosely out the small, cracked basement windows. He had built a sort of movable shoring of old boards against the coal itself, which he moved as the winter wore on and the coal supply dwindled. Thus the size of his lodgings varied from extremely cramped in the fall to spacious in the spring. In assessing his rent, my mother must have taken an average of the space he occupied throughout the year.

"What's new with the dinnysours?" he'd ask whenever I appeared. When first I'd learned about dinosaurs I had mentioned the matter to him, and he remained convinced thereafter that my studies at school were devoted exclusively to dinnysours. Aside from that, he never questioned me, and he was therefore the only member of my family I felt I could trust. And it was naturally to him that I came with my sex problems.

For the worst aspect of my father's accusation was the necessity of facing my mother. I realized that she would never be able to forgive the insult I had offered her. But I still had to inhabit the same house, to share the same dinner table, while we all pretended that I was normal, that I had not assaulted her most tender sensibilities with all the bravado of an amateur rapist. It was this mortification I confided to Uncle Jake in the coal bin that evening.

"I have to get control of myself," I said.

"Whyn't you just do it in the bathroom?" Uncle Jake asked vaguely, staring out the window, his breath fetid with beer.

"I'll go crazy if I keep it up," I moaned.

"Whyn't you get a girl?" he asked, after a moment's thought.

"I'm no good with girls," I said scornfully, implying they were beneath mature consideration.

Uncle Jake eyed me speculatively for a long moment. "This interfering with your study of dinnysours?" he asked.

"No," I sighed, "it's just—"

"That damn old fool!" Uncle Jake muttered.

"Who?"

"Never mind, never mind. Look, whyn't you just forget all about it?" Uncle Jake's eyes avoided mine.

Suddenly I felt uncomfortable. There was something unexpectedly and shamefully *shifty* in Uncle Jake's expression, something I had never seen in it before.

And there was the feeling of dread. I began to sense undercurrents in our house, or had I always sensed them but never before been able to understand them? Not that I understood them then. It was more a heightening of awareness, perhaps even the beginning of suspicion, that made my observations more acute. And in spite of my determination to control myself, to live cleanly, to avoid glancing at my mother's breasts when she bent over, to touch myself only when I urinated or bathed, to banish the erotic fantasies that flooded my nights—in spite of all this, my self-abuse did not end. In fact, it grew in frequency despite all my efforts. But I was determined not to shame my mother again. If I was doomed to become a sex fiend I could at least cling to one shred of decency. I would never assault my own mother, not even in fantasy. I would expend myself on erotic magazines and await the day I would be confined in a mental institution.

And yet I was becoming sensitized, aware. For example, I suddenly came to attach great importance to the frequent arguments and fights between my parents. They had always been common enough. But now, for the first time, I sensed tension beneath them, caught in their conversation pauses and gaps heavy with the threat of unspoken words. For the first time, also, I came to realize that there was, had perhaps always been, an oppressiveness about our house that made it different from my friends' homes.

Then, with vivid clarity, there was Jake's army. It commenced as simply another demonstration. There was the usual bawling in the street, the usual scurry as my father rushed to lock both front and back doors of the house, the usual silent tension within as he lowered the shades and waited patiently for the storm to pass. But this time the storm did not quite pass. I was peering from behind the window shade in the living room, and I saw it all.

Uncle Jake's army was drawn up in disarray on the sidewalk facing our house. Twenty or thirty misshapen bearded, deliriously drunken bums staggered back and forth to the tap of a snare drum played by one of their number. Uncle Jake himself carried a stained and faded American flag attached to a broken broom handle. He barked out his orders haphazardly and wandered about as if dazed. "Tenshun! Right face! Forward march! Three cheers for Chanky Check!" His army paid no attention to these commands but simply staggered back and forth to the drum.

By now the neighbors had gathered on their porches for this customary entertainment. They were laughing and shouting instructions. And, as always, Mr. Carmoody appeared at the door of his bakery to harangue the army. This was all part of the ritual. Mr. Carmoody was long-suffering behind his apparent outrage.

"This is the last time! This is the very last time!" Mr. Carmoody shouted.

Uncle Jake came to attention, saluted and shouted, "Form up, men! Form up!" Then he turned to Mr. Carmoody and demanded, "Are you addressing the Volunteer Army for the Aid of Chanky Check?" He paused and swayed drunkenly. "To hell with the Japs!" he cried. "Remember the *Panay!*"

"Bums! That's what you are! Bummers!" Mr. Carmoody's normally pallid face darkened apoplectically. "You give the street a bad name! You're bad for business! I'm telling you to get out! Out!" He waved his arms frantically.

"What'd you do in the war?" Uncle Jake demanded. "Go on and make fun of an old soldier!" He started to cough and spat hugely on the pavement.

"An old bummer!" Mr. Carmoody retorted. "I warned you! Don't say I didn't warn you!" And suddenly, unexpectedly, Mr. Carmoody rushed back into his bakery.

The neighbors tensed and so did I. This was something unusual, something not part of the ritual. It was ominous.

"Bolshevik!" Uncle Jake shouted after him. "Now, boys," he cried as he turned to his army, "let's show that traitor that we love this old flag. Let's all pledge allegiance right here and now!" He cleared his throat, brandished the broom-stick flag and led them solemnly through the oath. "I pledge allegiance to the flag of the United States of America . . ." The ragged chorus mumbled with him.

Halfway through the recitation Mr. Carmoody reappeared before his bakery. "Bummers, run!" he screamed. "The cops is coming to catch you!"

My uncle paid no attention to this disturbance. The oath of allegiance finished he cried, "It's him they'll arrest, for being a traitor! Carmoody, you're a foreign spy! Now, boys, let's dress that line to the right there—that's it!"

"This time they'll catch you!" Mr. Carmoody warned.

"Army of Volunteers! Tenshun! Let's show this traitor what real soldiers look like! Now, everyone—everyone, all together:

"My country, 'tis of thee,
Sweet land of liberty . . ."

As the strains of the song howled from the street a large black police van drove up quietly behind the army. If Uncle Jake saw it arrive, he gave no sign. If any of his army noticed it, they simply accepted it as their natural fate. They never even protested as the police prodded and hauled them into the wagon. Some of them even continued singing. And as the Black Maria drove away with its load of Volunteers for Chanky Check, Uncle Jake's voice could still be heard, wavering somewhat on the high notes:

"From every mountain-side
Let freedom ring!"

And my parents' voices, nagging, arguing, clawing at each other:

"You've got to bail him out. It's not right that your own brother should rot in jail just because you're too cheap to raise the lousy ten bucks—"

"Crap! I've been bailing him out for years! I'm fed up with it, I tell you! It'll do him good to be away from the bottle for a few days."

"You'd let your own brother just sit in jail—"

"Goddammit! Do you think I'm blind! Don't you think I know why you want him out?"

"Don't speak that way in front of the boy!"

"Why the hell not? You think every person in this whole neighborhood doesn't know my shame? He'll find out soon enough! Look who's worried about appearances! When you married into my family you did just that, didn't you— married the whole damned family!"

"Paul, go upstairs to bed . . . Well, read or something. Your father's lost his senses."

"Oh, I have, have I?" The voice shouted after me up the stairs, echoed hollowly within my room, its words muffled but their import terrifyingly clear.

And of course, of course—how had I ever forgotten it? Hadn't I played hooky that day? Hadn't I sneaked down the filthy alley back to the house? Hadn't I crept in through the kitchen window and tiptoed over to the basement door, and listened to them down there? The smells, the sounds, the tactile memories, rushed horribly from their recesses, speeded up toward the inevitable collision: my mother's face streaked on the forehead with coal dust, her stare of vacant surprise, disorder, everything in disorder, while I screamed, "Don't touch me! You're dirty, you're dirty!"

So deeply had I sunk into despair that I was unaware of any presence other than my own. I had not noticed or comprehended the appearance of two booted feet along-side me, had not heard their approach nor attributed reality to them, until the harsh beam of a flashlight blinded my eyes.

"What's wrong, buddy?" A harsh but not unkindly voice spoke from the blackness behind the light. "Somethin' wrong? You all right?"

I cleared my throat and wiped my eyes. "No—no, I'm all right. Would you mind—the light I mean."

"Yeah, sure." The light flicked off and I saw that a short, stocky individual attired in a drab green uniform was staring down at me. As my eyes grew accustomed again to the darkness I realized that he must be some sort of night watchman. His face was grizzled with age and the stubble of a white beard, his expression was one of cautious friendliness.

"Too much to drink?" he suggested.

"No," I answered without thinking, and immediately regretted it. Drunkenness would have been the most ac-ceptable explanation for my behavior. "I—well, I did have a few, and I was walking down the street, when some-thing came over me. I don't know what. I'm all right now."

"Sure, sure," he said quickly, relieved no doubt by my meek demeanor. "Listen, that can happen, ya know? I mean, that could happen to anybody. Uh—you want me to call an ambulance?"

"No!" I exclaimed. "I mean, no, really, I'm all right." I got to my feet and stretched my arms, and he backed off a few feet. He was obviously still considering the possibility of flight, of alarm. I grinned. "You want to know the truth?" I asked in sudden inspiration.

"Yeah?" he replied skeptically.

"Well—I used to live in this neighborhood. Right behind me, right behind this wall was my building. I haven't been up here for some time, and I just happened to be in the neighborhood, and I thought I'd walk by and see how the old place was getting on. And then when I saw it was all gone"—a catch in my voice lent unfeigned verisimilitude to my remarks—"I—well, it sort of hit me hard. That's the truth, believe it or not."

"Oh, I believe it, buddy!" he exclaimed, with real friendliness lighting his watery gray eyes. "I believe it all right. It happens all the time! Why, I've been a night watchman on and off for about ten years now—ever since I quit the Force—and you're not the first guy I saw broke down when he came back to see his old neighborhood. Believe me, you're not the first!"

I nodded with what I hoped was an expression of wise understanding on my face.

"Yeah, you'd be surprised maybe how many people come by to visit their old neighborhoods. And where are they? They're gone, that's where they are. Gone. All gone. There ain't no part of this city that's permanent. Up and down, up and down—put 'em up and tear 'em down, that's all they ever think about. They got my old neighborhood over in Brooklyn fifteen years ago. I know just what ya mean." He paused thoughtfully and inspected my uniform. "Uh—you with the city too?" he asked.

"Yes, I'm with the Department of Hospitals. I work night shift at Bellevue. I was just on my way home."

"Uh-huh." Another thoughtful pause. "Well, uh—would ya like a cup of joe, maybe? I got a shack down the block where it's warm, and I'd stand ya a cuppa joe."

It was his use of the phrase "cup of joe" that decided me. For that was what Harry always called a cup of coffee. And the words seemed to clinch an identity in my mind between this person and Harry. As I followed him down the block to his shack I reflected that New York contained an entire race of Harrys—all aged, stocky, grizzled, speaking with an accent that was definable only as "city," born of the city, wise in its ways, indestructible and indispensable. News vendors, night watchmen, tour guides, subway men, doormen—survivors, most of them, from less complicated eras, friendly natives ready to give succor to outsiders trapped in their jungle.

The shack was small and drab and wooden. A coffee pot percolated lazily atop an ancient coal stove. One entire corner of the single room was filled with sacks of coal. There was a roll-top desk, three wooden chairs, a bleak window, the whole illuminated by the harsh light of a bare electric bulb dangling from the corrugated roof.

"Have a seat," he said. "It's black, but there's some sugar."

As I sat he bustled around the desk and finally produced two plastic cups and an old coffee can full of sugar. "Keep it goin' all night long," he muttered as he poured. "Gotta keep awake on this job. You know how many time clocks I gotta punch around this development? Thirty-eight! Thirty-eight clocks! And they're pretty far apart. Simpson on the other side, he's got twenty-five. But he gets the same money. Well, here's how." He raised his cup and swallowed the scalding liquid as if it were cool.

I sipped mine and then stirred it cautiously. "Hard work," I acknowledged his complaint.

"Yeah. It's not so bad now, but when it gets really cold—" He shook his head grimly.

"Must be pretty lonely, too," I offered.

"Yeah. But you're not the first guy's come in here for a

cuppa joe. I get maybe one every other week. Mostly drunks. I can see you're not that kind," he added hastily.

"You get bored?" I asked.

"Bored? Are you kiddin'? Well, like I mean, I can see you might think a guy'd get bored in a job like this. But believe me, it's not so boring. Why, listen—" He drew his chair closer to mine and glanced around conspiratorially. "You wouldn't believe the things come up on an excavation site like this!" he said eagerly. "Do you realize that not two hundred yards from where you're sittin', back that way, they uncovered a dead man in the basement of one of these old tenements? It's a fact. Saw the body myself. He must've been murdered. I mean, why the hell would anyone bury a guy in the basement of a house if they didn't murder him first, get me? Uh, say—uh, anything wrong with the coffee?"

"No," I gulped, "I guess I'm just a little tired."

"Yeah," he continued with relish, "you shoulda seen that one! Rats must've got to him. He wasn't no pretty sight when they dug him up, believe you me!" He eyed me closely. "I'm not makin' you sick, am I? I mean, there's lotsa people can't take that sort of thing. You look a little sick."

I smiled feebly and finished my coffee. "I'm all right," I mumbled.

"Yeah," he went on introspectively, "I've seen a lot in my time. Seen 'em come and go."

"Did you—" Sudden inspiration excited my voice. "Did you ever happen to run into a Chinaman named Suskind? Used to live around here—"

"Suskind? Chinaman?" He pondered for a moment and then his face clouded. "You don't mean that nut that lived over in two-twelve? A sort of a big fat bald Chink that collected junk?"

"That's the one," I said cautiously, disturbed by the suspicion in his face.

"You a friend of his?" he asked carefully.

"Well—I used to see him around." Wariness was turning to anticipatory dread within me.

"Well," he said, "that guy—you say his name was Suskind? Must be the same one. He lived in this same building I was tellin' you about—with the corpse in it. And he had a shotgun. He was some kook, that one, let me tell you. They got the city marshal to get him out, and he took a pot shot at the guy! I mean, he didn't hit anyone, but like he was a nut. At first they thought he was just one of these people who won't go when the city says move— there's lotsa them around. But then when they dug up the body they figured it all out. They got him on a murder rap all right."

"No!" I cried out, all caution dispelled by this ghastly news.

He stared at me thoughtfully. "Why do you say no?" he asked quietly.

"Well," I said, trying desperately to disguise the panicky despair I felt, "he may have been a little odd, but I'm *sure* he'd never hurt anyone. That shotgun was for hunting rats in the basement."

"Yeah? Well, maybe it was. But that's not the way the Force saw it. Anyhow, they took him in."

"What—what happened to him?"

"Like what should happen to a kook like that? I mean, they sent him up to the happy farm upstate—the loony bin. Listen, he's better off there, believe me. You shoulda seen the conditions he was living in! They had to dig their way in! You never saw such a pile of junk in your life!" He got up and stretched wearily.

My mind reeled with the implications of what he'd said.

Suskind condemned for a crime that was my own, Suskind committed to the dreadful mercies of the state insane asylum, cut off from the research that was the breath of life to him, trapped like an animal among the maddened refuse of that very civilization he'd sought to comprehend! And falsely!

"You better have another cup," he said quietly. "Help yourself. It's time for me to make the rounds. I mean, you can stay here for a while if you want. You still look a little green to me. Be back in an hour."

I watched him gather up his flashlight, a clip board and something that looked like a large wrench, which I guessed to be his clock key, still too overwhelmed by this distressing information even to utter thanks for his offer. At the door he paused.

"Uh—there's a cop car comes around checking pretty soon. Same guys that nabbed this Suskind. I mean, maybe they can tell you more about it, if you feel like waiting." Then he was gone.

Even in my shocked condition I recognized the courtesy of his veiled warning. He was a part of that ancient brotherhood of the oppressed, who have learned not to pry, not to advise, not to concern themselves. If I had imagined for one second that I could disguise from the cool scrutiny of his wisdom my obvious alarm at his remarks, I was a fool. He knew that in one way or another I was implicated with Suskind and the discovery of Harry's corpse. It was no affair of his. But native decency had caused him to speak that word about the police which might put me on my guard. For once the Samaritan would be rewarded.

My mind raced as I poured myself another cup of coffee. A feeling of tremendous frustration and of urgency constricted my throat. Somehow I had to liberate Suskind. I could not allow him to suffer for my own crime, misdemeanor—call it what you will. The very fact that I had not been molested thus far spoke of the silent fortitude with which he'd borne his punishment. My name had never escaped his lips. Now it was my turn to act with generosity, self-abnegation—to sacrifice myself, if necessary, to redeem him. But what could I actually do?

These speculations were interrupted by the flashing reflection of lights against the windows of the shack. I did not need to think twice about them. The instinct of the hunted, now roused deep within me, warned that these were patrol-car headlights. I carefully placed my steaming cup on the desk, put the five one-hundred-dollar bills beneath it and slipped out into the darkness. I was inside the project area before the squad car halted.

Where was I to go? In all the city, where could I hope for refuge? As I clambered over piles of cement sacks, picked my way around girders, avoided excavations, I thought desperately. And only one possibility came to mind. I clung to it without examining it (would it bear examination?) as I ran once again down deserted side streets, plunged into the rushing bowels of the subway system and rode toward familiar territory.

The lobby of the building was deserted, but instead of risking the elevator I climbed the stairs. One flight, three flights— The pain in my chest (which I felt not as pain but as pressure) merged into the urgency of my situation and was drowned in it; I was surprised by the seeming weightlessness of my movement, the spring in my body. Then I was there.

I paused outside the door and could no longer avoid facing the implications of my action. What was I doing here? I was running from the police, from Stein, yes, but what did I hope for here? What tremendous welling of subconscious desire, confidence, desperation, led me to expect I would be welcome behind that door? I did not attempt to rationalize my feelings. I simply allowed them to flower. As I ran my fingers through my hair and attempted to smooth the wrinkles from my uniform I found my throat constricted with emotion, my heart racing with anticipation.

My hand hovered near the bell, and there it stayed, two inches from the worn brass button. For from within I now heard a dismayingly familiar sound. Yes, it was the solemn moan of a cello. Instantly I felt my stomach turn to ice. He was here—Tony Buono.

An old feeling possessed me in that moment—the sudden surge of sick jealousy. All the ancient demons rose to take possession of my soul. My imagination slipped into high gear and raced down unworthy alleys and byways. For an instant I teetered on the precipice of my former hysteria. And that instant was more revealing to me than hours of thought. It was not dead, then—had probably never been dead—in spite of all my efforts to kill it. In an instant of deep need the wave of my love for M broke over me and I knew I'd never escaped the fatal undertow of our union. I pressed the button with a trembling finger.

The music stopped, feet approached, the door opened. It was Tony. He was dressed in a worn and faded red bathrobe, his heavy chin was shaded with beard. He still clutched the cello bow in his left hand, and for one moment his face was fixed in a look of simple annoyance. "This is a hell of a—" he started brusquely. Then he recognized me. His eyes widened, his chin fell slack and his lips moved soundlessly. He backed away from the door, shaking his head as if trying to dispel a nightmare. "No," he mumbled, "no, please, no—" He held the bow out before him like a sword as he retreated into the flat.

I followed him and slammed the door behind me. His reaction to my appearance had startled me at first. I could find no explanation for it. But it was obviously one of deep, almost instinctual fright. I determined to take advantage of it. At the same time I experienced, again unreasonably, a great wave of relief. For from the first moment I was certain that M no longer inhabited this flat. There was the indefinable odor, the barren disorder, the haphazard atmosphere, of solitary bachelorhood about the apartment, which I recalled so vividly from my own days of solo occupancy. "What's wrong, Buono?" I asked casually.

"You—you're wrong—all wrong," he groaned. By now he had backed around a small table, which he obviously intended as a barricade. The pallor in his cheeks was replaced by a flush.

"How am I wrong, Buono?" I demanded, still advancing slowly.

Suddenly his heavy brows contracted angrily. "Because you're dead, that's how!" he blustered, waving the bow vaguely. "The announcement was in the *Times* months ago—" His lips shook again despite his effort to control them.

I had, of course, suspected something like this accounted for his reaction. How thorough of Stein, I reflected. "That report was grossly exaggerated," I said coolly, determined to press my unexpected advantage.

"Stop!" he cried. "Stop right there!"

"All right, Tony. See? I'm standing still. I don't want to

touch you," I said coldly, but with a certain amount of insinuation. "I just want to talk to you."

He'd shuddered slightly when I mentioned touching him. But my remarks seemed to calm him slightly. "You might show a little respect for people's feelings," he muttered resentfully. "What was it—some sort of insurance swindle?" Behind the bluster of this remark I detected a tone of pleading. "What's that outfit you've got on?" he asked suspiciously.

"This is the uniform I put on in the morgue," I said tonelessly, somberly. "I said that report was exaggerated. I didn't say it was a lie."

The remark had its proper effect. His cheeks paled again, and he bit his lower lip nervously.

"I *was* dead. I am not dead now."

"Go away," he groaned, his eyes darting desperately around the room as if seeking some way to escape. "Just go away—"

"Look at me, Buono," I continued coldly. "I have been dead. Now I am alive." I confess that I enjoyed this confrontation, enjoyed my feeling of power, enjoyed his superstitious terror. "I will tell you what is waiting for you out there," I continued relentlessly.

"No!" He raised his hands as if warding off a blow.

"Where is she?"

"She's not here—you can see she's not here."

"What have you done with her?"

"Nothing! Nothing! I swear to Christ, Webster, I never even touched her!"

"What are you doing in this apartment, Buono?"

"Oh, so that's it!" I had overplayed my hand. The appearance of a dead man at his door, the zombielike tone I'd maintained—all this had touched some nerve of in-

stinctual dread within him, some atavistic streak of superstition first awakened in his Italianate childhood. But my
inquiries were entirely too mundane for a dead man. Now,
unwittingly, I'd given him a straw of reality to grab. He
seized it desperately, and with growing confidence. "I get
it," he sneered. "You figure you're gonna get this place
back. Well, I got news for you, Webster. This is my place
now. I got a legal lease. I got a lease direct from the
landlord. You can't get me outa here. I got a lease!"

"Where is she?"

"Go on, go on to the rent-control board. You'll see it's all
legal!"

He was obviously so unnerved by his fear of losing the
apartment that he could not assimilate my question. And
here once again I noted that in fact it was not, after all, a
hiding place I'd been seeking; it was M. For I had no
interest whatsoever in his housing problems. "I am not
interes—"

"You gave up this place! You walked out! I'm paying
ten percent more rent than you did."

Was there no piercing his hysteria? I reached out suddenly and seized a pack of matches from the table. His
quick backward step told me he had not completely overcome his dread. I opened the pack slowly, displaying all
my movements with the precision of a card sharp. I struck
a match, then held it to my wrist until a ghastly stench
arose and my flesh turned black. "Now do you believe me,
Buono?" I demanded.

He was breathing deeply, his eyes wide with wonder.
"Listen, Webster," he said in a labored voice, "I don't
know what to believe about you. I don't care if you came
back from the dead or from Mars, you got no more right
to this flat! Understand? Go crawl back into your coffin or

wherever. And for your information, my lease is automatically renewable next year!"

I faced defeat. The housing shortage had overcome even the most deeply ingrained superstition. Suddenly, on inspiration, I drew forth Ritchie's gun. Its effect was exactly the opposite of what I'd hoped.

"You can't get the flat that way!" he cried. "There's a waiting list for all these places! It won't do you any good, Webster!"

"Shut up!" I shouted, now thoroughly annoyed. "I don't want your damned apartment. I want to know where she is."

His eyes narrowed suspiciously. "You know where she is," he said accusingly. "You know. You can't fool me like that. I know what you're after."

"No, you don't!" I cried. And this was a mistake. For there was that in my voice—a note of pleading, no doubt —which emboldened Buono.

Very calmly, quietly, without for a moment taking his eyes from me, he reached for the phone. I found myself frozen in helpless indecision as he dialed the operator. Did I have it within me to shoot him? I knew I did not. He knew I did not.

"Police!" he barked into the receiver; then as he waited patiently, triumphantly: "We'll just see whose flat this is, Webster!"

I waited to hear no more. M was in any event not there. I did not pretend that I was cruel enough to force him to tell me what he knew. In the face of his massive hysteria I knew myself to be helpless. I rushed into the hall and down the stairs, tucking Ritchie's gun back inside my smock. As I clambered breathlessly down the flights I found myself musing on my own social impotence. Faced with something even so simple as a man overwhelmed by the housing shortage, I had found myself incapable of penetrating to his essential humanity. But then, did Buono have an essential humanity? I pushed open the glass lobby doors and walked out into the street without a second thought, so engrossed was I in that problem.

Perhaps they'd been trailing me for some time. In any event, they must have been very confidently waiting outside the building all during my interview with Buono. Their movements were precise, professional, overwhelming. Strong hands gripped my arms. I felt myself lifted from the pavement and hustled toward the black ambulance so quickly, so smoothly, that I had no time even to think of crying out. And then, inside, there was Stein, waiting for me.

"Good evening," he said casually, placidly, as the ambulance doors swung shut, a powerful motor raced to life and the wail of a siren cut through the night. The guards who'd accompanied me into the vehicle had by now strapped me to a stretcher. One of them had a hypodermic syringe ready. "I do not think we will require that, will we, Professor?" Stein asked mildly. Then suddenly he leaned forward and grabbed my arm. "What is this? What is this? What have you done to yourself?" He was staring, aghast, at my burned wrist. "Quickly—the first-aid kit," he snapped at one of the guards.

I paid no attention to the bandaging, paid little heed to my surroundings. My mind was now a shambles. Ritchie's gun and its potential use never even occurred to me.

I observed the mechanical process of my return to The Foundation as a disinterested spectator, not even amused by the ironical fact that I was smuggled back into The Foundation in the same way I'd been smuggled out. We used the same underground hearse ramp, I was again placed on one of the wheeled corpse tables with a sheet drawn over my face and I was again trundled through halls and corridors. I reflected during the journey that there was someone or some group within The Foundation from whom Stein wished to keep my escape a secret.

But when at last the table came to rest and the sheet was removed from my face I received a surprise. For I had not been returned to my old tomb in Psy, nor had I been delivered to my original room. Instead I found myself in a comfortably appointed living room-library with doors opening into a bedroom and what I guessed was a private bathroom. It was a suite, and a residential one at that. It looked like any one of thousands of apartments that might be found among the older buildings of the city. The furniture was comfortable but by no means modern, the illumination was by table and floor lamps rather than being indirect. And under any other circumstances I would have been delighted by the solid wall of well-stocked book shelves, the large desk, the typewriter, the filing cabinets that filled part of the room. But my indifference was impenetrable.

Stein dismissed the guards as I crawled off the table and wearily slumped down into an overstuffed chair. "Well, you will want some sleep," he said warmly. "This entire suite is at your disposal. We have decided to take a completely new view of your case. But I will be discussing all that with you tomorrow." In spite of his even voice, his massive calm, I could tell that my utter indifference made him slightly nervous. "Well—" he said tentatively. "Well, I won't detain you any longer. Good night."

I made no reply. My eyes were closed now, and I was

already drifting into sleep as I heard him leave my room, softly closing the door behind him.

Sometime during the night I dreamed; the constellations burned brightly, gutted themselves, left the night a black velvet screen on which fantasy danced and cavorted. These were not dreams; they were visions, impressions, screaming whistle-stops on the route to madness. There was a human junk yard full of broken men, one of them a paraplegic who modeled artificial limbs, and another, most terrifyingly, a man who had no free associations. And there was one who was chairman of a convention of epileptics but in reality a spy for the Consulate General of the Holy Roman Empire, 551 Park Avenue. And some of this human junk was displayed at a children's zoo . . . But we were not entirely hopeless, for we were all informed by the tremendous anticipatory knowledge that we were evolving into pure spirit, all humanity rising nearer and nearer to some physical surface (where scum was concentrated) but about to break through, to be liberated from the physical into the spiritual. And behind us were untold billions of souls fighting for reservations on earth, in a vast and awful battle in which quarter was neither asked nor given . . .

Sometime during the night I awoke on the floor in front of the overstuffed chair, got up blindly and staggered into the bedroom, undressed and crawled into a wide and comforting bed in which I slept profoundly, dreamlessly.

I awoke considerably refreshed, my limbs relaxed. My bedroom was bathed in light that flooded through tall, curtained windows. I saw a white hospital smock lying across the foot of my bed.

My clothes! I glanced about desperately. Someone had

removed them during the night. And—no, I felt the familiar cold steel beneath my mattress where I'd hidden it. I was so relieved by this discovery that it was not until I'd got up, dressed myself in the smock and walked to the bedroom door that I realized this smock had no back. It covered me completely in the front and was fastened by straps tied behind, but it was nonexistent in the rear. I cautiously made my way to the open doorway and peered into the room beyond.

Here was the comfortably furnished living room-library of the night before. Overstuffed chairs, wall-to-wall carpeting, Van Dyck's "Smiling Cavalier" in a medium-priced reproduction adorning one wall, the long, low coffee table in front of a deep-cushioned couch—all this was so familiar that I barely noticed it. In any case, my attention was centered on the sound of the door opening.

Suddenly I felt a thrill of pure terror course through me. I stepped back, almost instinctively, to hide behind the bedroom door. For into the living room, at a careful, stately pace, wheeling a small table before him, walked Dr. Ritchie. He was clothed in a simple white uniform with a small, circular white hat on his head, and his entire attention was forcused on the table before him.

I felt my fingernails digging into my sweaty palms. What was on that table, beneath the square, white, neatly folded cloths? Ritchie's slow entrance, the slight creaking of the table wheels, the whiff of antisepsis that accompanied him, stimulated something akin to my old panic. The table came to rest in the center of the living room. Ritchie reached out his square, blunt hand to remove the cloths—

My groan must have been audible. I covered my eyes with my hands.

"What's wrong?" Stein's high, brisk voice cut through

my mounting terror. "Come out and see what we've got here!" he demanded jovially.

I dropped my hands and saw Stein standing over the table next to Ritchie, rubbing his chubby hands together, his excited face flushed in anticipation of the hearty breakfast for two that was now revealed.

"Come out, come out," he called.

I edged cautiously into the living room, making sure that my exposed backside was always protected by a wall.

"I could eat a cow, a whale, a hippopotamus," Stein announced, as he dragged the desk chair over to the table and seated himself. "Well, aren't you hungry?" he demanded while tucking a napkin beneath his chins, his eyes gleaming greedily at the array of chafing dishes, pitchers, china, silver and crystal.

I was not paying attention to him. My eyes were fixed in speculative horror on the silent, dreamily distant figure of Ritchie, who stood at attention behind Stein's chair, his eyes glittering strangely. Was it at all conceivable that Stein did not realize—? No, I rejected the thought before it was barely formulated. Stein must certainly know all the details of my escape. But had he merely degraded Ritchie to the rank of Steward by way of punishment? Did Stein propose to trust the food he received from those hands? And what depths of hate for me lurked behind Ritchie's immobile face? I was the cause of his downfall—

"What *can* be the matter, Professor?" Stein glanced at me, then at Ritchie, then back to me again. "Oh, I see!" he exclaimed with a slight grin. "You must excuse me, Professor. One becomes so parochial regarding one's own work and surroundings. One forgets, for example, that you are not familiar with symptoms of shock therapy. But in any event, you must not worry about Ritchie here." He nodded obliquely at the figure behind him. "He's a new man, aren't you, Ritchie?"

Ritchie frowned very slightly, his eyes glistened, and then he smiled inanely. "Yes, sir, never felt better!"

Did I detect behind those glassy eyes something striving to express itself? He seemed like a man bound with invisible chains, and yet—yet his facial expression was one of near-bliss. Never taking my attention from Ritchie, I sidled along the wall and into a chair facing Stein.

"Orange juice?" Stein poured himself a glass and then one for me. "You really must not fret about this, Professor. Ritchie was suffering from a deep-seated paranoia rooted in emotional displacement. Believe me, he is not listening to what we say. Our object in these cases is not punishment but cure. We have cleansed his frontal lobes—his memory organization. Look, I'll demonstrate." He drained his orange juice in one gulp, with a noise like a toilet flushing.

I sipped mine slowly, trying (and failing) to pretend that I could believe in Stein's diagnosis.

"Has uh—Jerry been acting up again, Ritchie?" Stein asked, as he dug his spoon into a grapefruit half.

"'Fraid so, sir. We can expect gas cases today. Phosphene, I reckon. Bloody barrage fell a hundred meters short. Got to hand it to 'em. The Boche is on his toes, all right!"

Stein slurped his grapefruit juice with each mouthful, pausing only to dab delicately at his lips with his napkin, which quickly became stained. "How's morale?" he inquired.

"High as a bloody kite, sir, if you'll pardon the expression! Can't get our lads down!"

I found my hand shaking as I tried to sprinkle sugar on my grapefruit. I could not bear to look at Ritchie standing

proudly at attention, a slight smile of grim dedication on
his lips, but Stein's table manners were such that I could
not bear to look at him, either.

"Ritchie here has seen some hard fighting," Stein announced. He started to spread butter on his bread and
continued until it was at least a quarter of an inch thick.
"Don't like toast in the morning," he said. "Crumbs get
stuck behind my false teeth." He belched deeply. "With
the Aussie uh—Fifteenth at Ypres, wasn't it, Ritchie?"

"Begging your pardon, sir, it was the Anzac Twentieth
at Gallipoli."

"Of course, of course. Brave set of boys. Good sense of
humor, too. Now, let me see, what was that song they
always—"

"It's an old outback song, sir." Ritchie grinned hap-
pily.

"Eggs? Bacon? Let me help you." Stein dished out
scrambled eggs and bacon from their chafing dishes, load-
ing his own plate mountainously, mine moderately. I felt
a twinge of annoyance. He even predicted my appetite. A
more sensitive man would have asked.

"Can you give us a chorus or two?" He spoke with his
mouth full of eggs and bread, crumbled bits of bacon
clinging slimily to his chin. "Do eat, Professor." He invited
my attention to the plate in front of me.

Ritchie cleared his throat. "With your permission, then,
sir." He started to sing in a rasping, carefree voice:

> "Oh, she can fuck, fight, ride a bike
> And climb a cherry tree,
> She's a broad brave colleen now,
> And she's the girl for me!
> She's got dimples on her ass
> Like the apples on a tree—"

"No!" The word exploded from between my lips with a force that surprised even me. "No! Please—I don't want to hear any more." In the sudden silence I looked up to see Ritchie watching me with embarrassment. Stein, his coffee cup halfway to his lips, had a look of innocent concern on his face.

"That will be all, Ritchie," he said quietly.

"Right, sir!" Ritchie snapped to attention, saluted, wheeled and marched stiffly from the room.

I pushed my plate away from me.

"You mustn't be depressed," Stein said genially, slurping up his coffee. "We have simply freed Ritchie to enact the role closest to his heart, the role he was best equipped emotionally to handle. We have made him a happy man." He poured himself another cup of coffee and dunked buttered bread into it. A thin film of yellow soon spread over the brown surface, and when he ate, soggy bits of bread fell and clung to his napkin.

My revulsion at the spectacle of Ritchie reduced to some role he had memorized from childhood attendance at the cinema had merged with the disgust Stein's table manners aroused, until my original trepidation was now effaced by simple but profound anger. I longed to strike out in some meaningful way at the placid, moonlike face across the table. I finished my coffee and lit a cigarette from a box on the table. I noticed without surprise that it was my favorite brand. "I wonder if you know all the details of my escape?" I asked casually. I had a bit of news for him calculated to destroy his smugness.

"Aren't you going to finish your bacon and eggs?" Stein inquired hopefully. "No? Well, waste not, want not, I say." He pulled my plate toward him and attacked it zestfully, maintaining silence while he diligently devoured the remains. Finally he glanced up, wiped egg from his chin and poured himself another cup of coffee. Did his face reflect the snare lurking behind my own conversational gambit or some cunning trap of his own devising? "What one always requires from breakfast," he said, "is repletion. The breakfast that does not fill is no breakfast at all. It is well enough to leave the luncheon or dinner table slightly hungry, but never the breakfast table. I make it a rule to eat a hearty breakfast."

"It was quite an adventure," I suggested.

"Your escape? Yes, I suppose it was. Actually, we know all the details of that. It is our policy to know. Ritchie's assistants have been cured, also, and delivered to The Institute. He, however, knows entirely too much about our affairs to take that chance, even after shock therapy. You are troubled by these results of your 'adventure'? Yes" —he puffed thoughtfully on his cigarette—"you seem to involve very many people in your affairs. Unlucky people perhaps. But you yourself seem to have surprising luck. Where is the gun?" Stein leaned forward suddenly, his huge eyes intent upon my tiniest facial expression.

"I lost it in the park." I lied as casually as I could. "How did you know there was a gun?"

"I did not. But I assumed that Ritchie was not unarmed, and our forensic expert guessed that two of the blows from which he and the attendants suffered were struck by the butt of a revolver." He paused.

I could tell he did not believe I'd lost the gun in the park. But why hadn't I been searched when I first arrived? Was it possible that the great Stein, the implacable, unswerving, meticulous Stein, had overlooked that little detail? I was sure he had. But one never knew with him. Was there anything planned about the omission? I

judged not. There was an undertone of nervous aggressiveness about him now that suggested a simple, uncal-
culated mistake. But it would be well to change the topic
of conversation, and I was still longing to disrupt his
masterful assurance.

"You know," I said reflectively, "when I ran across the
street into the park I was struck by a truck or a car, I'm
not sure—"

"What?" Stein sprang up, knocking over his coffee cup,
oblivious of the dregs spilling down his pants. "You were
hit by a vehicle?" The effect was all I could have
wished.

I nodded. "Sent me flying. I was unconscious for a
while—"

But Stein was no longer listening. He had rushed over
to the desk and was pressing a button on what appeared
to be an interoffice call box. "Send Nurse Williams up here
immediately," he snapped, "with emergency kit seven.
Clear X-ray room . . . I don't care. Use number five. We'll
be there in ten minutes, and I want it ready!" He remained leaning over the desk, staring at me. "You were
struck by a vehicle," he muttered, "and you've seen fit to
mention the fact only now. Do you realize that you may
have suffered internal injuries? Obviously the impact did
not affect your skeletal or muscle structure, otherwise you
would not have made it all the way to the Bronx. But
internally—" He shook his massive head regretfully, in a
manner calculated to convey unutterable sorrow not
simply for my thoughtlessness but for the thoughtlessness
of Fate, God, the universe. "After everything we've done
for you," he murmured. "You—you risk as if it was
nothing—the most scientifically valuable body in existence today, irreplaceable . . . Shocking, shocking!" His

eyes conveyed a reproach I could not meet. I found myself staring sullenly at the disordered remnants on the
breakfast table.

"Perhaps you do not realize," he continued relentlessly,
"just how delicate the balance of the body's mechanism
truly is. No, of course you do not. You *could* not!"

"It wasn't my fault," I protested. "I wasn't driving the
car, after all." I was conscious of the weakness of my excuse. I was aware that Stein did not even consider my remark worthy of a reply. But our mutual embarrassment was
cut short by the arrival of Nurse Williams, wheeling before
her into the living room a square, many-shelved table on
which boxes of instruments were stacked in neat array.

"Emergency kit seven, Doctor Stein" (hoo), she said.
She glanced at me with that intolerable smile. I suddenly
felt a savage longing to wipe it from her face.

"We meet yet once again, O ravishing daughter of the
Nile," I said solemnly but with as much leer as I could
muster.

She ignored the remark and busied herself preparing
various tubes, instruments and vials under Stein's silently
intent direction.

"How are the portals of pleasure today, child of delight?" I demanded.

"Look, Doctor Stein," she announced, in a tone of voice
that hovered on a precipice of pure disgust, "is this one
still nuts? I mean, after all, I'm not trained as a psychiatric nurse, and I'm not paid to look after types like him."
(hoo)

"He is perfectly sane," Stein muttered absently, fiddling
around with a blood-pressure gauge.

"Yes, bride of lust, I am perfectly sane," I whispered
throatily.

"Make him stop!" (hoo)

"Stop what?"

"Stop talking like that!"

Stein sighed. "Please, Professor—"

"Sticks and stones may break your bones, but words will only rape you, Williams," I chuckled.

My small stratagem to divert Stein's attention from the gun seemed to work perfectly. For now he became completely absorbed in my condition. He drew blood, he probed, he made me swallow batteries of radioactive tracers. I was conducted on the wearily familiar tour of The Foundation's testing laboratories and even found myself becoming, like Stein, so completely engulfed in this research (which revealed, incidentally, nothing graver than the bad bruise on my right thigh) that I too forgot about the gun. By the time we'd returned to Stein's suite, the breakfast table had been removed. I relaxed in an armchair and Stein posted himself behind the desk. Shafts of late-morning sunshine caught tiny motes of dust and turned them to gold behind his bald head.

"Last night, Professor," he said thoughtfully, "I told you that we were taking a completely new view of your case."

"It hasn't been noticeable," I muttered, yawning.

"I have to tell you something, Professor. Something . . ." He paused and removed his spectacles, drew out his handkerchief and began polishing them intently. "Professor, you need us as much as we need you. No." He waved a balloonlike hand at me. "Please do not interrupt. I suppose"—he cleared his throat sententiously—"I should begin at the beginning." He leaned forward, replaced his spectacles and stared at me. "I will put two questions to you and then aswer them. Question number one: Why do we need *you* specifically? Why *you* in the first place and *you* now and *you* tomorrow? Why not some other and perhaps more co-operative subject? Question number two: Why do you need *us?*" He smiled quizzically.

"Well then," he said, "question number one. A simple answer. You have been suffering from leukemia—I should say, you have been suffering from leukemia S. You are also not more than forty years of age. You were also, at the time of your arrival here, alive. This is a rare combination of circumstances. Very rare. Now, this is all very complicated, and I will not bore you with the details. But I will tell you that despite the years of effort that have gone into it, CNH research is still in its infancy. By breaking down and then re-creating the gene factor CNH—a biochemical factor—we are now able to restore life to an undamaged body, as your own case proves. But by an 'undamaged body,' I mean just that. We cannot, using CNH therapy, restore life to a body whose death has been caused by damage to the internal organs, such as would be the case with an accident victim, or with someone who died of any of the diseases that attack vital organs—I could mention cirrhosis, tuberculosis, peritonitis, in fact, the overwhelming majority of mortal diseases, all of which are mortal because of the damage they wreak upon internal organs. Now, under the classification of damage must also come the damage of old age. Hardening of arteries, heart faults, brain dysfunctions. CNH does not repair damage. So who is the ideal experimental subject? Of course, he is someone who is not old and who dies of a nondamaging event. Suffocation, including some forms of gassing, a thrombosis that caused no heart damage, electric shock—all these might be suitable. But there is one other qualification. For serious experimental work it is essential that the subject be under control both preceding and following actual death. Now, it is true that hundreds of people die—or, more availably, are executed—every day in one of these acceptable ways. But," he added regretfully, utterly missing the irony of his words, "they die outside our jurisdiction. The tiny percentage that might arrive here would be—*are,* in fact, already in a moribund condition, making premorbid pathology impossible. Of course, we could make thorough studies of potential subjects during their lifetimes. Then we would gamble that some of them would die young enough, and of these that a still smaller percentage would die of a nondamaging cause, and of these that a still tinier fraction would be brought here. But nondamaging death before middle age is always a surprise, and death occurs out there, not in here. Peter and Paul, our computers, inform us that in order to get *one* suitable subject we would have to initiate such studies upon not less than five million people. And that is why our experiments had been conducted upon animals until your arrival. Mind you, The Foundation, at no matter what cost in money or time, would have undertaken the necessary research. But your case offered us a providential short cut."

"I'm happy to have been of service," I muttered.

"Leukemia S!" he exclaimed, completely ignoring my sarcasm. "It's perfect! No damage to organs or tissues, a death slow enough to enable full statistical and chemo-pathological research. It may, simply put, be likened to a kind of internal suffocation caused by the breaking down of the blood and its growing incapacity to carry oxygen to the organs. It is susceptible to transfusion and CNH therapy, but rare, oh, so rare! Try to understand our position. Here you come, a young man suffering from a nondamaging fatal disease, to place yourself under our care. You are

a statistical improbability of the highest order! Indispensable! That is why we decided to proceed with the first
stage of experimental proof, using you as the subject. And
it is the vast amount of research knowledge we have acquired about your unique chemo-bio-psycho-pathological
condition that makes it imperative for us to continue with
you. Have I answered the first question?" He beamed at
me with unbearable kindliness.

"The first stage?" I asked drily. "I have to die again?"

"A mere formality!" Stein cried impatiently.

"To you, perhaps. But why again?" How easily we slip
into the logic of insanity!

"That," Stein sighed, "brings us to question number
two. Why do you need us?"

"I can't imagine."

Stein clasped his hands behind his huge bulk and
slowly walked over to the window. He peered out into a
cloudless sky. "Tell me, Professor," he said at last, "is
there nothing we can do for you? You know, there are few
organizations in the world to compare to The Foundation.
Perhaps we could help you in your work somehow? In
some personal matter or other?"

I felt uneasy at this sudden turn in his monologue. This
was, as far as I could recall, the very first time Stein had
ever offered to help me, indeed, had ever suggested that I
might find assistance useful in any extramedical sense.
Why had he offered? A thousand suspicions clamored at
the door of my mind. But I refused them admittance.
Why? Because there was indeed something with which
The Foundation might aid me. If Stein was opening the
door to some sort of bargain or trade, I must seize the
opportunity.

"Have you ever heard of a man named Suskind?" I

asked, trying to maintain a casual quality in my voice as I would if bargaining with a used-car salesman.

"He is mentioned as having occupied the same premises as you at the time of your arrival here," Stein acknowledged. He did not turn to face me but continued to stare out the window.

In as brief but as clear a manner as possible I outlined Suskind's plight and the reasons for it. I made it very clear that I expected The Foundation to effect his release from the asylum to which the police had committed him. Stein did not respond immediately but kept silence for a moment, as if waiting for me to go on.

"That is your only request?" he asked quietly.

"It's the only one you can help me with," I replied.

"I see, I see," he muttered thoughtfully. "Tell me, Professor—you were found by us outside one of your earlier places of residence at the time of your recapture. Had you any special purpose in going there?"

"That's none of your business!"

"No need to get angry, Professor. I was just wondering if by any chance there was anything else we could do for you."

"Nothing! Not a thing!"

"Very well. Now then, I wonder if you would cooperate with us in one small matter. It is a question of rehearsal." He turned toward me, his face reflecting momentarily the aroused suspicion on my own.

"What do you mean, 'rehearsal'?"

"Some time ago, Professor, while you were pretending to be in a catatonic trance, I explained to you the importance of a concise, controlled, publicly witnessed demonstration of this experiment. This involves the participation of doctors, assistants, television and other news media, a coroner—"

"No!"

"Please, Professor, let me continue. I am speaking only of a rehearsal. Certain matters—technical details—can only be properly worked out in a complete—let us say a full dress—rehearsal."

"There's no point in rehearsing something that isn't going to take place, Stein!" I cried. "You let the cat out of the bag long ago. You can't force me to co-operate. You can kill me, you can overpower me and kill me, but you can't prevent me from making a botch of things after you revive me. I'm telling you right now that if I wake up dead some day, what I'll have to say will ruin you—ruin you! I don't know what it'll be, but I'll have them investigating you and your assistants and The Foundation, I'll convince them it was all a fraud, I'll—"

"Webster!" Stein shouted suddenly. His face may have mirrored my own rage or expressed his own. His breath was short and his hands were tightly knotted at his sides. It was the first time I had ever heard him call me by anything so personal as my last name. "Please be sane!" His voice sank to a hoarse whisper that issued through clenched teeth. "There would be no need in any case to overpower you, as you put it. This is only a matter of convenience."

"Well, rehearse with a dummy then—"

"I was not referring to the rehearsal. I was referring to your condition."

"My condition?"

"Yes. I will answer question number two for you now. You need us, Professor, for the very simple reason that you will die again—normally, I mean—of leukemia S within a matter of weeks, perhaps a month. I told you CNH therapy was not a cure." His voice was quiet now, as close to apologetic as it was able to come. The words fell softly into stillness. His face for one brief moment anticipated the look of stunned desperation I was unable to mask.

"I don't believe you," I lied, unable to look at him. "I have no symptoms at all, I feel fine—"

"You mean, don't you, Professor, that you feel no pain?" He glanced at his wristwatch and walked to the door. "We have tentatively arranged the rehearsal for this afternoon. Sleep Time will be tonight."

"Sleep Time?" In the whirlpool of despair that now threatened to engulf me, I grasped irrationally onto the least important debris in his remark.

"Not a phrase I would have chosen. But our public-relations people are fond of it. I'll be back in a few hours for your decision about the rehearsal, and about Sleep Time. And I will see to the Suskind business immediately." His hand was on the doorknob.

"Just a minute!" I cried out desperately. "Suppose I refuse to co-operate?"

"Professor, a refusal on your part to co-operate in an experiment so vital to the progress of the human race, a refusal that would also in fact be a choice of suicide, would be a clear demonstration of insanity. If such is the case we would not abandon you. The Foundation is, after all, devoted to treatment and mercy. We would certainly attempt treatment—probably through shock therapy. After that, for the small time remaining to you, you would certainly be free to leave us. Good morning, Professor." He made a slight bow and left.

I sat for a long time staring blindly at the door. Fear at the ring of truth behind his words (for I believed him utterly, instinctually, regarding my condition; he had never lied to me), impotent rage at the threat of shock therapy in the event of my refusal (the spectacle of Ritchie's inanity had been, I now realized, deliberately paraded before me), hysteria at my own helplessness (had he, in fact, left me any possibility of choice?)—all these were mere emotional shadows projected onto the solid, almost tangible wall of my despair. After what may have been a matter of minutes or a matter of hours, I got up slowly and walked over to the windows.

Far, far below, a few people strolled through the park. Cars crept sluggishly past on the street. There was a world of normal human beings—or as normal as our society permitted them to be—awaiting, all unknowing, an announcement that would spell calamity for them. Did they deserve that? But perhaps I'd better explain.

First of all, you must believe me when I say that I no longer feared death *per se*. Pain was now a stranger to my flesh, and the prospect of nonexistence evoked in my spirit not fear so much as regret—regret for the interruption of my work, regret for the few pleasures I might still enjoy. My experiences had exhausted me, I supposed, very much in the same way as someone dying (consciously aware that he is dying) of an incurable disease is exhausted. And I found that the prospect left me only numb, weary—and regretful. For the certainty of death almost always finds us prepared for it. Just as the human fetus is extravagantly and subtly prepared for the act of birth, so the dying man (I speak, of course, of nonviolent death) is prepared by nature for the act of dying. When man thinks of death he panics because he imagines it occurring in conditions of mental and emotional health or vigor. But usually death invites us to leave a banquet table already barren, when we have been surfeited by the stuff of life and are weary with the feast. The old or the desperately ill are not afraid to die. Fear of death is strongest in the young and healthy. By co-operating with Stein's experiment I would in fact be condemning mankind to a greater fear of death than that which they now suffered. But there was a more important consideration.

Stein had hinted at Foundation support and help in my private work on *The Theory of Place and Decay*. I had not responded to this hint, but an interesting line of speculation was aroused by it. With Foundation support I would be able to expand and deepen my work infinitely. I would be able to amass overwhelming research material, command vast, controlled experimental data. *And I would have all the time in the world, perhaps all the time of infinity, in which to complete the work.* For if Stein was correct (and I had no reason to doubt him), then barring some accident, I need never taste of permanent death. I myself—and perhaps this generation of men, perhaps the next—would face, at last, the life everlasting. The fact that men might have to die every so often was, I was certain, merely a small obstacle. Stein and his successors would soon overcome even temporary death. And as this realization settled into me—as the vista of endless time opened before me—I was gripped by a sort of nauseous boredom compounded of helplessness (the endless choice of *possibilities* in a life without end threatened madness) and lassitude (nothing could seem urgent, nothing important when time lost its meaning) and vertigo (the road ahead stretched away into an open-ended system as large as space-time itself). I glimpsed, however fleetingly and superficially, the meaninglessness of life without death. Without death, the effort of living seemed hardly worthwhile.

And there was yet another chilling prospect that Stein's words uncovered. He had said his experiment was "vital

to the progress of the human race." On another occasion
he had referred to the great freedom which resurrection
had presumably conferred upon me—would confer upon
all mankind. I have tried to explain the great prospect of
boredom that this "freedom" opened before me. But there
was another, and perhaps even more vital matter.

For I understood what Stein implied. By "freedom" he
meant mere freedom from fear, from the psychic dread of
death. By "progress" he meant nothing less than human
evolution itself. He saw me at the very apex of evolution,
for the next step in this "progress" was to be the conquest
of death and of the fear of death. Humanity, to Stein, was
an endless procession of pilgrims drawn in the faceless
style of Rockwell Kent, marching slowly but inevitably
and triumphantly from the remotest past toward some
glorious future, bearing banners on which Stein's name
would be emblazoned.

But true freedom is freedom *from* evolution. The concept of humanity's becoming something it is not is an ancient trap. It is the abominable lure that a snake first
offered to our remotest ancestors—for that is the central
meaning of the myth of Eden. And this same lure has now
been built into the very structure of the world. But the
trap is obvious to anyone willing to look upon life objectively.

Make a test. Go to the nearest zoo and visit the ape
house. Stare continuously and dispassionately into the
eyes of a large gorilla as he shells his peanuts and spits at
spectators. You cannot fail to realize, if you will but take
sufficient time, that behind those sunken, tortured eyes,
behind that brutish, hairy forehead, *someone is at home.*
Who? But the realization and the question are perhaps
too terrifying. Make this experiment and see if you are not

terrified. Now, how do you avoid the realization and evade the question? Why, simply by concentrating all your psychic energy, all your rational mind, on a spurious issue. It is a question of misdirection. The magician in our minds, when confronted by something too awful to contemplate, by a sort of sleight-of-hand focuses our attention on something else. The first thing you must do is sell yourself the Lie. The Lie is simply that you have not seen what you have seen but instead have seen something totally different and very absorbing. You have seen the outer husk of a most *improvable* object. By concentrating on the potential physical improvement of the beast, you avoid facing the question of the Who within. Or at least obscure it. The science-swindlers and religion-fakers would have us believe that progress, self-improvement, will make the gorilla, the world, every individual in the world, a fitter habitation for the Who within. But the Who never demanded this.

The simple truth is that evolution has been sold to the gorilla just as it has to man as a means of *insuring* the imprisonment of the Who within by the misdirection of all our energies to the improvement and refinement of the prison. And the reason is fear—fear of the eventual escape and triumph of the Who. The task of mankind is not to become; it is to unbecome. The most unbecoming among us are closest to true freedom.

And all this and more was the price mankind would have to pay for the life everlasting on that triumphant day when Stein revealed his godhead. Yes, of course, godhead. For after Stein's discovery, what would remain for God but to abdicate and creep into the dustbin of human memory? No concept of God could survive the fact of human immortality.

And what of the psychic impact of all this upon the race? Would men retain sanity in a life everlasting? After all, I have a remarkably strong mind, a tenacious grip on reality, a keen comprehension of the thin border between truth and madness, and I found myself reeling. Resurrection would not only deepen man's fear of death, eliminate meaning from life, permanently imprison the soul; it would also most probably madden the race.

What then could I do about it all? As the morning grew into afternoon, I did not delude myself. Stein had referred to me as a statistical improbability, not an impossibility. And although he claimed uniqueness, although he claimed to be the sole originator of, repository for and authority on his discovery, he would not always be so. There would one day be another me, another Stein. This discovery could not be hidden indefinitely. In the long run Stein or someone like him would succeed. But simply because we cannot stave off eternity forever is no reason why a dedicated man should not win whatever battles against it he can. And what was my life if not a long dedication? I had the means of winning one battle at least. Beside that fact details became irrelevant. In fact, they became grotesquely amusing. I would co-operate with Stein so far—and beyond that I would be in absolute control of the situation. Having made a decision I suddenly found myself free, light, almost exhilarated. Stein had been playing cat-and-mouse with me. I saw no reason why the game should not continue—with the roles reversed.

I had been drowsing in the armchair for perhaps an hour when Stein returned. I did not hear him enter but snapped out of my reverie to find him standing before me like some particularly fat and loathsome vulture over its prey. He was swathed in a white smock. Behind him two technicians stood next to a wheeled table. Behind them Nurse Williams appeared.

"Well, Professor, have you decided to help us with this rehearsal?" Stein's manner was a jovial denial of the anger he'd shown not four hours earlier. More than that, he managed to convey the greatest confidence that I would in fact co-operate, at the same time that something indefinable in his manner suggested that if I did not ride the table to the rehearsal I would ride it to shock therapy.

"I will co-operate," I replied pleasantly. It was my turn now to savor knowledge *he* did not possess. As I climbed onto the table I flattered myself that a flicker of suspicion flitted obscurely behind Stein's eyes. Let him worry! I was also interested to note that Nurse Williams smiled at me in an unmistakably friendly fashion. Evidently my coarse jokes had been forgiven.

"Now, we leave here at exactly eight twenty-five P.M.," Stein said. He fiddled with his watch. "I'm setting it at eight twenty-five now so that we'll have a time check. Let's go, then."

I was wheeled out of the apartment and into a long, shadowless corridor. An elevator awaited us with doors open.

"Good timing," Stein muttered to the operator as we entered. Then we descended in silence. When the elevator reached its destination and the gate slid open, Stein again glanced at his watch. "Williams, please note that elapsed time was four and a half minutes."

I saw Williams enter the fact in a little black notebook.

I was wheeled through further corridors, past steel doors, beneath red lights, with my vision limited to the passing globes of white fluorescence in the ceiling.

The wearisome journey terminated in the wings of the operating theater. And here my eyes were blinded by a glaring light, my ears confused by a babble of innumerable voices.

"Move arc number one two feet to the left!" someone was shouting.

"That brings it into camera frame!" a distant voice protested.

"Frank, lower the scrim a few feet . . . more . . . more . . . that's it."

"Flood number four is out! Goddammitall, can't *someone* do *something* about those outlets?"

"You're casting a shadow right over area B now—"

"Williams," Stein's voice, close at hand, cut through the others, "ten minutes have elapsed since we left his apartment. That's five minutes too many. Make a note that table and elevator are to be prepared as of eight-fifteen. That will give us a five-minute margin of safety."

"What's going on here?" I asked apprehensively.

"Oh, it's just the stage manager and his crew," Stein replied. "Now, I'm going to leave you, and we'll commence the rehearsal when I give the word." He passed outside the limits of my vision.

When my eyes grew accustomed to the brilliant light, I saw that I was waiting at the edge of a large, round platform in the center of which stood an operating table surrounded by a maze of immensely complicated machinery. The walls were so impeccably white as to suggest they were made of plastic; the floor was of stainless steel. And swarming over this area was a small army of technicians. Some were adjusting arc lights while others held up meters to test them. Others were steadying a large black screen that was lowered from a platform suspended below the ceiling. Several men were going about with tape measures, while overalled electricians tinkered with a maze of cables that festooned the platform. It was a reassuring sight. Stein could be planning no sudden move before all these witnesses.

"Scrim in frame, now! Up, up, up . . . that's it! No shadows in area B now, but I'm getting flare in area A."

"Frank, tilt that reflector a bit higher . . . higher still, please—"

"Number four is still out! Someone—please—can't we get a little co-operation here?"

I confess that excitement slowly stole over me now, all the old magic of the theater—the terrible tensions, the quivering nerves, the desperate dedication and uncertainty, that always attend a first night. Of course, I had never had any theatrical experience. But I had read very thoroughly in the history of the drama as a part of my research. I found myself being swept into the general enthusiasm, found that my stomach tingled with what could only be symptoms of stage fright. I was determined to play my part perfectly now. I practiced lying rigidly on the table, my eyes shut, my hands folded upon my chest, in what I thought a suitable counterfeit of a dead man's position.

Three sharp hand claps exploded amid the babble of voices, which were instantly silenced. I heard Stein's voice sounding from a distance.

"Patient enters from stage left and is wheeled to stage center."

As the table rolled forward I closed my eyes and assumed my role. I wondered if make-up would not be necessary under these terribly bright lights.

"Thirty seconds for applause," Stein called. "Now we enter from stage right. Gentlemen, if you please."

I squinted one eye open and saw Stein advancing toward me with a group of white-smocked doctors and technicians. There must have been two dozen of them.

"Would you mind taking that again, Doctor?" a voice called from the higher balconies of the theater. "You're walking too fast. We can't track properly."

As Stein and his group reassembled at stage right I twisted my head around and saw several huge television cameras in the top tier of seats.

"Enter, gentlemen," Stein called, as he and his group walked once again—this time at a very stately pace—toward me. When they reached the operating table they bowed to the vacant auditorium. "I think two minutes for applause here," Stein called.

Thirty seconds of applause for me and two minutes for them?

"Positions, please!" Stein called.

His band of technicians and doctors rushed to their places, some attending to the complicated machinery around me while others poised over my body. They were in fact hiding me from the cameras. I was about to protest when a voice called from the balcony.

"The three doctors standing in area A completely mask the patient. Can't they stand at either end of the table, Doctor Stein?"

"They have to transfer the patient," Stein replied. "Of course, instead of a side lift they could try a shoulders-and-feet lift. Let's try that."

As I was lifted from the wheeled table onto the operating table I reflected that Stein was at least honest. He was not willing to sacrifice the drama of this moment to the

base egos of his confederates who hoped to hog the lime-
light.

"That's much better," the balcony voice announced.
"Now, are those the final positions for the operation, Doctor?"

"I have already explained that there is no actual operation," Stein called. "There is a blood transfusion and the
connection of these various tubes, breathing apparatus,
CNH factoring machine, etcetera. But we do not actually
cut the patient. He will be under this oxygen tent almost
immediately."

"Yes, yes, of course, Doctor," the voice answered.
"But—"

"Please get to the point!" Stein interrupted.

"Well—wouldn't it be possible to make just some
small—maybe unimportant—cut? I mean, it would make
a terrific zoom shot. Nobody can resist the sight of flesh
being cut open."

Stein frowned thoughtfully.

"I don't mind," I announced suddenly. "Provided it's
only a small cut."

Stein glanced at me then with the only truly *friendly*
glance I recall ever having received from him. "Spoken
with courage!" he exclaimed. Then to the balcony, "All
right. We'll make a surface incision upon the abdomen. It
will take about two minutes. We'll have to suture as soon
as actual treatment starts—"

"That's all right. I can pan over to that whatchamacallit
behind you."

"That is the respiratory system," Stein said tersely. "I
assume I will remain in frame?"

"Right in the middle, Doc, just as we arranged."

I smiled bitterly. So Stein had already arranged that he

would not for one moment be outside camera frame? How his colleagues must hate him! But then the oxygen tent was placed over me, and I was cut off from further proceedings for some time.

I waited nervously. My big moment was coming. Would I be expected to say a few words to the audience? I had best prepare something.

But before I had a chance to order my thoughts the oxygen tent was removed. I saw Stein poised above me with a look of great benevolence upon his face. The star and central attraction even now? I suddenly raised myself up, turned full toward the cameras and smiled. I waved my hand broadly.

"No, no, no!" Stein exclaimed angrily. "You won't be in any condition to make such a gesture. Just stay put, if you please!"

"Well, if you want to be a camera hog!" I replied testily.

"Will the patient be able to respond, Doc?" the voice asked hopefully.

"No, of course not!" Stein growled.

"He's upstaging the entire show!" I cried.

"But that's ridiculous!" Stein said testily. "The patient will be conscious but completely incapable of movement of any sort!"

"You'll make sure of that, won't you!" I replied.

"Oh, please," he groaned.

"Well, what we'll do, Doctor, is zoom in on the patient's face in that case."

"You will?" Stein's temper was paper-thin.

"It's the high spot of the show."

"I would not use those terms. In any event, I should think the most realistic thing that might happen would be—well, say I was to put my hand on his forehead and say—very simply and quietly, mind you—no dramatics about it—but perhaps say something like, 'Awaken to life, Paul Webster!' "

"No, no, no, Doctor! That's really overdoing things, don't you think?"

"Perhaps so," Stein acknowledged. "Perhaps if I said something a bit simpler, such as, 'Good morning, Paul Webster.' How about that?"

"Let's try it."

We did a run-through. After Stein's announcement I fluttered my eyes open slowly and, I thought, very effectively. Then I smiled the peaceful smile of one who awakens to a hope beyond hope. Stein fought to stay in the shot to the end. But in the end he lost.

"I'm sorry, Doc, but nothing can beat that face. We'll open on you, of course. We'll do it just the way you rehearsed. But at the end we've simply got to zoom in on a tight close-up of Webster's face."

Stein grumbled assent, and I did not even attempt to hide the smile of triumph that rose to my lips. It was my first victory over him.

Of course, even though I had joined enthusiastically into the proceedings—been caught up in the excitement, so to speak—I did not long remain entranced. The full beauty and irony of this situation was that it would never take place. But this was a secret I kept well hidden. I continued to make suggestions for improving the performance, delightedly savoring the magnificent fraud I was perpetrating upon all of them. But as we went through the routine several more times, even this began to pall. It was with relief, finally, that I at last heard the call for break.

Stein joined me in the wings. He was obviously weary,

but well satisfied with the rehearsal. "Well," he said, "that last run-through was perfect. I'll be seeing you directly, for the first stage."

This offhand remark completely dispelled the lingering wisps of my stage-struck bemusement. "The first stage," I repeated.

"Yes, of course. I'll be putting you to sleep within an hour." Stein turned to go, then paused as an apparently random thought crossed his mind. "By the way, Williams, will you please conduct Professor Webster to his ex-wife now?" Then, while the shock of his words still strangled me, he walked quickly away.

"Wait! Wait a minute!" I heard my own voice cry out as though it were a stranger's.

"Just lie back and relax, Professor." (hoo) Nurse Williams pushed my shoulders gently back down onto the table.

"But wait—wait a minute, please!" My cries might just as well have been uttered within a padded cell. I saw two attendants grip my rolling bed and felt myself being wheeled briskly down a corridor. Nurse Williams walked alongside, her face a mask of pleasant innocence.

"What's my wife doing here?" I demanded. I tried to raise myself on the table, but one of the attendants forced me back again.

"Why, she's been in role therapy for oh—months now" (hoo), Nurse Williams remarked.

"Why wasn't I told? Why didn't that fat maniac—"

"Professor, please! There are patients on this floor. You never asked."

"Of course I didn't ask!" My shout echoed hollowly, futilely, down endless vaults of gleaming indifference. "How could I guess? How could I know?" I groaned, my

voice cracking hysterically now. Then I suddenly remembered Tony Buono's sneering implication that I ought to
know where M was. This was what he'd meant. I was
wheeled into an elevator, which began a slow and silent
ascent. "Please, Williams . . . I'm not ready . . . I've got to
have time to think—"

"But we do want to see her, don't we?" (hoo)

"I don't know if—"

"But we did try to reach her during our escape, didn't
we? Isn't that where we were found?" (hoo)

I felt my eyes fill with tears—not only tears of frustration, fear, rage, but also a sudden flood of suppressed
emotion. Yes, yes, I did want to see her, had wanted desperately to see her, talk to her, touch her—for how long?
For months, years. "Yes, yes, I do want to see her, but she
won't want to see me because of the buttons and the beer
and everything—we weren't very happy—I mean, we
were happy once but not then, not afterward—it was all
my fault . . ." I babbled hopelessly, trying to control my
voice. I felt Williams's hand on my shoulder.

"Now, we certainly don't want to see her in this condition, do we, Professor?"

"No—I mean, yes—" I shut my mouth and tried to
force my breath into a natural rhythm. The elevator came
to rest, its doors slid silently open, and I was wheeled into
another long corridor. "Williams," I asked, "why is she
here?"

"I'm afraid I'm not too familiar with the details. Doctor
Stein says her personality spectrum has suffered a shift.
He says she's making excellent progress. He says—"

"I don't give a damn what he says!" I snarled. "What I
want to know is—"

"I really can't tell you any more, Professor."

I felt the table come to a halt.

"Well, here we are." (hoo)

I had a moment of panic. I was not ready for this meeting, not in control. "Look, Williams—"

"Now, we certainly don't want to be wheeled in, do we?" Williams interrupted. "Let's get up and walk in by ourselves and not alarm her. Doctor Stein said to tell you that she doesn't know anything about your case. If you tell her you've been uh—resurrected, it may be too much for her mind to bear at this time. Doctor Stein said he trusted in your affection for her and your good sense. We won't disappoint Doctor Stein, now, will we?"

I had gotten off the table. Nurse Williams was brushing at my shoulders as if trying to flick lint from the ridiculous white smock I wore. Even amid the turbulence of my unstable emotions at that moment, I found myself reflecting that this action, performed in a place where not the slightest speck of dust, let alone lint, was conceivably present, must mirror something deeply instinctive within the female psyche.

"Now, she's right inside this door. We'll wait out here." (hoo)

We were outside a closed door. I glanced apprehensively at the impassive faces of the two attendants, indecisively at Williams. She smiled encouragingly. I placed my hand on the doorknob, half-expecting it to melt beneath my touch and reveal all this as a dream.

As the door swung open I felt my heart race wildly. I shut my eyes tight, held my breath and then opened them again. Once again, as so often in the past, I was half-convinced I was the helpless victim of an unending nightmare. For the room I entered was, down to the last detail, the living room of our old apartment near the University.

There was the sagging couch, there the easy chair, there the lamps, the tables; the carpet, stained in exactly the same place; even the clutter of ash trays and magazines seemed a perfect replica. I had the sense of entering another dimension, into the past. Of course, I understood. Had not The Foundation overnight constructed for me a very plausible replica of an Egyptian tomb? This would have been a simpler task. And it did not escape me that M had evidently revealed her personality to be most at ease in these our formerly shared surroundings. That was hopeful.

She was standing, dressed in an old bathrobe, playing her violin, with her back to me. Her head inclined toward a score sharing the table before her with several quart bottles of beer. She had evidently not noticed my entrance.

"Hello," I said, my voice quivering.

She continued playing. She had not heard me.

I cleared my throat. "Hello!" I said.

"Just a minute, Paul," she muttered, intent on the music. Then with a flourish the piece was finished. She turned and smiled, placed the violin carefully on the table and poured herself a glass of beer. "I've been expecting you," she added pleasantly.

Her face had changed hardly at all. Perhaps a bit heavier beneath the chin, perhaps there were a few additional lines in her forehead. Still that strange composition of features, that suggestive montage, exuded Passive Pursuit. But her manner stirred a faint quiver of apprehension deep within me.

I hadn't planned anything. My mind had been in too much of a turmoil to make cool assessments. My first impulse, which even now burned my cheeks, was to rush

forward and take her in my arms. But the coolness, the
pleasant, friendly coolness with which she'd greeted me,
dampened that instinctual impulse. And in the split second of my hesitation, this opportunity vanished, to be replaced by crowding doubts. After all, considering what I
had done, why should I expect more than mere friendliness—in fact, why should I expect even that? Instead of
the sickening sensation of hollow regret which rose within
me I ought to be experiencing gratitude that she could
find a smile, a pleasant greeting, with which to acknowledge me.

"You haven't changed much," I said.

"What's that silly thing you're wearing?"

"That's a hospital smock or something. One of Stein's
little tricks."

"How have you been?"

"Oh, I've been— No, I haven't. Lonely—I've been
lonely."

"Want a beer?"

"No, thanks." My mind was heated with the fever of
despair. There was so much I wanted to explain. And yet,
bearing Williams's warning in mind, what could I do? "I
understand a lot more now," I offered.

"That's good. I don't."

"I mean—" Suddenly words seemed inconsequential. "I
mean, it was all my fault!" I blurted out. I couldn't go on.
The very sincerity of the friendly interest in her eyes
struck me dumb. What in the world was I saying? What
in the world was I thinking? "I'm sorry," I mumbled. I
stared at her helplessly.

"Poor Paul," she murmured. "It was only partly your
fault. It wasn't anybody's fault, really. People are what
they are. If they know who they are, that is," she added,

frowning introspectively. "You didn't know who you were, and I didn't know who I was. But now I've got a chance to find out."

"What do you mean, you've got a chance to find out?"

"Well, here. Don't tell me you don't recognize this place?"

"Yes, of course I do—"

"I feel so—secure here! They call this role therapy. And it's working already—"

"My God, I know what they call it! It's just one of Stein's devices to destroy people! They'll—"

"I'm glad to see you've still got a temper."

"I'm sorry. I'm not angry, believe me. I'm frightened—for you."

"But there's nothing to be frightened about. Doctor Stein has been wonderful. You don't know what a depression I was in when they found me. The past few years—well, they haven't exactly been a barrel of beer for me. Now I've got a chance to breathe."

"But you don't know—"

"But I do know! Doctor Stein explained it all to me. When I get out of here I'll be able to live in the real world—as myself instead of some shadow of myself."

"They'll change you."

"No, they won't. That's just the point. They'll give me the strength to be myself instead of trying to make me into someone else. Like you tried to do."

"I guess I will have a beer." I watched as she poured each of us a glass. When she handed it to me the tips of our fingers touched.

"I'm glad you're going to get well," she said, raising her glass in a toast.

I followed suit automatically, the bitter irony of her

words constricting my throat so that I almost gagged on the beer. "Stein told you?"

"Yes. I don't see why you hate him so. You owe your life to him. He's a wonderful man!"

I glanced at her sharply, trying to detect just how much emotional freight those words were hauling. But my twinge of jealousy was stilled by the transparent coolness of her expression. Her admiration for Stein was purely theoretical.

"What about us?" I asked quietly.

"What about us?"

"Would you—I mean—I'm very much in love with you. Love—I'm in love with you," I whispered haltingly.

"I know. You always were. Even when you divorced me. I knew you'd still be in love with me."

"Don't talk like that!"

"Like what?"

"I mean—you're so cool, so distant—"

"I'm sorry. I have to be. For now. I can't—I just can't afford to let myself disintegrate again, Paul. I'm not strong enough."

"Well—I mean—what about after all this?"

"We'll see. Maybe after all this you won't want me any more. Can't we just wait and see what happens?"

I fought back the tears. Wait and see what happens? I knew what was going to happen. But these were thoughts I had to suppress. For of course, as I talked with M, as I intuited and sensed her state of being, I found that Stein was, as always, right. I could not possibly burden her fragile equilibrium with my own worries, could not intrude the demons infesting my landscape into her painfully ordered world. But even if my own case appeared hopeless, I might still be able to warn, to save her.

"Listen to me," I said quietly. "I've been in The Foundation for months now. I know all about it. It isn't what it seems. They might even give you shock therapy and then your memory, your whole personality, would just vanish. No, don't interrupt. I've seen what they can do here. I don't think they'll do that to you. But they'll—they'll diminish you. That's what they do to people here, they diminish them. They diminish them until they fit into the little tiny places waiting for them out there—"

"But it was Out There, as you call it, that I couldn't face—"

"Do you want to? I mean do you want to fit into it, accept it, feel secure in it on its own terms?"

"But that's just it. I'll be able to do all that on my terms."

"No, you won't. What's out there is something you can never be part of on your own terms. You can only be part of it if you let your soul die, little by little or all at once. Most people can do that and never even feel it happening. You couldn't. I tried—God knows I tried—and I couldn't. Now, don't interrupt, please. I know what I'm talking about when I mention the soul—don't ask me how or why, I just do. People like us—maybe there are very many people like us, I don't know—we simply feel it too much when we try to smother our beings, our—well, there it is again—our souls. So we wreck everything around us, wreck our entire external lives, just because of some instinct for salvation. It's that instinct Stein will kill in you. That's what happens here. That's what they do superbly well here. They do it here when they can't do it out there."

M smiled understandingly, benignly. In the calm superiority of that smile I read defeat even before she spoke.

"Poor Paul! Still all tangled up with Out There, and Them. How is the Theory coming along these days, by the way? I forgot to ask."

"Fine, fine," I mumbled.

"Look, Paul, I simply won't have you worrying about me like this. You've got to concentrate on getting better! That's what I'm going to do. I mean, maybe you're even right about Out There, but there isn't any other There, is there? It's the only There we've got. And I'm—tired, yes, that's it, I'm tired of not being able to live in it. I'm tired of trying to invent ways to escape it. When I leave here I won't have to do that any more. Maybe you'll like me better then."

"Like you better!" I cried. I jumped up and enfolded her in my arms, burying my face in the warm place where her hair met her neck. "I love you now, here, just the way you are, the way you were—"

She accepted my embrace but did not respond to it. She patted my head fondly, but not with any discernible passion. I drew away, quivering with frustration. For now, at this moment in time, I faced utter and complete defeat. And I could not tell her that this moment was, as far as I was concerned, eternity. In any event, I could barely bring myself to look on that serene face. My mind was stunned, my emotions frozen.

"Sorry to interrupt, but we really must be getting back now" (hoo), Williams said. So deeply enmeshed had I been in my hopelessness that I hadn't even noticed her entry. Behind her I could see the guards waiting.

And—I confess it—I was glad for the intrusion, glad to be forced to leave this scene of disaster. "Good-bye," I muttered, unable to think of anything more important to say.

"Well, I'll be seeing you again soon, won't I?" M asked, with that damnable smile of content.

"Oh, I'm sure we'll see quite a bit of each other" (hoo), Williams intruded briskly. I stared at her with pure hatred.

"Yes." I summoned as casual a tone to my voice as I could muster. "Well—so long." And in an act of sublime inanity I found myself shaking hands with M! With her other hand she was already pouring herself another beer.

I followed Williams from the room, fell into step before the guards and retraversed the chill corridors, the impersonal route of defeat.

But as I walked along I found myself growing eager, even impatient, to confront Stein again. For you must understand that the frustration, the bitter surge of despair, that my encounter with M had aroused had only convinced me that I was right. Stein had to be stopped— stopped for the sake of humanity, stopped for M's sake, for my own. I thought gratefully then of the icy steel automatic beneath my mattress.

He was awaiting me, white-smocked and smug, standing beside the desk, on which lay an assortment of gleaming steel instruments among which a hypodermic syringe was prominent. He was busy with a square black plastic box and did not turn when we entered. "You may leave us alone now, Williams," he said over his shoulder. "The Sleep Room has been prepared. Would you mind checking it over once again?"

"Certainly, Doctor," she replied, and immediately left with the attendants, closing the door behind her.

I felt a thrill of hope at this unexpected stroke of fortune. I had not imagined I would be left alone with Stein.

And from the depths of grim hatred, ironical humor rose to my lips. Stein did not know it yet, but I was in control now. How often he'd played upon my hopes and fears! Now I would give him a slight taste of that treatment before I put a final end to this affair.

"Everything ready for Sleep Time?" I asked casually.

"Yes—except for this damned thing. Ah! There we are." He turned and smiled benignly. "I have Mr. Suskind for you, right here!"

I suddenly recognized the box as a tape recorder, and once again my calm was splintered by fevered suspicion. "That was not what you promised!" I exclaimed. "You were to get Suskind out of the asylum!"

"Please, please, Professor!" Stein raised his hands, palms outward, in supplication to heaven. "This is a message from Mr. Suskind. He was interviewed last night in his present place of confinement. I advise you to listen before jumping to conclusions."

"How do I know it's really him?"

"Precisely why we used a tape recorder. You will grant, I think, that no one could possibly imitate his accent in such a way as to fool you?" He clicked a switch on the machine and then walked over to the window to stare thoughtfully down at the park below.

"*Hello, Paul!*" The tape crackled to life, and even in the first two words of greeting I discerned the true Suskind. My suspicions vanished as I concentrated on the message. "*Velly glad to hear you awright. Have been velly wollied about you. Doctor Stein says you gonna be up and alound velly damn quick. Fine. Fine. He said you velly much wollied about me, too. Please not to wolly. Please not tly to get me outa here. Paul, you understand I am velly happy here. Velly much aflaid first, then velly happy.*

Here I come to glips with essential ploblem our society. This is one big tlash heap—but tlash heap of humans, Paul. This much better than cataloging garbage, better than statistics of disposal. Here evlybody disposed of finally. Working like mad. Have awready made thlee hundled pages notes. Matelial velly fine, velly fine. Study glaphs who gets committed here, who gets disposed of first. You maybe suplised some of my findings. Possible solution population explosion thlough disposal of people in places like this one. Consumer society consume humans, too—all velly intelesting. Begin to see how society like ours can go on folever—ploduce, consume, ploduce, consume—same with people like with cars and lefligelators. You lemember Liverside Dlive, Paul? Ha ha. I like to lemember old times too. But velly busy up here. Plomise not to tly to help me, Paul, please plomise. Lemember Liverside Dlive! When you up and alound maybe you come visit me? Velly welcome. Visitors' days evly Fliday. Good-bye for now, Paul—and mazel tov!"

I cannot begin to describe the impact these words made upon me. First there was the glad recognition. By the time the message had ended I found my eyes filled with tears just at the sound of that well-remembered voice. Besides that, there was the feeling of immeasurable relief that Suskind was happy, busy, prospering in his own way. But conflicting with these generous emotions was an undercurrent of despair that pressed on my consciousness. It had something to do with the element of defeat that even Suskind's reassurances could not gloss over, something to do with the pitiable horror of the very gladness with which he accepted his new surroundings. Was this, then, the best the world could offer to that noble mind?

Stein turned now, and walked back to the table. "You

see," he said quietly, "The Foundation keeps its promises."
He carefully rewound the tape.

I walked over to the windows. So hectic, rushed and disoriented had the hours been that I had barely noted their passage. But it was night now. The darkness of the city below was sprinkled with bright windows, honeycombed with tracings of light, the feeble evidences of man's defiance of the outer black. Beyond this window my fellow men pursued their lives in the desperate hope of catching them one day—perhaps a futile, frustrating occupation, but one that was not yet disturbed by immortality. There in the gathering night men were still secure in their idyl of life and death, the recurring cycle with the termination that gave it meaning. I turned to watch Stein.

His huge face wore an expression of serene, contemplative piety. "I am glad to see, Professor, that at last you are calm about it all. I knew—always knew—you were basically dedicated, courageous and sane." He picked up the hypodermic syringe and started to fill it from a glass vial of colorless liquid.

"You are on the very threshold of success now, Doctor, aren't you?" I asked quietly. "Nothing stands in your way. Certainly I don't stand in your way. My ex-wife doesn't stand in your way. Nothing human stands in your way." If he noticed the tightness of my voice he did not show it. All his attention was concentrated on the syringe, which he held up to the light, squinting at it like a man aiming a rifle.

"Excuse me a moment," I said.

"Where are you going?" he asked absently, favoring me with a glance.

"To the bathroom," I lied.

"Good, good. A general evacuation would be desirable at this moment."

I passed him, walked into the bedroom, reached beneath my mattress and drew forth the cold automatic. It weighed heavily but comfortably in my hand. I inspected it and switched off the safety catch, then returned to the living room. What were my feelings at this supreme moment? They were no longer hope, joy, hatred, despair, or even fear. No, my emotions had been exhausted, or perhaps they simply no longer communicated to me. I was beyond and above all that now. Only triumph—detached, contemplative, implacable triumph—that is what I felt.

"I thought you were going to the—" he started, and then stopped suddenly as he saw the weapon in my hand, its insolent snout pointing at his huge belly. "I see," he muttered with a deep sigh.

"Do you see, Stein?" I inquired. "I don't think you see. I want you to tell me what you see. Or perhaps I should tell *you* what *I* see. I see a madman tampering with the universe. I see a crazed buffoon playing with human minds, human souls. I see men—all men, everywhere—driven mad by the emptiness of life without death, see their souls shrivel and die in their immortal bodies. I see a perverted, twisted genius—yes, I grant you that, genius—facing its own ruin right here and now in this room. Suppose you tell me now what you see?"

During my little speech Stein had been staring at me and shaking his head slowly as if he could not believe his ears. His bearing implied it was I who was mad. "I see a man abandoning his fellows," he said quietly.

I laughed once, harshly. His audacity never failed to astonish me. I jerked the automatic slightly, insinuatingly. "Don't tell me you're afraid to die, Doctor?" I demanded.

"That is insulting," he said quietly.

Was there no shaking his reserve? I longed to see him abase himself, just once. "Your final error was in bringing my ex-wife into this. It wasn't your only mistake—simply your last one."

"It was you who brought her into the situation," he said gruffly. "And I might add that her condition is in large part your responsibility. Killing me won't solve any problems there."

"What makes you think I'm going to kill you?"

"You have a gun pointed at me. The safety catch is off." His voice was annoyed now, definitely annoyed.

"Do you perhaps think you deserve to die?"

"No more than any man." His voice was impatient now, trembling on the verge of anger.

"But you're already mostly dead, aren't you? Your emotions are dead, your body is a waste of corpulence, your personal life is a stench and a decay already."

"I did not imagine you would sink to this!" he muttered.

"When you torture people you have to imagine that they'll sink to almost anything, Stein. But of course, you wouldn't realize that. In your coldly intellectual world—"

"Coldly intellectual!" he shouted, his face flushing darkly. "For God's sake, pull that trigger and get it over with! Coldly intellectual! Coldly intellectual!" In his rage he seemed to forget the automatic pointing at him. He tossed the hypodermic syringe onto the desk and waved his arms in grotesque despair. "Coldly intellectual! Do you realize nothing? Nothing at all? Don't you understand what you're doing? Don't you understand that if CNH therapy can revive an undamaged dead body, then the rest is mechanics—mere mechanics!" The vitality of his hoarse whisper almost gripped me. "Damaged organs can be replaced, don't you see? Already we can replace some.

It is only a question of time, a few years perhaps, before we'll be able to replace them all. Then if someone died of kidney disease, heart ailment, even brain tumor—yes, interesting experiments on those lines are already being held in Moscow—why, by replacing the damaged organ in conjunction with CNH therapy, we will be able to restore life to almost anyone! And when I speak of replacing damaged organs, I include those damaged by old age— yes, even veins and arteries and nerves. It is only a question of time now. Not only can life be restored, it could be preserved, perhaps indefinitely." His voice was slowly rising. "This is the breakthrough that humanity has been awaiting since the dawn of time! This is the first step toward immortality! It means the death of death—yes, and the death of God and the gods, the end of heaven and hell. There will be nothing left to fear. Mankind will be free for the first time in its history!" Spittle trickled down his chin. "The infinite comes within our grasp! The universe becomes our toy! Time loses meaning—eternity is our goal!" He stopped abruptly. His eyes narrowed, and he wiped his mouth on the sleeve of his jacket as he said in an awe-hushed whisper, "You could have been the first immortal! And even if you died permanently—not today, that is practically a statistical impossibility, but years from now—even then you would have been remembered for all time as the first man to return from death. People until the end of time would have recalled you with gratitude, love—you might have become a new religion. When you speak of cold intellect, remember that in this matter imagination boggles at the limitless potential!" He straightened and stared at me reproachfully. "Well, get it over with," he demanded.

The sweet taste of triumph must have communicated

itself to my smile, for Stein averted his gaze from my face with an expression of distaste. But I was not yet finished.

"I ask you again why you expect me to kill you. You decline to answer? Very well. You expect me to kill you because you know in your heart you deserve to die. But I have no intention of killing you, Doctor."

"Then—you understand now—you see it—you're convinced?" He could not suppress the eagerness in his voice.

"Yes," I remarked reasonably, "I see it all very clearly now. But I'm going to leave you behind to ponder it a bit more—to ponder your failure, Doctor. You see," I added, pointing the gun at my head, feeling the cold breath of its snout against my temple, "I am convinced."

For one tiny fraction of a second I enjoyed the look of amazement, of dawning anguish on Stein's face. Then I squeezed the trigger.

Instantly I was drowned in roaring blackness that exploded with the impact of a sledge-hammer against my consciousness, and I collapsed. And at that ultimate moment, everything within me surged to the surface, broke through the icy calm I had maintained, rushed through my fading consciousness with a shriek of despair. My emotions a torrent, a screaming torrent, beating against my mind, clamoring No! *No! No! No!*

For in my frigid hatred, my lofty triumph, my detached confidence, I had forgotten that vivid, seething mass of *life* within me. As cunning as my action had seemed, as rational, as inevitable—so now, in the instant before the dark, I knew it to be insane, hopelessly insane. I did not want to die! I did not want to die! It was a mistake! A terrible, awful—

I could only have been unconscious for a few minutes. For when I awoke Stein was again next to the desk filling the syringe, Nurse Williams was standing beside me and I was resting on the couch. "He's coming around now, Doctor." I heard her voice as from the end of a long, hollow corridor. My mind reeled in confusion, grappling desperately to find its bearings. The explosion, the roaring blackness, the despair, the fright, the gun. The gun! I saw it resting impotently on the desk. Stein was finished with the syringe now, and he approached me with it held aloft. His face was not unkind as he bent over me.

"You really do want to live, after all, don't you?" he asked gently.

"Yes, yes!" I moaned. "I want to live! That gun—"

"Be calm. It was loaded with blanks. You don't think we'd let you harm yourself, do you? We allowed you to keep it the way one leaves a rattle for a baby—it was a comfort to you. And in the final analysis it was the last way of convincing you that you really want to live."

Perhaps because of the shock to my mind, perhaps because of the weakness I felt in my flesh, my bones, my consciousness, I found myself crying. Crying with relief that my insanity had not succeeded, crying with gratitude for Stein. His omnipotence, his vast understanding, his overwhelming kindness, reduced me to simpering awe. "Yes, yes," I moaned brokenly, "I want to live."

"And in knowing now how much you want to live, you understand how much all men want to live."

"Yes—"

"And by dying a few times you can help them—and yourself—live forever."

"Yes, yes! I'll help! I'll help!"

"Now I believe you will. Now I truly believe you will.

Now I have confidence in you even after your recovery!" Stein spoke with pride in *me*.

As he loomed above me his face seemed to fill the room, the universe. There was something awful, majestic, in the vast reassurance of his presence. Even though it seemed idiotic I found myself muttering, "Stein, who are you . . . who are you?"

Stein smiled. "Well, Professor, as far as you're concerned I guess I am the Resurrection and the Life."

As I felt the needle prick my skin (but not the pain of it), as my eyes grew immediately heavy with a fading linger on Williams's bulging hips curving past Stein's immense body, from some remote and misty region of memory a phrase from the Greek crept into my fast-dying consciousness. It glimmered feebly just as blackness enveloped the world:

Ζώη μου, σᾶς ἀγαπῶ

About the Author

ROBERT CONROY GOLDSTON was born in New York City in 1927. During his childhood he lived at different periods in New York, Chicago and Los Angeles, although he also traveled extensively with his family throughout the United States. During the Second World War he served with the Quartermaster Corps in France, Belgium and Germany. He attended Columbia University during the postwar years. Since 1950 he has spent a great deal of time in Europe, living in France, Italy and Spain. He is the author of three previous novels: *The Eighth Day*, published in 1956; *The Catafalque*, published in 1958; and *The Shore Dimly Seen*, published in 1963. He has also written a history of Satanism and several children's books. He was awarded a Guggenheim Fellowship in 1958. Mr. Goldston now lives with his wife and six children in Vermont.